Lovely
Reckless
Redemption

Printed

Subscribe!

Please Subscribe to Abbey Easton's newsletter to get access to exclusive bonus content and be the first to know about exciting news and book updates!

www.authorabbeyeaston.com

Content Warning

Due to the suspense elements of my books, there may be content that some readers may be sensitive to. Most content is not explicit or graphic, but for a full list:

CLICK HERE

Lovely Reckless Redemption

ABBEY EASTON

Prologue

DAWSON

Three Years Ago

I LIVED FOR THE one day a week I saw her.

This prison that had been my home for the last four years had sucked the very soul out of me. Maybe it was the fact that I never committed the crime I was convicted for, but everything about being here felt so...wrong.

When my mother was attacked on our family ranch, I had found her broken and bleeding body. It was my hand that had idiotically picked up the knife that she'd been stabbed with. When my brother saw me, cradling our dying mother and holding a weapon, he drew conclusions that weren't true.

I would've never hurt my mama, but I hadn't been able to save her, either.

Some days, I prayed I wouldn't wake up in the mornings. I always did though. Again and again, I worked my designated prison job. I read books. I made art and worked my body in the gym to its breaking point, but it all barely kept my head above the depression and sadness that consumed me.

It was only the days she came to see me that breathed some life back inside my hollow and cold chest. She was a ray of sunshine on my constant dark and dreary life inside this hell hole. The only thing that I looked forward to.

She smiled as she walked in and my dead heart awakened in my chest.

Faye Liles has been my friend for a very long time. It was still hard for me to grasp why she put up with me, but ever since we were in middle school and I defended her against the class bullies, she'd stuck around. We'd always been close friends. She was everything that I wasn't and she was never afraid to put me in my place.

But things were...changing for me since I was locked away. I had never felt anything for her other than close friendship, but she was the one constant thing in my life these days. When I saw her now, something felt different. She was becoming more than my best friend...she was becoming my *everything*.

I'd never tell her that, though. Faye deserved so much better than a man like me, and I had nothing to offer her. We'd made a promise a long time ago, anyway.

She would always be my friend, nothing more.

As Faye sat down on the opposite side of the glass partition separating us, something was off about her familiar, warm smile. It didn't touch her eyes. She inhaled deeply, pulling back her shoulders before grabbing for the phone and putting it up to her ear.

2

I paused before I picked up the receiver on my own side. "What's wrong?"

She blinked, her fake smile faltering. "What do you mean?"

"You can't hide from me, Faye. Something's bothering you."

Her lips narrowed as her eyes widened. My fingers tightened around the bulky plastic phone, wishing I could reach out and touch her. I had never ached to touch Faye, but I longed for the feel of her. I couldn't remember the last time I hugged her, and I cursed myself for taking it for granted. I hadn't known it would be the last time.

"It's nothing." She shook her head. "I'm not spending the little time I get with you complaining."

My jaw throbbed as I clenched my back teeth. She was always checking up on me, asking how I was feeling and how I was doing. Friendship goes both ways.

"You can tell me, Faye." I gestured around the cold, gray visitation room. "Please, if you're willing to come to this God-forsaken place every week, the least I can do is be a good friend to you."

"You are a good friend."

I wasn't. I didn't know if I ever had been. I never appreciated her like she should've been. Yet here she was, sticking by my side. "What's bothering you?"

She pulled in another small breath. "My mother made a surprise visit to Cypress Falls."

I scowled. Faye grew up under her toxic mother's roof in our small, river-side town of Cypress Falls. Her mama was constantly bringing new men and taking them into her home, around her young girls, without a care of how it affected them.

That woman was nothing but selfish, in my opinion. The day Faye's mama left Cypress Falls ten years ago with one of her

3

low-life boyfriends was probably the best thing that had happened to Faye and her little sister, Ellie.

"What did she want?" I asked, voice tight.

"I think she wanted to get the land Ellie inherited from her daddy."

The noise that left me was something between a gasp and a growl. "How did she even know about that?"

Faye and her sister hadn't been in contact with their mother since she left town as far as I knew.

Faye shrugged. "She lived in Cypress Falls most of her life. She still has friends there and word gets around."

"I'm so sorry."

She shook her head. "I feel bad for Ellie. I didn't even have to talk to the woman, but Ellie just lost her daddy and our Mama comes sniffing around looking to get something from her." Faye bristled. "She's done enough. I just want her to leave us alone."

I put a hand on the glass partition that separated us, the upset look on her face breaking my heart. I'd been there when Faye was under her mama's care. I'd seen the way that woman treated them, as if her daughters were nothing but nuisances. She'd try to control everything they did, especially Ellie, who she'd used since she was a baby in beauty pageants like her own little doll. Faye was always looking out for her little sister, trying to take care of her because their mother chose not to most of the time. It had been too much for two kids to deal with, but they had. They'd come so far to build a life for themselves despite their mother.

"Ellie has you, Faye. She'll be fine. She's strong. So are you."

Faye bit her lip. It was weird the way the small things Faye has done since we were young have suddenly changed for me. The way she bit her lip now, it had my stomach tightening and my heart feeling things it never had before.

It's being in this hell hole. That's all. I just miss her.

I chanted that mantra over and over as I tried to chase away the unfamiliar feelings she suddenly stirred up inside me.

Faye's eyes flicked to my palm pressed up against the glass. Slowly, she picked up her hand, placing it over mine on the other side of the glass. My skin prickled, yearning to just...feel her. The slight warmth of her hand against the glass sent a shiver down my spine.

Get a hold of yourself, this is Faye. Your best friend.

"Thanks," she whispered into the phone, her gaze cutting back to mine. "I miss you, Dawson."

My eyes closed briefly. Her words cut down to my very bones. I missed her, so much.

Maybe more than I should.

When I opened my eyes again, my heart dropped as an officer cued that our visitation time was already up.

Faye let her hand drop from the glass with a long sigh. "It always goes so fast," she said.

I nodded. "It's never enough time."

Her face broke out into a bright grin, though the sadness lingered in her blue eyes. "But I'll be back next week! I promise not to be so gloomy then, okay?"

I let out a low grunt that I meant to sound like a laugh, but didn't quite make it there. "Gloomy is not a word I'd ever use to describe you."

Her nose crinkled as she laughed—a breathy, beautiful sound that had my heart skittering against my ribs. "Well, I've felt a little gloomy this week. But next week I will be back to normal." She winked. "I promise."

Back to normal. If only I could go back to normal. My life inside here was anything but that.

5

I tried to give her a grin. "Next week."

"I'll see you, Dawson. Take care of yourself."

Then, she was gone. Much too soon the tiny bit of relief she brought with her every visit dissipated as I sunk beneath the cold and dark depression once again.

As I watched her walk away toward the door, the only thing I could think of was that she was the one thing keeping me here, anchored to this earth and this life no matter how much I hated it.

All I had to do was survive another seven days until I could see my sunshine again.

Chapter One

DAWSON

Present Day

I GLARED OUT THE Jeep's windshield. Too many people were wandering around Main Street. At any other time, to any other person, the sight was picturesque. The sun cast a warm glow on the tidy straight sidewalks. Tall, historic brick buildings were nestled tightly against each other, lining the street on both sides and housing local businesses.

It was the middle of January, but only mildly chilly in the small, Southern town of Cypress Falls. It had been unusually cold lately—even for winter—and the nice weather had drawn everyone out of their houses. Unfortunately.

I grimaced at the package sitting on my passenger seat. It never ceased to irk me that no one would come collect packages up in the hills at my cabin. A price I had to pay for my solidarity, it seemed.

The orders for my small art business had gone above and beyond what I'd expected. When I started posting my work on social media for fun, but after one of my posts went viral, it had turned into a means to support myself. Though I was thankful for the opportunity, having to come into town at least once a week, if not more, wasn't what I signed up for when I moved to my secluded piece of land.

Gritting my teeth, I finally forced myself out of the vehicle, package in hand. As I locked the Jeep, I popped the collar of my dark leather jacket, hunching over against the slight breeze like it was a bitter wind.

The closest parking spot was three blocks down from the post office, and I trained my eyes on the ground as I hurried along the sidewalk. Not many people minded me, but a few did a double-take to get a good look before dawning a sharp scowl that rivaled my own.

I wasn't welcome in this town anymore.

I thought I'd been okay with it, but the looks of disapproval, even after all these years, made my chest twinge. Living here all my life, you'd think that people would forgive and forget. I hadn't done what I'd been accused of, but it seemed that doing prison time for a crime I didn't commit wasn't enough penance for these people.

Relief hit me as I came to the post office. The bell above the door chimed as I slipped inside. Mallory, glanced up from behind the service desk, her eyes lighting up as they often did when I came in. She was young, just out of high school and mostly oblivious to my not-so-great reputation because she was so young.

Gazing around the small space, I relaxed slightly. The bustle of the streets hadn't touched here. I was the only customer.

"Hey, Dawson," Mallory greeted me, pushing back her long, wavy blonde hair. "Another one? That's two this week."

I quickly sat the box on the counter. It already had its shipping label and was ready to go. The only thing I needed to do was drop it off and leave. Such a freaking waste of time.

"Well, the customer paid for expedited shipping," I said, voice low.

Mallory took the package, eying the large fragile labels on every side of the box. Shipping out physical art canvases was tricky. It had taken me a few times to get it right, but now the paintings usually arrived without damage.

"You ever going to tell me what you sell?" Her brow arched.

"No."

Her lip puckered in a small pout. "Hmm...what could Dawson Evans possibly be mailing out all the time that's always so fragile?"

I shrugged, a bit annoyed at her prying.

My social media pages were public, but I sold my art under a pseudonym. The people of Cypress Falls didn't need to know what I did. It wasn't their business and the fact that the oldest son of the prominent and wealthy Evans family was making his living painting and making art of all things would zip around the town's gossip mill in the blink of an eye.

"See you, Mallory," I said, raising one hand and turning to leave.

"I'm gonna figure it out one day!" she called as I opened the door and exited the post office.

I stepped out onto the sidewalk, the hair on the back of my neck standing on end as I sensed someone's eyes on me. Every muscle coiled with tension as the heavy door fell closed with a thump.

I turned my head, meeting the cool gray eyes of my younger brother.

When we were kids, I used to see softness in Knox's eyes. He was always following me around, and though it was annoying at times, I had always seen good things when he looked up at me: curiosity, a bit of mischief, and also...love.

But that was before our mother was attacked and ultimately passed away from her injuries. It was before my brother had testified in court against me and put me in prison for hurting our mama even though I had nothing to do with it.

Now, the only thing I saw when he looked at me was cold steel sharp enough to stab me in the back.

I slowly slipped my hands into the pockets of my jeans, my eyes sliding to the girl standing beside him. Her black hair was pulled up in a messy knot at the top of her head. Her black sweater with white skulls matched her Chuck Taylors. Shiloh Bennett wasn't someone I expected my brother to fall for. He was about as straightlaced as they came. A flannel-wearing country boy with a cowboy hat obsession. But they'd been together over a year and seemed genuinely good for each other despite seeming like total opposites.

The side of my lip pulled up in more of a snarl than a smile as I glanced back at my brother.

"Don't worry, I'm just passing through. Wouldn't mean to impede on your territory."

Though it had been proven that I was an innocent man, Knox didn't trust me any more than he could throw me. I didn't care much for him either these days, though. When I first got out of prison, he didn't want me anywhere near him or our family ranch. He hadn't been the whole reason I hid away in the hills, but he was definitely part of it.

Something flashed across his face. A flicker of...anger? Guilt, maybe? It was gone in an instant, anyway. Knox had been perfecting his stony façade for years.

His lips thinned slightly before he spoke. "You're free to go wherever you please, Dawson."

I clenched my jaw, again cursing the fact that I had to come to town today. If there was one thing that could sour my already grumpy mood...it was this.

I shrugged and looked away like I was completely unbothered. Yeah, now I was free. No thanks to him though. If I hadn't been granted a new trial on appeal, I'd still be locked up behind bars because of him.

I couldn't stop myself from being an asshole to him. He stirred up this hate in the very pit of my stomach, like stoking a smoldering pile of ashes made from all bridges he burned when he chose to throw his own flesh and blood brother in prison. It didn't make it right, but I couldn't look at him and not feel the searing pain of betrayal.

It might make me a bad person, but I wanted him to feel a fraction of the pain that I did.

Knox pulled on the brim of his worn cowboy hat until it covered his eyes as he let my comment go without a response.

"I'm actually glad we ran into you," Shiloh piped up, changing the subject.

All the interactions I'd had with her the few times I'd seen her at our family ranch hadn't been great ones. But ever since my brother met her...he seemed different. Hell, last time we spoke to each other he'd even tried to apologize, but I wasn't having that. It was too little too late.

She curled her arm around Knox's, stepping closer to him until she was pressed up against his side. She drew in a deep breath as she lifted her chin and pulled back her shoulders.

"Knox and I have been talking a lot...about you," she said. She glanced up at Knox, and he squeezed her arm tight. "We wanted to ask you something."

"What the hell are you talking about?"

Knox pushed back his hat and met my eyes again. "We're getting married...and we would really like you to be there."

I threw my head back and laughed, a cold bitter sound. I hadn't expected that request.

My brother and I had barely spoken for the better part of six years. Now, he wanted to invite me to his wedding? Knox might've changed in the last couple years, but not that much.

I ran a hand through my hair, my laughter dying as quick as it came on. "No." I shook my head. "I don't think I'll be welcome."

I could imagine it now; it wasn't just the uncomfortable tension between me and my estranged brother, but also the rest of the town. Knox was quiet by nature, but he was well-known in the town of Cypress Falls. People respected him. They actually liked the guy. Their wedding would be filled to the brim with people, and the thought of being in a crowd like that made my skin crawl.

"I know things have been hard between you and Knox, but we do want you there. And not just for a wedding. We didn't want this to be just about us. We want to give back, too."

I frowned. "What do you mean?"

"We decided that our wedding isn't just for us. We want to make it into a fundraiser for Paws and Pastures."

Paws and Pastures Animal Haven was both the only vet clinic and animal rescue in the area. It was run by the Roberts family. I'd known their only son, Axel, in high school. It had been a long

12

time since I'd set foot on the property out there, though. My family always brought our ranch horses there, and they'd taken amazing care of them.

"How charitable of you," I said, truly meaning it, but still hesitant. "I'll have to decline, though." I could donate money anonymously, I was sure. My presence wasn't necessary.

A silent beat passed. Knox hardened his expression, jaw working. "I think it's time we move on, Dawson."

The anger came on instantly, dousing any sense of softness I felt for my brother and his charity wedding.

"Move on?" I hissed. "Move on with what exactly?"

"We need to move on with our lives. We need to move on from this hate."

I swallowed another honorless laugh. That was ironic coming from Knox, of all people. He was the one who hated me first. Hated me enough to not believe me. Hated me enough to put me behind bars for the rest of my life.

I stepped toward him, and his body straightened with tension as he pulled Shiloh behind him. I scowled. I would never hurt her, but it was obvious he still didn't trust me.

Knox and I were about the same height, but I was stronger than him now. If prison taught me anything it was to be disciplined with my physical health. A habit I'd kept up with.

Pinning my brother with a level stare, I hoped he felt the heat of anger that flared from the core of my being.

"I can't just move on with my life, little brother," I snarled. "You destroyed mine."

I didn't wait for his response. I turned on my heel, walking away from my brother and his now fiancée. All I had left were shambles of the life I'd once had. That wasn't something that I could just move on from.

I couldn't ruin Knox's life like he ruined mine, but I would never forgive him.

Chapter Two

DAWSON

I STOMPED ON THE sidewalk, hands clenched tight as my long legs carried me farther and farther away from my brother. Cursing under my breath, I stared down at the clean concrete in front of me, and realized I was heading in the opposite direction of my vehicle.

My blood was on fire. How could Knox really think that we could move on? He had ruined me. He ruined our family. Our mother was gone, but we didn't even have each other now. And that was on him, not me. He had been the one that thought he saw something that night. He was the one who believed I would do something so heinous despite my word and the lack of evidence.

My nerves were fried as I wandered aimlessly, not knowing where to go but knowing that I wanted to be far away from Knox Evans.

I halted suddenly, almost at the end of Main Street where most of the local shops and businesses were. My eyes cut across the street where one small shop in particular stood out. It wasn't different from the other orange brick buildings that surrounded it, but the moment I saw the wooden sign for Southern Sunshine boutique, some of the tension inside me eased.

There was only one person I ever wanted to see when I came into town. The only person I trusted.

Faye.

I crossed the street before I realized it. Faye and I had known each other since middle school. Technically, we'd been in the same class since kindergarten, but I'd never talked much to people. I suppose deep down I've always had a bit of loner in me. But then, she'd come into my life.

As I approached the shop Faye owned, where she sold Bohemian-style clothing and trendy graphic T-shirts, my stomach sank. Behind the large glass display window, the store was dark. The sign hung on the window of the door read, "closed, but still awesome."

My stare bore into the sign, trying to make sense of it. It was in the middle of the afternoon on a Wednesday. The shop should have been open.

I took a step back, craning my neck toward the windows on the second story of the building. The curtains of the tall windows were drawn. There was no sight of movement. I frowned. Faye lived in that apartment above her shop.

I rounded the corner of the building, entering the alley on the side and not stopping until I reached the back of the building where there was a small strip of gravel for parking. The space where her car was normally parked was empty.

Strange.

Taking out my phone, I sent her a quick text. When she didn't answer right away, I gave her a call, letting it ring until I was sent to voicemail. I reluctantly slipped the phone back in my pocket.

Something made a noise behind me; a soft, high-pitched whine that had me looking over my shoulder. I turned, facing the most pathetic looking creature I'd ever seen. I was pretty sure it was a dog, though it barely resembled one anymore. The spine was poking through the dirty, light brown fur. Almost every bone in his hips was visible, and his ribs protruded with every labored breath.

The dog stared at me. His caramel-colored eyes were wide and exhausted, but also...curious. A small spark remained within them as he cocked his head to one side, his tail flicking back and forth slowly.

The way he looked at me stirred an old memory I'd buried long ago. My gut twisted.

I stuffed my hands in my pockets, shoulders curling in as I tried to chase away the childhood recollection of the one and only dog I'd ever owned. The best dog.

"Go away," I said, my tone harsher than I intended.

The dog gingerly eased his hips down onto the gravel of the alleyway as if I'd just instructed him to sit.

I gritted my teeth. "Go on, get out of here!" I waved a hand, hoping to shoo him away.

The dog barely flinched. His tongue lolled out as he panted. It was cold, but also dry. By the emaciated look of him, he hadn't been fed. He had to be dehydrated too.

I looked away, reminding myself that this dog was not my problem. My eyes caught back on Faye's building. They flicked back up to the second story windows where her one-bedroom apartment was. I wondered if she'd come across this dog.

I shook my head. She hadn't. Faye would've never left him out here. She would've cooked him a homemade meal and taken him in. He would be living like a king if she'd found him.

Reluctantly, I glanced back at the dog. His ears flopped forward framing his face to make him look like a puppy even though he had to weigh at least fifty pounds. Well, he was probably supposed to weigh fifty pounds.

"You must be one unlucky dog if you're running into me here." Despite myself, I crouched down, placing my elbows on my knees. "What are you doing out here all by yourself?"

The dog's tail wagged harder, thumping off the ground. My heart clenched with both sadness and maybe a little fondness. I stretched a hand out toward him, palm up. The dog stood, but his tail never stopped wagging as he slowly made his way toward me. His nose, which should've been wet and cold, was dry as he sniffed my palm.

He looked worse up close. I scratched him behind the ears, my fingers tangling in mats and layers of dirt and grime.

"Did someone leave you? Or are you just lost?" I felt dumb talking to an animal who couldn't respond, but the dog licked my hand.

I didn't want a dog. I've never wanted another dog. But as I stood up and stared down at the pathetic, starving creature, I couldn't leave him there. The very least, Faye would have kicked my ass if she ever found out I left this dog to fend for himself.

I sighed. "Come on, buddy."

I turned, heading back down the alley toward Main Street. I didn't have to turn to know that the dog was behind me. His nails clicked on the concrete as we made it back to the sidewalk. He followed me all the way back to my Jeep. I opened the back door and waited for him to jump in.

When he didn't, I whistled and patted the leather seat that he was about to get disgustingly dirty. But the dog stood there, his tail wagging as he shifted on his feet.

It hit me, then, that he probably didn't have enough strength to jump up. I gritted my teeth, pissed at whoever decided to abandon this poor dog on the street. Squatting down, I carefully scooped him up and placed him in the Jeep. He curled into a ball immediately laying his head down, letting out a small huff I could've sworn sounded like a relieved sigh.

As I got back into the driver's seat, I checked my phone again. Still no text from Faye. I threw the phone into the cupholder, wondering where she was and if she was okay. It wasn't like her to disappear in the middle of the week without saying something to me about it.

I buckled in and cranked the engine, glancing at the stray dog through the rearview mirror. His tail whacked against the seat as his eyes met mine.

"Don't worry. I'll get you some help," I promised.

I drove north for less than ten minutes before a quaint little farm on the edge of town came into view. The sign at the end of the driveway read, Paws and Pastures Rescue and Veterinary Clinic. I cruised down the long dirt driveway. In the distance there was an old farmhouse and a barn with multiple pastures. The drive led toward a smaller building with bright red siding and a black tin roof.

I parked in front of the vet clinic, the sound of bleating goats mixed with the barks of dogs as I stepped out of the Jeep. It'd been a while since I set foot on the Roberts farm and vet clinic, but it hadn't changed at all. They had all sorts of animals, mostly rescues, that lived with them. They took in everything, from donkeys to cows to horses. Chickens roamed freely, and a sense of familiarity settled around me. I opened the back door of the Jeep and carefully scooped up the dog in my arms. He wasn't nearly as heavy as he probably should be, and as I approached the red building

I remembered the times I'd come here as a kid with my mama to drop off sick horses. We'd been pretty close with the Roberts family at one point as they helped us with the animals on the ranch and had a son around my age. The dog's tail wagged again, thumping against my arm and he put his chin on my shoulder, as if she trusted me completely.

The dog's ears perked up as barking intensified closer to the vet clinic building. The kennels were in the back and were usually overwhelmed with dogs and cats. When I'd known the Roberts family, they always seemed to have a lot on their plate, but were always more than happy to sacrifice for the animals in their care.

When I entered the building and stepped inside the waiting area, an older woman looked up at me from behind the front desk. I groaned inwardly, recognizing her. Mrs. Watson had been working at the vet clinic for as long as I could remember and wasn't the kindest woman. She was known to love keeping up with the town gossip. Her wire-rimmed glasses slipped down her nose as she gaped at me.

"Good heavens," she squeaked, her gaze shifting to the animal in my arms. "What on earth did you do to that poor thing?"

My gut clenched as hard as my jaw at her judgmental tone.

"Is Axel here?" I asked, ignoring her question.

Mrs. Watson pressed her thin, wrinkled lips together. She pushed her glasses up and frowned. "Dr. Roberts is available, yes."

I tried my best not to snap at her. "Can I see him?" I asked with forced calm.

She didn't respond, but stood from her chair and turned toward a door that led to the exam rooms in the back.

The dog shifted in my arms, and I scratched him on his side. About a minute later, a tall man with sandy blonde hair and gray scrubs strode out the same door that Mrs. Watson had disappeared behind.

Axel Roberts had graduated high school with me, and though I wouldn't call us best friends or anything, we had been friendly throughout our school years. He was the only person I considered a friend other than Faye. His father owned this veterinary practice before he took it over.

Axel's lips tipped up as he saw me, but the smile disappeared completely as he took in the dog.

"What happened here?" At the sound of Axel's voice, the dog lifted his chin from my shoulder, swinging his head around to look at him.

"I found him downtown in an alley."

Axle sighed and reached toward the dog, letting him sniff the back of his hand before petting his head. The dog's tail wagged, and that hint of a smile returned to Axel's lips. "Well, at least he seems in good spirits." He gestured toward the back door and turned. "Come on, let me take a look at him."

The small exam room was small but clean, and I carefully set the dog down on the tall metal table. Axel immediately got to work examining him. I stayed close even though there was a chair sitting against the wall.

"I didn't know that you were still in Cypress Falls," Axel said as he carefully checked the dog's ears and mouth.

I wasn't much for small talk, but I could make an exception for Axel. I had been avoiding everyone in Cyprus falls, including him, though he didn't deserve it.

"I didn't know that *you* were still in Cypress Falls." That wasn't exactly the truth. Annabelle, my little sister and the person currently running our family ranch, had mentioned that Axel had officially taken over his father's practice over a year ago, but last

21

time I'd talked to him in person, he'd been headed out of town. Axel was never a fan of the small town life. He'd escaped to live in a bigger city, at least for a few years after high school.

Axel glanced up at me, his blue eyes clouding over. "Yeah, well, things don't always work out the way you plan."

I wanted to ask why he had come back to this little town that had nothing to offer him. But I already knew the answer. Axel was the kind of guy who sacrificed. He always had been. I think that's why I found myself drawn to him. He was just...trustworthy. Loyal.

Annabelle said that his father was getting older. They'd had Axel late in life, and when he couldn't continue on with the practice, he'd asked Axel to come back. Axel had come, even though he had always felt trapped here.

I shifted on my feet. "I know a thing or two about the unexpected things life can throw at you."

Axel lifted his brows. "I reckon you understand that better than anyone."

I nodded, and we held each other's gaze for a moment before Axel patted the dog on the head and grabbed his stethoscope. "I know I wasn't here when it happened," he said quietly before he put this stethoscope in his ears. "But I want you to know that I never believed it. When I heard what happened to your mama, I knew you couldn't have done it."

I placed my hands on the metal table and leaned against it. Hearing those words hit deep within me, easing a fraction of my broken spirit.

"Thank you," I said, my voice thick.

We fell quiet again as Axel continued his examination.

"Well," Axel looped his stethoscope back around his neck. "He looks pretty rough, but he should pull through."

My chest eased. "He's going to be okay?"

Axel nodded. "He's obviously malnourished, but we'll give him some fluids and medication for fleas and ticks and other parasites. He doesn't seem to have any broken bones or open wounds. With some good nutrition, rest, and a good bath he'll be a whole new dog. You should be able to bring him home today."

I blinked down at the dog still curled up on the examination table. He looked so broken, thin and frail and dirty. But despite all that, his tail wagged when his wide puppy-dog eyes met mine. *Was I really going to take him home with me?* Taking in a dog was a lot of responsibility: training him, walking him, giving him the time and attention he'd need. I didn't know if I was ready for all of that.

"Unless...you don't want him?" Axel asked slowly.

I shook my head and cleared my throat. "No, no I can take him."

He could stay here at the rescue, but who was ever going to want to adopt this mangy, sick looking dog? I didn't doubt that the dogs here were well taken care of, but this dog needed to heal, and the best place for that wasn't in a kennel. I couldn't leave him here all alone.

Axel smiled. "Good."

I stayed and waited as Axel treated the dog. Mrs. Watson even gave him a good bath, and by the time Axel was finished with him, he indeed looked almost like a new dog. He was still much too skinny, but at least he was clean, and he already seemed a lot happier.

Axel brought him out walking, slowly, on a leash with his tail swishing my side to side. It seemed like that was always on the move. I smiled as I stooped down to pat his head.

"Ready to go, bud?"

The dog's mouth pulled up, almost looking like a wide grin.

"He likes you," Axel mused.

"One of the few who do, I guess." I straightened, and Axel handed me the leash.

"I'd like to see him back in about a week to make sure he's doing well. I'll have Mrs. Watson send you an email of his care instructions and food plan. We have some food here in the office that will be good for him you can take too."

I nodded, reaching to shake his hand. "Thanks."

"Don't be a stranger, Dawson," he said, taking my hand. "And I don't mean because of the dog. Maybe we could get together sometime and grab a beer."

I blinked at him, stunned. I couldn't remember the last time I'd been invited to go out for a beer. "Uh, I'll think about it."

I wasn't sure how to take it, I'd gotten so accustomed to being alone.

"You know my number." He grinned before he turned, heading toward the back again.

Mrs. Watson got me set up with everything the dog needed, albeit a little begrudgingly. Once I got the dog situated in the back seat of the Jeep again, I checked my phone one last time before heading back up to the hills and my cabin.

There was still no word from Faye.

I sent her one more message, and then I turned on the Jeep, cranking the heat more than usual. The dog was shivering in my back seat. I couldn't imagine how cold he'd been on the streets, especially at night.

As I started making the steep, precarious climb up the narrow roads to my cabin, I tried to process the events of the day. Not only had I come face to face with my estranged brother, but somehow I'd taken responsibility for a dog, of all things. I glanced at him in the back again.

"You better hope I'm making the right call here, bud. I can barely take care of myself these days, let alone another living thing."

The dog's tail thumped against the seat at my words, either totally oblivious to my earning, or simply just happy to be warm.

I sighed, and as I pulled into the drive on my property, I glanced one more time at my phone. There was still no reply from Faye. As I parked the Jeep under the car porch on the side of the cabin, I couldn't keep away the sinking feeling that something was wrong.

Chapter Three

FAYE

I PULLED MY CAR up to the gate, stomach in knots. My knuckles turned white around the steering wheel as I shifted in my seat. This day had both come so fast and not fast enough. Now that it was here, I still wasn't sure how to feel or if this was even the right choice.

All the paperwork had been filled out, though, and now all I had to do was wait. They said he'd be out quickly, but after a few minutes, I feared that this wasn't going to happen. When I was contacted six months ago by someone claiming to be my father, I hadn't believed it.

My entire life was spent fatherless. My mother was someone who cycled through men quickly, never staying with one for long before either they left her or she moved on. So much so that I'd believed she didn't know who my father was. She had never told me his name; she simply acted like he didn't exist. As if I had just appeared one day without one.

For so long I'd been envious of my little sister—my half sister technically—when she got to spend summers and some weekends with her father. We shared a mother, but had different fathers, and I never got the same escape Ellie did from Mama and her endless string of boyfriends who often treated us like trash. When I was younger, I would daydream about a man stepping into my life, claiming me as his daughter, and taking me away to live somewhere happy and peaceful.

I never expected it to happen when I was almost thirty-six. And I definitely didn't expect that man to be contacting me from a prison cell.

There was a reason my mama acted like he never existed. And it wasn't because she didn't know who he was.

When that first letter arrived at my small town clothing boutique, I thought it was a sick joke. But something nagged at me, not letting me ignore it. My mother had left Cypress Falls with some man she'd been engaged to about thirteen years ago, leaving us behind. Ellie and I weren't in contact with her, but I'd managed to find her Facebook profile after some cyber digging and was able to message her. After demanding answers, she'd confirmed it herself.

Marc Lawrence was my father. A man who had spent years behind bars, and the man who was finally getting his freedom today.

The last six months I'd slowly gotten to know this stranger who was half of me. We'd communicated through letters and phone calls and eventually, visits at the prison in person.

I jumped at sudden movement at the prison gate, snapping me out of my daze. The gate opened, and he stepped out onto the sidewalk, blinking against the bright rays of sun. Though he was well into his fifties, his salt and pepper hair was thick, and he was tall and muscular. The years in prison had worn deep lines into his

27

face, but there was still a remnant of how handsome he used to be. He had a hard, square jaw beneath the overgrown silver-streaked beard. I could see what my mother saw in him. Although, it didn't take much to charm my mother.

My father stood for a moment, his chest expanding in a deep breath as he looked up into the blue sky. He didn't have anything with him except for the dark pair of jeans that looked a size too big and the long sleeve blue shirt that was slightly too tight. He didn't even have a coat, even though it was the middle of January and unusually cold.

When he lowered his chin, his gaze snagged on my car. His lips broke out into a wide smile as he sauntered toward my vehicle. My heart thundered in my chest as he rounded my car and opened the passenger door, the winter chill blowing in making me shiver.

"Hey, Sunshine," he said, the sweet nickname making my own lips pull up. "Part of me can't even believe you showed up today."

He settled himself in the passenger seat, pulling the door closed behind him and sealing the heat back in. We'd talked about this day for months, but now that it was actually happening, it was hard to comprehend.

"Of course I came."

He'd spent fifteen years inside, and I was the only person he had left. The only person who would still speak with him, at least.

Marc, my father, smiled, his eyes sparkling. "You know, these last few months getting to know you have been such a privilege. I never had any other children." He paused. "I mean, I had a stepson at one time, but I reckon he never thought of me as a father. I'm probably not what you were expecting in a dad, but I—I'm proud to call you my daughter."

A warmth blossomed in my chest. I fiddled with the thin, gold ring on my finger, looking away as the heat rushed up my neck and into my cheeks. This wasn't how I'd imagined meeting my father would be, but still, it was surreal. I'd never thought those words would ever be spoken to me, and they lit up a dark and barren place inside me.

What my father had been convicted for wasn't a small offense. There was some nuance to it, but he'd caused the death of the woman he married after he left my mother. It had been an accident, but he'd said he'd been in a bad place back then—a different person. I believed him. The man I'd gotten to know the last six months and the man sitting beside me seemed like he couldn't hurt anyone.

People could change.

"Thank you." I didn't know what else to say to convey how much it meant to me.

Marc reached over and patted my hand, sending a gentle jolt of surprise and warmth coursing through me. His touch carried a mixture of tenderness and a quiet reassurance. There was an unspoken acknowledgment of all that had been missed, and a sense of belonging filled the spaces within me that I hadn't even known were empty.

"I've missed so much, Sunshine, I know that. I want to make up for every moment I wasn't there."

I cleared my throat against the lump of emotion constricting it.

"We have plenty of time now," I said. I shifted into drive, peeking over at him as I raised a brow. "Are you ready to go?"

He nodded and reached for his seatbelt. His gaze caught one more at the gates and the expansive prison beyond it. "I've never been more ready to go anywhere else in my entire life."

29

THE DOOR TO MY upstairs apartment creaked like always as I opened it. The familiar scent of cinnamon and peonies met my nose when I walked inside. My heart was still racing as Marc entered behind me. I couldn't believe my father was inside my home.

It was a bit awkward, but I didn't feel...unsafe. Though I truly believed Marc, there was a place in me that was nervous to let him in my home. I'd done some extensive research in his case and spoken with his counselors and officers at the prison and they had nothing but good things to say about him, confirming what I'd gotten to know about him.

This was risk, but he was my family. I was all he had left and I couldn't walk away from my own father.

He glanced around the space, which wasn't anything impressive. The one-bedroom apartment sat right on top of my boutique. I hung my keys next to the door as we stepped into the small but tidy kitchen that was open to the living room. It had one bedroom off to the side and one bathroom. The perfect size for one person, and I had grown fond of decorating the space and making it feel homey and cozy.

Marc stepped farther into the room, his eyes snagging on the gray sectional that was made up with sheets and comfy pillows for him to sleep on. A vase of fresh pink flowers was sitting on the coffee table. I had bought an assortment of travel size toiletries that were neatly placed on top of a pile of folded blankets and a towel.

A smile pulled up the side of Marc's lip. "You spoil me," he mused. "You know, I don't want you to feel forced to let me stay here. I can always get a hotel or something."

I crossed through the kitchen and put a hand on my hip.

"What hotel are you going to get in Cypress Falls?" I asked, raising a brow. Cypress Falls was small, nestled along the Blue Cypress River in Northern Alabama. There were no hotels within a thirty mile radius. The small motel downtown wasn't exactly the best accommodations, either, and had seen better days. I wouldn't make him stay there.

Marc waved a hand. "Oh, I'd figured it out."

I shook my head. "Don't be silly. You're more than welcome to stay here for as long as you like. Besides, we have a lot of time to make up for, remember?"

My father nodded, and he looked away. But not before I glimpsed the sheen of tears misting over his eyes. "Thank you," he said. He coughed to cover the quiver in his voice. He turned toward the windows that looked out over Main Street, peeking out of the tall panes that let in ample amounts of sunlight.

I placed a hand on my chest over my heart welling with emotions. "You don't have to thank me."

Marc shifted on his feet and nodded. He cleared his throat, changing the subject. "So, the store you own is on the first floor?"

"I've been in business for almost five years now."

When I first started the small boutique, I never imagined that I would fall so much in love with it. Fashion was always something I enjoyed, though growing up we didn't have a lot of money for clothes. I remember scouring the racks at thrift stores and finding hidden treasures in certain pieces.

The boutique was really an experiment at first; a way to use my degree in business and marketing and to try my hand at something I'd always thought would be fun. It wasn't easy by any means, but it was rewarding beyond what I expected.

I never imagined that after five years I'd be designing my own graphic tees and have a thriving little shop of handpicked clothing that brought me so much joy.

I approached my father and glanced out the window at the quaint and quiet streets of Cypress Falls; a place I'd once been so excited to leave and get away from growing up, now held a special space in my heart.

A delivery truck was sitting on the street below us, and the warm and fuzzy feeling in my stomach disappeared like a sinking stone.

"Oh my God," I hissed, glancing at my watch.

I turned and grabbed the compact planner sitting open on my desk, groaning. It wasn't like me at all to forget something like delivery day. I'd been so distracted, it slipped my mind completely what day it even was.

"You okay, Sunshine?" Marc asked, shooting me a concerned glance.

"I am so sorry." The planner flopped onto the desk as I put it down, anger at myself surging through me. "I have to run down to the shop real quick. I have a shipment coming in today."

Marc glanced back at the truck and then at me. "Do you need some help?"

"No, I got it." I didn't have to pull out the inventory today. It just needed to be dropped off. "It'll only take me a few minutes."

"All right, then. Give me a holler if you change your mind."

I gave him a smile and rushed to the door. As I hurried down the steep steps to the first floor, I silently scolded myself again for being so distracted. I never forgot about delivery days. I had written it down.

Then again, I never closed the shop in the middle of a work day, either. That hadn't been part of the plan.

My sister Ellie used to work for me sometimes, but since she became a full-time author, she couldn't make working for me fit into her schedule. It was difficult for me to delegate—and give up control—especially to someone I didn't know extremely well. So, I hadn't taken the time to find someone to replace her.

I flew through the back door of the Southern Sunshine boutique, the soft sounds of gentle knocking making me pick up my speed.

How long has he been knocking on my door waiting to drop off my inventory?

Guilt grew inside my chest as I ran through the small but trendy shop. Racks of dresses and shoes and purses were on display in every usable nook and cranny. Everywhere I looked were pieces of merchandise that I'd personally selected for the way they inspired me in some way.

The color palette was neutral, yet unique, with handmade macramé on the walls and natural wood grain display tables. I didn't want to be just another shop, but I wanted to give my customers an experience when they shopped here. A vibe.

A vibe I couldn't enjoy much right now as I skidded to a halt near the front of the shop.

Through the glass door, a man was standing with his hands cupped over his eyes as he glanced into the dark interior, his boyish, handsome face screwed up in confusion. He was tall, his chest and arms almost too muscular looking for a delivery man. When his eyes met mine, he blinked, his face clearing. I stared at him apologetically as I unlocked the door.

The cold air blew in, ruffling my hair and making me glad I hadn't had time to take off my jacket yet.

"Is everything okay?" He frowned at me with concern as he stepped inside, pulling a dolly loaded with boxes in.

"Yes!" I said, my breath heavy from running all the way down here. "I'm so sorry, Julian."

He paused inside the door as I let it fall shut. His cheeks were pink from the cold, making me feel bad again for making him wait for me out there.

"I was trying to call you, but you didn't answer your phone," he said, pulling out his cell phone from his pocket.

I stared at the phone, eyes widening. "Oh my God." I slapped a palm against my forehead. "I totally forgot I left my phone in my room all day today."

Forgetfulness was becoming the theme of the day, making me feel even more off.

Julian blinked at me, then he shook his head as pocketed the phone. "Shocker. You need to get better at that. I was worried. I don't remember the last time you closed the shop in the middle of the day."

I crossed my arms over my chest. I didn't love having my phone on me all day. It probably wasn't the best idea, since I used it for work often, but that's exactly why I didn't like having it with me twenty-four seven. It was always going off with emails and social media notifications, and I didn't need the constant distraction. I preferred paper, which was why I often carried around my planner rather than my phone. But even that I'd left at home today.

"Today has been...overwhelming."

Julian tilted his head to the side. He wasn't originally from Cypress Falls. He was fairly new to town, still a bit of an outsider, but he'd been delivering for me the past year and a half. We'd become good friends in that time. I wanted to be as welcoming to new people as possible, and Julian was nice, open, and always wanting to talk.

"What aren't you telling me?" he asked with a knowing stare.

I shifted on my feet. "Nothing."

He narrowed his eyes. "If I know anything about you, it's that you're a bad liar."

"Well, I..." I didn't know why I was so nervous about saying the words out loud. "I picked up my father today."

His eyes widened as understanding set in. "Seriously?"

I nodded.

"I didn't realize that was today." Julian stepped closer, placing a heavy hand on my shoulder. "Did you...pick him up from the prison? All by yourself?"

"Yeah." It embarrassed me how small my voice sounded.

My father wasn't the first person I'd visited from prison, or the first person I welcomed back into my life after being behind bars. But it was different this time. Dawson had been innocent when he was put behind bars those few years. I couldn't say the same about Marc.

Julian's hand tightened on my shoulder. "That's...a lot, Faye."

It was. Julian had been the only person besides Ellie who I confided in about Marc. I hadn't meant to tell him, exactly. He had been dropping off a delivery shortly after I'd received confirmation that Marc was really my father.

My mother still wasn't in the area any longer, thank God, but she'd finally called me after I'd pestered her and left her numerous messages about Marc. She'd called me on the boutique's phone to tell me the truth. Julian had walked in on me bawling my eyes out. It had been extremely embarrassing, but luckily no one else had been in the store at the time. I'd needed someone to spill my overwhelming feelings to about learning that a man who'd been in prison for years was my real father, and Julian was simply in the right place at the right time. That's the only reason why he knew about today and who my father was. Other than my sister, I'd kept this news quiet.

"I know," I said, biting my lip. "It's a lot but I think that maybe this will be a good thing. I have always wanted to know him. Maybe this is my chance."

Something flashed across his face, but it was gone in a moment. "Where is he?"

"Upstairs."

His jewel green eyes flicked up toward the ceiling. "Right now?"

"As we speak." I hoped he was okay up there by himself. He wasn't a child, but this was a whole new environment. A whole new life.

"Aren't you...nervous to be alone with him?"

I had thought about this before I decided to take him into my home. Marc had done bad things in his past—very bad things—but he had done his time. He had never been in trouble in the prison, and they had nothing but good things to say about him. Wasn't that the whole point of being in prison, anyway? Rehabilitation?

"I can't judge people for the things they've done in the past. Especially not when they've paid for it." I shrugged. "I don't know how to explain it but...I just have a good feeling about him."

Julian ran a hand through his thick, wavy hair. "You're a better person than I am."

"No." I shook my head. "I'm not."

He glanced back up at the ceiling, a muscle popping in his jaw. "Just be careful, okay?"

"Thanks, but I'm a big girl." His concern was sweet, though. "I don't want to throw the time I get with him away. I've gone my whole life wondering who my father was... This is my chance."

Julian sighed. "I get it." He reached for the dolly again. "I'll just put these in the back and be on my way. You enjoy your time with your dad."

Your dad. Hearing that had my stomach flipping. I'd never had a dad, and the thought always startled me. "I will."

Julian finished up and dropped the boxes off in the back stockroom. He gave one last goodbye, and I locked the door behind him when he left, watching him load the dolly into his delivery truck before hopping in the driver's seat.

When he was gone, I turned and I ran up the stairs two at a time back to my apartment. I skidded to a halt in front of my door, trying to catch my breath before I opened it. Marc was sitting on the couch, and he glanced up at me curiously. He cocked his head to the side.

"Everything all right?"

I nodded and held up a finger. "I forgot that my phone has been charging in my room all day," I said, before heading to the door on the left-hand side of the living room.

Sure enough, there my phone was, sitting on my nightstand with the tiny light in the corner blinking incessantly as if scolding me for leaving it behind yet again.

I pulled off the charger and unlocked the phone. It had been a long time since I'd left my phone for so long. My heart skittered as I opened my text messages and missed calls. I had a few unimportant ones, but my eyes immediately latched onto his name.

Dawson Evans. He had texted and called a couple times. I bit down on my lip.

Dawson was probably the one person besides my sister who I would stop anything for and help. We'd been friends for a long time, and have been through so much together.

Yet, I was keeping a secret from him.

37

I hadn't told him about finding my father. I hadn't breathed a word to him about what I was up to today.

It was a weight on my shoulders the past six months. I spoke to Dawson almost every day, but I didn't know he would react to this new development in my life. Part of me was afraid to know. Dawson could be quite...protective of me.

I opened a new text message and typed a quick reply.

Sorry, I forgot my phone. A lot has been going on today. Can I bring you dinner later?

It was barely sent before his reply came in.

Sure.

I stared at the one word answer, waiting for him to bombard me with questions about what I had been doing and where I'd gone. He'd obviously noticed that the store was closed by his earlier messages. I hadn't expected him to be in town today. He wasn't here often.

I pocketed the phone and went back out into the living room. Marc was still sitting on the couch. I glanced at the TV, which was off.

"You're welcome to watch something, if you like," I offered.

He smiled. "I kinda like the quiet."

"All right," I said, shrugging as I headed toward the kitchen. "Well, if you don't mind, I would like to get dinner started."

"Faye," he said, sounding exasperated. "You've done enough. You do not need to cook."

I waved a hand at him dismissively. "I don't mind cooking."

I slid off my ring and placed it on the small jewelry dish by the sink. My grandmother's ring was nothing but a cheap green stone set in a gold-plated band that had little roses carved into it. I was glad it hadn't been worth anything so Mama let me keep it after she passed when I was ten. Grandma was more of mother to me than Mama ever was and used to watch me when I was little. So the ring was special. I always took it off before I cooked or did dishes so that it wouldn't tarnish.

Marc tried to argue again, but I turned and put up a hand. "Please, I have everything I need to make dinner. I like cooking, anyway."

Marc continued to frown at me, but then he nodded, giving up. "Fine, but at least let me help."

He stood from the couch and walked into the kitchen. I wanted to argue that I didn't need help, but it would give us both something to do.

As we made dinner, we talked. A lot of the nervousness left my system as my father and I worked together, peeling potatoes and mixing together ingredients. It had been a long time since I'd cooked for anyone but myself, or sometimes Dawson, and there was a sense of belonging between the two of us that I hadn't felt before.

Marc wasn't the father I had imagined, but maybe he was the father that I needed.

I GRIPPED THE STEERING wheel, my knuckles blanching as I realized that I'd forgotten my ring on the jewelry dish.

This day just kept getting better. Not only was I exhausted from the day, now I had to drive through a damn rain storm without my emotional support ring.

I'd been in a hurry to leave after having a nice dinner with Marc, because it had started raining. Of course. Halfway up the hill toward Dawson's cabin it really started to come down, the rain turning to a mixture of water and sleet the farther up I traveled. Pulling in a deep, even breath, I tried to get my nerves under control. Driving in the pitch darkness and the rain had my nerves on edge, but so did the fact that I needed to face Dawson and fill him in on everything I was keeping from him.

The winding road was barely a road at all. I drove slow and steady, ascending up the hill that felt more like a mountainside. I decelerated, rounding another sharp bend in the treacherous path that became even more craggy as I ascended higher than any other homestead on the hill. Dawson had built his cabin as far away as possible from the small town, somehow without leaving it completely.

He was funny, needing to get away, but staying close enough to his family to be there at the drop of a hat. It was a good thing, though. His father had gotten into a horrible accident last year, and he'd needed to be with him in the hospital a while. He had his issues with his family—especially his brother—but he loved them with everything he had, even if it hard for him to show it.

I gnawed at my lip so hard I almost broke the skin as my windshield wipers worked on overdrive. Rain and sleet pelted my windshield making it almost impossible to see. My nose wrinkled against the smell of the meatloaf and mashed potatoes that filled the small cab of my sedan from the backseat. The leftovers from our delicious dinner, but my stomach churned against the meal sitting my stomach like a rock.

My anxiety finally dialed down a notch as I recognized a hollowed-out tree trunk near another sharp curve. I was close now, and I yearned to be out of this car and off of this stupid road and in the comfort of the cabin. My foot pushed harder on the gas as the curve started to straighten out, more than ready to be done with this drive.

That's when it happened.

The doe came out of nowhere, a streak of ghostwhite in my headlights as I slammed on the brakes. I shouldn't have done it, but it was as if I had no control as I jerked the wheel to swerve out of the way. It wasn't much of a motion, but it didn't matter. The moment my arms moved, I started spinning.

Chapter Four

FAYE

ONE MOMENT, MY VEHICLE was careening out of my control and the next, a shuddering crash that rattled my bones. The horn blared, piercing my ears as a burst of pain erupted on the side of my head. My heart rammed against my ribs, and I blinked as the world around me flickered out before gradually coming back into focus.

Oh my God.

Freezing cold air blew against my skin. My arms trembled, one hand was covering my head, like I'd reflexively tried to protect it, while still gripping the steering wheel for dear life as my eyes surveyed my body. My head did hurt dully, but in the dim light inside the cab of my car, I didn't see any blood.

A relieved breath escaped me as I glanced out the windshield. Nothing but trees surrounded me, branches pressed right up against the glass. The doe was nowhere, but neither was the road. I closed my eyes for a brief moment, trying to comprehend what had happened. Thankfully, I hadn't spun off the side of the hill.

This high up, the drop was steep and deadly. My pulse raced, pumping adrenaline through me. I winced as the horn continued to blare, making it even harder to focus.

"Faye!"

My name was a panicked cry, sounding strange and foreign in the familiar voice. A voice that was always calm, no matter the situation.

Dawson.

He was suddenly at my window, reaching right through and touching my cheek. A light flashed in his other hand, and I squinted against the brightness. I hadn't realized until now that the window's glass was completely gone. Shattered. Little drops of icey rain hit my cheeks.

His eyes were almost black in darkness. "Faye, are you okay?"

I drew in a shaky breath, trying to make my brain function through the shock. "I'm okay." I was almost certain that I was, and the wild look on his face made me want to assure him.

His hand moved to my chin as he cupped it carefully and lifted my face to meet him square in the eye. "Does anything hurt?"

I blinked, finding it difficult to concentrate. "My head...just a little."

His jaw hardened. "Can you tell me where? Does your neck hurt?"

I lifted a hand and gingerly touched the side of my head. It was tender, but wasn't bleeding. "Right here. And no, my neck doesn't hurt."

"Look at me," he instructed.

I listened immediately as he moved his flashlight over to my right eye. I squinted, but he barked at me to keep my eyes open and on him. He looked so...serious. More so than usual. His gaze was deep and assessing as he moved the flashlight back and forth in my right eye, and then my left.

"You're positive your neck doesn't hurt?" he asked again.

"Yes."

He lowered the flashlight and reluctantly pulled back, releasing my chin. He stared down at the driver's side door, inspecting it with a grimace. I realized for the first time that he'd been leaning into the car at an angle. There was a massive tree trunk blocking most of the door.

"You're wedged in there pretty good." He jerked his head toward the other side of the car. "You're surrounded by the trees. I couldn't get to the other side at all."

I glanced at the thick trunk my door was molded around. I wasn't sure how I'd managed to spin right into the forest of trees relatively unscathed, but I gave my gratitude to the old tree and prayed that I hadn't done it much damage.

My eyes met Dawson's again. "I can climb out the window."

"I'll help you."

It wasn't a question, and he didn't wait for permission before he leaned in through the window.

I unbuckled my seatbelt, and the horn finally sputtered and died out. "Thank God," I whispered, my ears ringing.

"Be careful," Dawson warned as I pulled my legs up. My muscles were sore, and I winced as I shifted myself up toward the window. "What hurts?"

"I'm fine."

"Like hell you are."

His long arms wrapped around me, and he basically pulled me out of the window all on his own. I didn't fight him as he hooked an arm under my knees and cradled me against his chest. I barely felt the rain and sleet falling, slowly soaking my clothes.

Despite the cold, heat crawled up my skin, blooming on my cheeks as his smell enveloped me: the scent of woodsmoke and pine and spice. The comforting smell had my tight muscles easing, though I couldn't stop my shaking completely.

"I can walk," I mumbled, not at all wanting him to let me go.

"So can I."

Dawson didn't let me go as he trekked uphill, somehow managing to hold the flashlight and myself.

It was hard to see through the dark and the rain, but we managed by the single beam of light. I'd spun a good way off the road. I shuddered as we made it back to where I'd swerved away from the doe. Deep tire marks grooved the dirt.

"What the hell were you doing?" Dawson hissed, as he rushed us toward his cabin.

I winced as he jostled me, a deep, pulsing ache building inside my head where I'd hit it. "What do you think? I was taking you dinner. It's not my fault the deer got in the way."

"You hit a deer?"

"No. I hit a tree."

He growled. "I texted you not to come. I left a voice message, too. It's not safe for you to drive all the way up here in the rain when it's dark."

My stomach flipped. I'd left my phone at home with Marc. On purpose this time. He didn't have a phone or anything like that yet, and I didn't want to leave him stranded at my apartment without one.

"I forgot my phone," I lied.

Dawson shook his head back and forth. "I have no idea what I'm going to do with you."

He slowed as the dim outdoor light of the cabin came into view. Relief hit me, my skin numb from the icy rain.

45

I squirmed in his arms as he approached the beautiful wrap-around porch. Only a couple years old, the cabin had a modern yet rustic appeal. Its cedar façade emitted a warm glow against the backdrop of towering pines. Glimpses of the cozy interior peeked through the oversized windows.

"Let me down. We're here."

"Not until I get a look at you in some good lighting."

I sighed, not having the energy, or desire, to argue with him.

He ascended the steps of the porch, barely pausing as he stuffed the flashlight in his pocket and opened the cabin door with me firmly in his arms.

Walking inside was like walking into a warm bath. The heat from the wood stove in the back corner instantly seeped into my skin and through my wet clothes. I hadn't realized just how cold I was.

The cabin was a decent size, not too big or too small. Dawson carried me across the threshold and straight to the open concept kitchen on the left side. He flicked on every overhead light in the space and then sat me right on top of the island countertop.

"What are you doing?" I squirmed against the cold granite under me.

Dawson stayed close, taking my chin again and forcing me to look up into his face. There wasn't a glimmer of a smile there. Nothing but his serious, set mouth and assessing stare.

"Taking a look at you," he said, his voice low.

I pulled in a deep breath as he brought his other hand up, cradling my face as he slowly, carefully ran them up my jaw and cheek until they crept up into my hair. I winced as his fingers ran along the sore spot on the side of my head.

His eyes flashed, the dark brown smoldering like embers. "You got a nasty knot, Faye," he grumbled, tilting his head to inspect the spot more thoroughly.

"I'm fine," I insisted.

"You'd say that even if you weren't."

I rolled my eyes. It was probably true.

"Any vision changes?"

"No."

"Nausea?"

"No."

He finally seemed satisfied and moved on from my head, running his hands down my neck and to my shoulders. My skin prickled as he felt his way down both my arms. His touch was tender, but thorough as he inspected. His closeness, and the fact that his hands were literally all over me, had my heart rate kicking up again.

Dawson and I had always been friends, but...he wasn't exactly the worst looking guy. It was no secret that he was handsome. Tall and muscular with that stupid sharp jaw that could cut glass and the most beautiful, luscious dark hair I'd ever seen on a man.

But I didn't do romance. It was something I'd decided a long time ago.

I bit my lip, my stomach pitching as he took both my hands in his, pulling them close to his face.

"What are you doing?" I blurted out again, my voice embarrassingly high pitched.

He paused, his eyes flicking up to meet mine. "I'm checking to make sure you don't have any more injuries."

I cleared my throat. "I don't."

"No?" He raised a brow. His gaze went back to my hands. He held both of them, my palms up, out right between us. "What is that then?"

I sucked in a sharp breath as he flipped my hands over, displaying a deep gouge on the back of my left hand.

"Yikes," I breathed.

"The adrenaline masks the pain."

I winced. *Great.*

Without more explanation he went back to inspecting. His fingers ran down my sides, barely touching me, but the ghost of his touch had me shuddering anyway.

"Do your ribs hurt?" he asked, his forehead wrinkling in concern.

An embarrassed flush crawled up my neck again, and I looked away, fixing my stare on the living room wall on the back, opposite side of the space. There was a large painting hung there that I'd always loved. It was of these very hills the cabin was on, as seen from a distance as if the artist was looking up from the town of Cypress Falls.

"Just...a bit sore," I confessed.

"It doesn't hurt when you breathe, doesn't it?"

I shook my head, instantly regretting it as my head pulsed with a pain I tried really hard not to show on my face.

When he seemed satisfied that my ribs weren't fractured, he moved on, slowly and gently making his way down to my legs, as if making sure they definitely weren't broken, either. They were not.

"See? I'm still all in one piece."

He scowled. "Luckily. You very easily could be in much worse shape."

I stifled a chill. The sight of my car broken and bent between those trees would haunt my dreams.

"Don't move," Dawson said, and before I could ask why, he was gone.

He rushed up the staircase opposite the kitchen, taking the wooden steps two at a time. There wasn't much up on the second level, two bedrooms and a bathroom. I almost never saw him go up there because the main bedroom was on the first floor.

A couple minutes later, barreled back down with what looked like a large duffel bag.

He started back toward me, placing the bag on the counter beside me.

"What is that?"

His brows narrowed as he unzipped the bag and opened the stop flap. "My first aid kit."

My mouth fell open as I gawked at all the medical supplies. The thing was packed with sterile, crinkly packages of everything you could think of: gauze, bandages, alcohol wipes, and other things I couldn't identify off the top of my head.

"That's the most intense first aid kit I've ever seen."

He frowned. "It's a long way to the hospital from here. You never know what can happen, I like to be prepared."

Obviously. I couldn't believe I'd never seen that bag before, I was over at least once every week or two. Maybe it was a good thing that I hadn't, though.

"Did you learn how to use all of that during your medic training?" I asked, intrigued.

He started pulling out packages here and there. "Most of it, yes."

It felt like ages since he'd left for training in the army, but also like it was just yesterday. When we graduated from high school, we'd gone our separate ways for a few years. I'd gone to college down in Tuscaloosa, and he ended up moving to Texas for a while. I was excited to finally get away from my mother and he was excited to join the army as a medic. It was something he'd always been interested in, serving in the armed forces and getting away from Cypress Falls and his family name and making a life for himself.

49

We'd always kept in touch those long few years. I was so proud of him when he finished his medic training.

He hadn't gotten to do too much else, though. He hadn't served long before he'd been asked to come home and help with the ranch. He'd left the army as soon as he completed his contract, even though he originally planned to continue. Part of me was thankful he'd come home sooner rather than later, but I knew he was always disappointed he hadn't gotten to serve longer.

"Put this on your head." Dawson jolted me out of my thoughts, holding a cold pack out to me.

I took it, placing it against the pulsing bump on the side of my head.

"Do you ever miss it?" I asked.

He ripped open some kind of single-use wipe. "Miss what?"

"Being a part of the army. Being far away from here."

His eyes met mine, and something stirred behind them. "Sometimes."

He began swiping the cut with the wipe, and I tensed, expecting a cold sharp sting. While the wipe was cold, it didn't sting like alcohol.

"Sorry," he said. "I need to get this cleaned out and make sure there isn't any glass in it."

The pain was more in my head than anything, and I nodded. He made swift work of cleaning out the gash.

"I don't think you need stitches," Dawson said as he carefully bandaged the wound. "But you need to keep it clean, okay?"

"Okay."

When he finished, he stepped back. I instantly missed his warmth. It hadn't taken him much time to clean and bandage me up, and I realized we were both still wearing soaking wet clothes.

I shivered.

Dawson's frown deepened.

"You need to keep those bandages dry."

I raised my hands, holding them awkwardly away from my body so they didn't touch my clothes.

He sighed. "No, you need to take those clothes off."

"Excuse me?" I scoffed, narrowing my eyes at him. "It's not very gentlemanly to ask a lady to take her clothes off." I tried to sound light, but his statement made my stomach flip.

He rolled his eyes. "You're shivering. I'll go get you something to wear, and you can change...in the bathroom."

He was of course simply being practical.

Dawson had been in my life since we were in middle school. At that time, I was constantly being picked on because of the reputation my mama had around town and for being dirt poor. Dawson had stepped up and defended me one day, seemingly out of the blue. I wasn't sure why he'd done it, he was rich and handsome and everything that I wasn't. Yet he stuck by me and the bullying died down until it stopped completely. But he'd done more than chase off some school bullies...he'd made me feel less alone.

Sometimes, being close with someone like Dawson made things...complicated. Because right now, after he pulled me from the wreckage of my car and carried me back to safety, my heart was fluttering in a dangerous way that had my defenses on alert. Which was weird, because he was my friend and I hadn't felt something like that for him in a long time. But a lot had happened today already and maybe I *had* hit my head way too hard.

A long time ago, Dawson and I had made a deal. We promised each other that we'd only ever be friends. Nothing more, nothing less. I intended to keep that promise, no matter what.

Friendship was something that lasted—it meant something. Even though Dawson was undeniably handsome, there was a firm line that we never crossed.

I could admire when a man was good looking, even kiss them on occasion if I felt the urge, but I'd rather be alone forever than let any guy into my heart.

Even Dawson Evans.

Chapter Five

FAYE

Sixteen Years Old

MY HANDS CLENCHED AROUND the opened paperback book as something shattered inside the house. They weren't killing each other, though it sounded like it. Mama and the new "love of her life" had been screaming at each other for over an hour now, and I hoped it would end soon. Not even Jane Austen could distract me from the chaos.

My mama screeched something intelligible, and my teeth sunk into my lower lip. At least Ellie was off with Ty and Knox and far away from this tiny, crappy house and all the fighting. I glanced at my watch, my stomach sinking.

Dawson was late.

We'd planned on going to the movies earlier, and he was supposed to pick me up over fifteen minutes ago. Of course he was late tonight, of all nights. I needed to be far away from this house too.

My ears perked as an ominous silence settled inside. Holding my breath that maybe they were finally done, the front door was suddenly yanked open. I startled as Carl, Mama's current boyfriend, stumbled out cursing onto the porch. A lit cigarette almost down to the butt dangled from his lips.

I pulled my legs up onto the lawn chair where I sat, training my gaze on my book, though I watched his every move through the corner of my eye.

He patted his pants pockets, mumbling obscenities under his breath directed at my mother. I prayed that she wasn't about to come out and continue the drama on the front porch for the world to see. The town already had enough opinions about her, they didn't need any more fuel.

Carl's eyes caught on me, doing a double-take as if he hadn't noticed I was sitting a foot beside him. His lip curled in a grimace as he found the carton of cigarettes deep in his pocket and pulled one out.

"Your mama is a crazy bitch, ya know that?" He shook his head, replacing the carton and grabbing the lighter from his shirt pocket.

My eyes flicked from my book, meeting him directly for the first time. "Funny, that's not what you said when you shared her bed last night."

My eyes widened at my own words. I wasn't sure what made me say them, but it was true. Carl had been around for a few months, and he and Mama were embarrassingly loud in the bedroom. Ellie and I had to sleep with headphones on these days.

Carl froze, his beady eyes narrowing on me. He took out the lit cigarette butt still pinched between his lips and pointed it toward me. "Your mama is passin' on her smart mouth, I see."

He flicked the smoldering butt in my direction. It landed on the thigh of my jeans, and I dropped my book on the ground as I hurried to brush it off. It had already singed a tiny hole in the fabric. My heart dropped. These were my favorite pair of jeans. It had taken me months of constant thrift shopping to find just the right pair.

My eyes misted over as I glared back up at Carl. I hated him. I hated all the good for nothing men my mother brought into our house. All they did was say they loved her when she opened her legs and then treated her like crap in the morning.

Carl chucked low as he lit the new cigarette. "You keep that up, and you'll never be able to keep a man."

My teeth clenched. "Maybe I don't want one," I spat.

Carl laughed again, louder this time. The sound grated on my nerves, making me flinch. He took a long drag, and before he could open his vile mouth again, a black pickup turned the corner onto our street.

Relief hit me, but it didn't ease the deep ache in the pit of my stomach. I grabbed my book up off the ground and bolted, putting as much distance between me and Carl as possible. I hurried to the end of our front yard, my toes teetering on the curb as Dawson pulled the truck up and slowed.

I didn't wait for him to make a complete stop before I yanked open the door and climbed inside.

"Whoa," Dawson said at my hasty appearance.

"Just go," I said, embarrassed how thick with emotion my voice sounded as I secured my seatbelt.

"What's wrong?"

I shook my head, forcing my gaze straight ahead out the windshield, highly aware that Carl was standing on the porch, watching.

Dawson didn't press, and as he continued driving down the street, my tight chest eased the farther away we became.

I didn't notice we'd arrived at the tiny, local movie theater until Dawson parked and said my name. I blinked, glancing around the small parking lot filled with vehicles. We were already so late for the movie, I didn't know if there was a point in trying to go anymore.

"Faye," Dawson said my name again, and I looked at him. His face was pinched in worry.

"Where were you?" I asked, voice sharp.

It wasn't Dawson's fault that I'd been ambushed by Carl, but a part of me wanted to put blame anywhere but myself. If Dawson had been on time, I would've been here instead of there.

Dawson's lips thinned. He scrubbed the back of his neck. "One of the horses got out of the pasture and we needed all hands on deck to get him wrangled back in."

My heart sank, and I closed my eyes briefly. Of course he was just helping out at the ranch, like always. "Oh," was the only thing I managed to reply, opening my eyes again.

Dawson's brows furrowed as he studied me. "I'm really sorry for being so late," he said.

I shook my head. "It's fine. Family is more important."

Dawson's warm hand reached for mine, gently squeezing it. "I want to make something clear, Faye," he said, voice low. "What you and I have is something special. You're my best friend. We might not share blood, but I consider you family, too."

I swallowed against the lump in my throat, nodding. He was the only person besides Ellie that I was close to. My best friend. My family. Did there really have to be a difference between the two?

I let out a long, heavy breath and leaned toward him, resting my forehead against his chest. He let go of my hand and slowly rubbed my back. I closed my eyes, melting into his comfort. His steadiness.

Dawson had a way of making me feel so...cared for. Protected. Sometimes, when we were close like this, there was a tiny flutter in my heart...an inkling of something that I never dared to acknowledge.

If there was one thing I'd learned from my homelife, it was that romance was temporary. I'd seen that displayed for me my whole life with my mother. Love like that wasn't real. Friendship was real. Friendship lasted. The thought of ever losing Dawson...I wasn't sure if I'd survive that.

"You gonna tell me what upset you?" Dawson asked, his voice rumbling low in his chest.

I exhaled, forcing myself to pull back from his warmth. His hand stayed on my back, not letting me go too far.

"It's nothing," I said, shaking my head. He didn't need the details of how small a man could make me feel. How insignificant.

And knowing Dawson, he'd probably go right back there and punch Carl's face in. As much I liked the idea of seeing Carl in pain, I wouldn't put Dawson in that situation.

Dawson frowned, not convinced. "Faye—"

I held my hand up, cutting him off. "Can you promise me something, Dawson?"

He stared at me, but then he sighed, relenting. "Promise what?"

I curled my hand into a fist, keeping up my pinky finger and holding it out to him. "Promise me that we'll always stay friends. Best friends. Nothing more, nothing less."

"Nothing more?" he said, sounding confused. "What do you mean?"

Of course he'd be confused. I wasn't telling him about stupid Carl and how much I hated men like that and most of all, I wasn't telling him about the tiny flutter in my heart. The flutter that I didn't trust. The flutter I would ignore until it died completely.

I shoved my pinky closer. "I don't care if we've never felt anything not platonic between the two of us. I just need you to promise that this won't be anything more than it is right now. We're friends. *Family*. Promise me nothing will ever change."

It was very important to me to know that Dawson would never leave me. No matter what, I wouldn't ever become like my mama, always looking for love, but never keeping it. No matter how much my heart fluttered in the presence of a guy, I wouldn't ever look for romance. I didn't need it.

Not if I had Dawson.

His stare focused on my little finger, the confusion lingered in his eyes, mixing with a smidge of worry, but he didn't push me on it. Instead, he wrapped his around mine, squeezing tight.

"I promise."

Chapter Six

DAWSON

Present Day

I COLLAPSED ONTO THE couch, tired to my very bones. Blowing out a long breath, I glanced down at the seat next to me where the dog lifted his head from the fuzzy blanket he was buried in and yawned.

He hadn't made a peep the entire time. Not when the sound of Faye's horn blaring through the quiet night made me immediately jump up and run out of the cabin, heart hammering. Not when I'd burst back in through the door, carrying an injured Faye in my arms. He hadn't even moved while Faye and I changed into warm clothes.

If you didn't know he was half snuggled under the blanket, you probably wouldn't have even noticed he was here. He was pretty chill for a dog. And I think he was also exhausted, soaking up his recovery time in a warm place with a roof over his head.

I patted him on the head, and his tail thumped against the couch. It was interesting how the simple act of petting something soft and warm could calm you. I'd forgotten that effect dogs had on humans.

"Oh my God. Dawson, is that a *puppy?*"

The sound of her voice made me look up. I'd been waiting for her to change and finish in the bathroom. Now, she stood there in the living room, staring down at the dog with round, bright eyes.

My breath hitched. Her dark, shoulder-length hair had almost dried, giving it a slight wavy texture. She wasn't wearing a smidge of makeup, but she didn't need it. Her pale skin was flawless and smooth, her lips narrow and perfectly shaped. I'd given her one of my shirts and a pair of sweats to wear. She'd tied the shirt up stylishly on one side and pulled the sweats high on her waist. Even though they were way too big for her, she managed to make them look good. Really good, actually.

I shook my head, wanting to knock away unwanted thoughts about how amazing she looked in my clothes. Since getting released from the nightmare of prison, I had thought my feelings for Faye would go back to normal. Most of the time, it was easy to slip back into our usual friendship. But those feelings that had stirred up during those years locked away were hard to forget.

I cleared my throat. "How's your head?"

No matter how distracting her looks were, I couldn't forget what had happened a mere hour ago. Her superficial cuts and bruises didn't worry me as much as her head injury. It didn't seem too serious, but I was concerned about a concussion at the very least.

Faye's nose wrinkled as she rolled her eyes. "It's fine," she said, for what seemed like the thousandth time. She stepped closer to the couch, falling to her knees to be eye-level with the dog. She cradled his face in both of her hands. "Now, where did you get this sweet little thing? Why didn't you tell me you had a puppy?"

I shifted on my seat, eyeing the dog who looked like he was in heaven as Faye cooed and stroked him lovingly. His tail was in overdrive.

"He's not really a puppy anymore."

She gave me a side-eye. "Every dog is a puppy, Dawson," she corrected me. "Where did he come from?"

She leaned in and kissed the dog on the snout. He made a pleased little yip of delight as he pushed his nose closer to her. He looked absolutely smitten. I couldn't blame him.

"He found me while I was in town today. He didn't have a home, and I couldn't get him to go away."

She lifted a brow, scratching the dog behind the ears. "So you took him in?"

"I couldn't leave him there. It's freezing and he looks like he's been through enough."

She dragged her hand down his protruding backbone and pressed her lips together. "He does look thin. Is he all right?"

"He will be. I took him to Axel. He said he'll be back to a healthy weight in a few weeks if I follow his directions."

"Good." A small, relieved smile pulled at her mouth. "What's his name?"

I paused at that. I hadn't thought about a name. There hadn't been a ton of time between getting him home and settled in and Faye crashing her damn car. My jaw clamped tight at the reminder of it. She shouldn't have tried to come here tonight. I should've looked at the weather before I told her to come over.

"Dawson?"

My eyes snapped back up to her deep blue ones. "What?"

"His name?"

Oh, yeah, that. I shrugged.

She frowned. "You didn't give him a name yet?" She rubbed the dog under the chin. "You need a name, don't you?" The dog made that weird happy squeaky yipping noise and she chuckled. "Yes, you do...hmm." She pursed her lips as she thought. "What would be a good name for a dog?"

I rolled my eyes. "It's not rocket science. Anything will be fine. How about Buddy?"

"Ugh, no." She shook her head. "Way too generic. This sweet puppy is anything but generic, right?" She leaned in and pressed her nose against the dog's. He licked her chin, and she laughed again.

"How about...Meatloaf?"

I grimaced. "What?"

Her eyes brightened. "Oh, yes! Meatloaf would be perfect. How do you feel about Meatloaf?" she asked, smiling at the dog who let out a soft bark in response.

Faye beamed. "He loves it."

"You've got to be joking."

"I am definitely not. Meatloaf loves his name, and I do, too."

"I'm not naming my dog Meatloaf."

"It's too late." She shrugged. "He's already accepted it."

I shook my head in disbelief. "Maybe you are concussed."

"Whatever." She kissed the top of Meatloaf's head before she turned more toward me, sitting back on her feet. "Speaking of concussions, what exactly are we going to do about my poor car?"

I tensed. "I'll have to see if I can get Mel to come out here and see if he can possibly tow it out."

She tucked her hair behind her ear. "I can call him."

"I can take care of it."

Her teeth caught her bottom lip, making my stomach tighten. "Do you think you can drive me home tonight?"

"You should stay the night here."

Her spine straightened at that. "I can't stay here tonight."

A frown tugged at my mouth. "Why? I'm not sure how comfortable I am with you being at home alone after a car accident with a head injury."

She hadn't stayed over at the cabin before, but I had extra rooms. I tried to ignore the way my heart flipped at the thought of her staying the night. I had to focus on her health and keeping her safe. Nothing else.

Her chest rose and fell, her breathing suddenly rapid. "My head is fine. I'm fine."

"And what if you *do* have a concussion? Do you want me to bring you to the Emergency Room?"

She shook her head, a lock of her hair falling over the side of her face. "No."

"Then you shouldn't be sleeping at home alone. If you stay here, I can keep an eye on you and look for signs of any more serious trauma."

One of her hands fisted into Meatloaf's fuzzy blanket. Her eyes misted over with unmistakable tears, sending a pang to my heart.

"I—I have to go home tonight," she said, voice almost a whisper.

"Fine. I can go home with you and sleep on your couch."

That didn't seem to solve the problem, either. "No," she squeaked, looking horrified. "You can't come over."

I leaned forward, placing my elbows on my knees and forcing myself not to reach for her, even though my hands longed to. She looked so distressed, but I'd touched her way too much already tonight.

"What's going on?" Maybe she was in pain, but that's not what I saw in her eyes. When she looked at me, I didn't see hurt...I saw fear. *What isn't she telling me?*

So, I waited. Faye looked down at her lap, almost squirming under my silence as I waited for the reason why she absolutely needed to go home tonight alone.

"I have something I need to tell you," she eventually said.

The hair on the back of my neck rose. Whatever it was, I didn't think I was going to like it.

"What is it?"

She looked up at me, eyes glassy as she swallowed hard. "I can't stay here tonight because...because my father is currently at my apartment waiting for me to come back."

I didn't move. I didn't even think I was breathing as I stared at her and tried to make sense of what she'd said. As far as I knew, Faye didn't have a father. It had been something that bothered her since forever. I think that with all the shit she dealt with from her mother, she wanted to know if she had one decent parent out there. But, her mother would never tell her who he was.

She rubbed the end of her nose that had started to turn as pink as the tops of her cheekbones. She was always so quick to blush.

"I know, it's crazy," she said, after I failed to respond. "Six months ago I got a letter from this man claiming to be my father. I wasn't sure what to think at first, but I decided to engage, and we sent a few letters back and forth. Everything he said started coming together and making sense, so I confronted Mama about it, and she finally, *finally* told me the truth." Her voice tightened, and a single tear slipped from her lashes and ran down her cheek. "It's true. All that he said. He was—he is my father."

My brain did its best to retain all those words that had rushed from her mouth in a nervous sputter. I simply couldn't make sense of one thing, though.

"Six months ago? Why are you only telling me now?"

If Faye had found her real father, I would've been the first one to be ecstatic for her. I knew more than anyone how much she wanted this...finally finding him after all these years. Wasn't that supposed to be good news?

The look on Faye's face told me that it wasn't the happy news that it sounded like.

"Because I didn't want you to worry."

I clasped my hands together, squeezing hard until my knuckles ached. "Why would I be worried?"

She needed to spit it out and tell me what was going on. This back and forth wasn't my pace. I wanted to rip off the bandage nice and quick.

"Because he's been in prison a while...I just picked him up today."

My stomach roiled, but I tried my damndest to remain calm. It wasn't merely the fact that her father had been in prison—I needed more information before I judged. It was because she had to deal with the fact that her father was in prison and she went to pick him up alone.

Did she feel like she couldn't trust me with this information? She didn't have to face it all by herself. That's what friends were for. That's what I was for.

I fell back against the couch, sighing in both frustration and relief. "You don't need to keep secrets from me, Faye."

"I'm sorry."

"Don't be sorry. Tell me the truth. I want to be there for you, and I can't do that if you keep big things like this from me. It's what friends do."

The color on her cheeks deepened. "I know."

"If you know that, then what was the problem?"

Her eyes darted away briefly. "I was afraid...afraid you'd find out what he did and totally lose it."

Lose it? My heart rate kicked up again. "What did he do?"

"It was a long time ago. He did his time, and he changed."

Her words did nothing to calm my suddenly soaring pulse.

"Tell me what he was convicted of, Faye."

She gnawed on her lip again. Her hands had moved away from Meatloaf as she wrung them together in her lap, almost tearing the bandages away. "It was an accident. An accident he spent the last fifteen years paying for."

In one smooth motion I reached for her, grabbing her hands and pressing them between mine so she wouldn't do any more damage to them.

Her eyes widened as she blinked at me. I was leaning in, our faces only inches apart. "Tell me, Faye," I whispered.

She was still for a beat, her entire body taut like bowstring before she opened her mouth and said the words that had my stomach plummeting.

"He killed his wife."

Chapter Seven

FAYE

His hands were warm as they gripped mine, but his eyes were ice cold. His face paled as he understood the thing I'd kept from him all these months. I waited for him to respond, but he didn't. He stared at me until I felt like I wanted to crawl out of my skin.

"I know, it sounds bad..." I started.

The corner of his lips curled up in what I could only describe as a snarl. "Bad?" Dawson shook his head, his voice sharp as a razor's edge. "You just told me that you have a murderer in your home right now. And you expect me to bring you back there?"

I flinched. "He already paid for his mistakes."

Dawson dropped my hands. They fell limp in my lap as he sat back on the couch, looking away. "It's not safe."

"You don't know that."

"No? I think that if someone is okay with taking another life, that it's probably not a good idea to take them into your home when you live completely alone."

Embarrassment and anger flared in my blood. I'd already had those thoughts; grappled with the safety of my decision. But I'd taken all the information I had—the good comments from the prison and the trust that I'd built with him the last six months—and ultimately went with my gut.

"This is exactly why I didn't tell you," I said between clenched teeth. "You'd think that *you*, of all people, would understand and not judge someone for being locked away behind bars."

His dark eyes flashed as his jaw clenched. "The difference here is that I was innocent."

"And who's to say he isn't? You *know*, Dawson. You know what it's like to be convicted of something you didn't do."

"Is he denying it?"

I paused, my hands fisting in my lap, sending a spike of pain across my skin from the cuts there. "He told me it was an accident."

Dawson let out a long, heavy breath. He ran a hand through his thick hair, pulling gently before he let his arm fall back to his side. "Did you at least look up his case? Read the court documents? Anything?"

"Of course I did." It stung that he doubted that I would. He knew me. Glancing down at my hands, at the bandages he applied, I steeled myself for the rest of the conversation. "He was convicted of voluntary manslaughter. He served a fifteen-year sentence, but the evidence wasn't completely cut and dry."

The woman he married after he left my mother wasn't very stable. She seemed to have a lot of mental health issues, and my father admits he drank too much at the time. He said it wasn't a good relationship and he should have left before things got out of hand, but he loved her. He wanted to help her, but didn't know how and he chose to numb the pain with alcohol."

I closed my eyes, seeing Marc's face clear in my memory, the devastation on his face as he told this story months ago behind that prison glass. He fought through tears to explain his side of the story.

"He said they fought too much. It was well documented because the neighbors often called the cops. No one was ever arrested or charged with laying a hand on the other...until the night it happened. My father came home from the bar, intoxicated as usual, and his wife was livid. He said he can't even remember what they were arguing about, but that she tried to hit him, he pushed her away and she fell. He said he didn't push her hard, but she hit her head on the edge of the counter and she—" I cut myself off, not able to make myself say the word. "He was scared, and he didn't call for help right away, and she didn't make it."

The quiet was heavy. It was almost as if neither of us were breathing, the only sound was the softening crackling of the woodstove. Eventually, Meatloaf let out a low whine, and I patted him on the head. Poor thing had been through enough, he shouldn't have to deal with us fighting.

Dawson scrubbed a hand over his face, looking absolutely exhausted. "It's...hard for me to accept that you're letting someone who was responsible for the death of another human—whether purposeful or not—stay at your home without any protection."

"I understand, but I...I couldn't leave him all alone when he has family—when he has *me*."

"People lie every day, Faye."

"I know."

His eyes softened. "Even if it was an accident...prison changes people. Not always for the good."

"I have a feeling about him, Dawson."

"Feelings don't make fact."

69

"I had a feeling about you. When you were in prison and every-one was against you, I—I knew that you weren't a bad person."

A series of emotions flickered across his face so quickly I couldn't decipher them all. He pinched the bridge of his nose, screwing his eyes shut. "I'm trying to look out for you. That's all."

I nodded. "I know, but I also need you to trust me."

"I trust you." His jaw hardened. "I don't trust *him*."

Fair. I glanced at Meatloaf, and he gave me a wide-eyed puppy stare and licked my arm. My thoughts were all confused and jumbled. I hadn't expected any of this: the car accident, hitting my head, being stuck here in the dark and rain. Meatloaf was the only thing that made me feel the smallest bit of comfort.

Dawson was coming from a good place. He was trying to look out for me. "If I really needed you to bring me home, would you?"

"Of course," he almost growled, obviously irritated. "I won't keep you here against your will. I'm not a monster."

No, he wasn't a monster no matter what he thought of himself sometimes. A sad smile pulled on my lip.

"But," he continued. "That doesn't mean I'd leave you alone with someone who could be a threat to you."

"Dawson," I said around a sigh.

"I need to make sure you're safe."

Always the protector.

I trailed my nails absently down Meatloaf's neck and back, inwardly wincing at the sharpness of the bones of his spine.

"Okay," I said, finally making a decision. "I'll stay the night." Relief flashed in Dawson's expression. "But you're taking me home tomorrow. And I need to use your phone."

He pressed his lips into a thin line, but he didn't question me as he reached into his pocket and pulled out his phone. I took and dialed my own number.

My father didn't answer the first call, which had my stomach twisting with nerves. I tried not to freak out. I hung up and typed a quick text.

Hey, it's Faye. Please answer the phone.

I sent the message, and waited a few beats before calling again. "Hello?"

Relief flooded me at the sound of Marc's voice.

"Hi, I'm glad you answered."

There was a short pause. "Is everything okay?"

I bit my lip and glanced at Dawson who seemed like he was biting back a few choice words. It would be an interesting meeting when the two came face to face, which was probably going to be sooner rather than later if I knew Dawson.

"Not exactly. I'm fine, but I had a bit of an accident getting to my friend's house tonight."

"Accident?" His voice spiked with concern. "What happened?"

I licked my dry lips, desperately needing a glass of water. I hadn't drank anything since dinner, which seemed like ages ago now.

"It's a long story. It's getting late, and I'm going to stay the night at my friend's house. He'll drive me back down tomorrow so I can figure out what to do with my car."

Marc let out a sigh. "I would come get you if I could."

"I know." He didn't have a vehicle yet. "I really am fine. Dawson has extra bedrooms, and I'll be perfectly comfortable here. See you in the morning."

I waited for him to disconnect the call, but he didn't. "All right," he said, his tone tight and uncertain. "Be safe. Always take care of yourself, Sunshine."

I fought a smile. The similarities between Dawson and Marc were a little unsettling at the moment. "Don't worry." I glanced at Dawson, catching his eye. "I'm safe."

I hung up and Dawson raised a brow. "Well, at least he pretends to be concerned about your safety. I'll give him that."

I rolled my eyes so hard I'm surprised they stayed inside my skull. "Whatever, you got what you wanted. Now, where am I going to sleep?"

He jerked a thumb behind him toward the staircase. "There's a free room up there, if you want it."

Looking at the stairs, I pursed my lips. I hadn't been up there much, if at all. We always stayed downstairs. While I was sure the room was cozy like the rest of the cabin, the thought of being all alone up there made me uneasy. Dawson's bedroom was on the main floor. I wasn't sure why it bothered me. I slept alone every night, but maybe everything that had happened today had me feeling out of sorts. I looked back at Meatloaf, considering making him my cuddle buddy for the night.

"Although," Dawson interrupted my thoughts. "I would prefer to keep an eye on you tonight."

My head snapped toward him. "Keep an eye on me?"

"Yes, you're going to be sore as hell tomorrow as the adrenaline wears off. If you start feeling worse, I'd like to know. We can sleep on the couches. Is that okay with you?"

I pursed my lips, considering. It seemed better than sleeping upstairs all alone, so I eventually nodded. "But I get to cuddle with Meatloaf."

He raised his hands. "I wouldn't dream of taking him from you."

I carefully made up the couches into our cozy, warm beds for the night while Dawson stoked the woodstove in the corner of the room and put a few more logs inside. The heat was welcome with my tight muscles. Sometimes, being in the living room so close to the stove could be too stuffy and hot, but not tonight.

The bitter chill from outside didn't touch this room.

After adding extra pillows, the couches were comfy enough, and I gingerly lowered myself down next to Meatloaf, who had only moved for a few minutes to get a drink of water. He seemed very pleased with the added blankets.

I was about to pull a blanket over us when Dawson's movement caught my eye, distracting me. He didn't sit on the other couch, but instead, left the living room.

"Are you hungry?" I asked, craning my neck to glance at him from over the back of the couch.

He was halfway to the kitchen and paused. "Huh?"

I tilted my head to the side. It hit me that I hadn't fed him like I promised. "The dinner I was supposed to bring you...we left it in my car."

"Oh," he scratched the back of his neck. "I ate before you got here. I was hoping you had gotten my message and weren't coming."

"Then what are you doing?"

His eyes flicked toward the staircase. "I was going to go upstairs for a little while. Is that okay?"

I frowned. "Upstairs? What are you doing upstairs?"

"I'm doing some work up there."

My eyes narrowed. "What kind of work?"

He scrubbed the back of his neck, but his lips twitched like he was suppressing a smile. "Maybe I'll show you sometime."

"Dawson William Evans," I mock scolded. "Are you hiding something from me?"

"We're all hiding something, Faye." He winked, though I didn't find it endearing at the moment.

"I told you my secret," I said, pursing my lips. "It's only fair that you tell me yours."

I wasn't sure what he could be hiding.

"Oh, I'll tell you…just not tonight." He flashed a wicked grin. "But if you'd rather have me stay down here with you, I will."

He was infuriating sometimes. It was probably something silly, like he was painting a room or something.

"No." I shook my head. "I wouldn't want to get in the way of your *work*." I put air quotes around the last word, making my annoyance clear.

He chuckled softly. "I'll check on you soon."

"Wouldn't want to bother you." I rolled my eyes.

"Mmmhmm." He was still laughing softly at my petty attitude as he started toward the stairs. "I'll be back down later."

"Fine." I huffed, folding my arms across my chest.

His footsteps thudded up the stairs as his laughter died away. I considered following him, but I really was comfortable, and a dull throb had started in all my muscles. Meatloaf shifted and laid his chin on my leg.

I stroked his soft ear. "I'd rather stay with you, anyway," I whispered.

I fought it as long as I could, but the heat radiating from the woodstove and the soft blankets and Meatloaf curled up against me had me losing the battle, and before I realized it, I'd fallen into a deep, heavy sleep.

Chapter Eight

FAYE

A soft whine and wet nose on my cheek woke me.

I reached for the dog before I even opened my eyes, scratching him under the chin and carefully pushing him away from my face.

Prying open my heavy eyelids, Meatloaf's toothy grin solidified in my vision. I smiled despite what felt like a very early wake-up.

"Good morning," I rasped, voice hoarse from sleep.

Meatloaf's whole body wiggled in time with his tail wags. His front paws dug into my upper arms, and I groaned at the pulse of pain. The soreness hadn't kept me up last night, but as I slowly sat up and shifted Meatloaf off me, I had to bite my tongue to keep from crying out. It felt like a very big, burly football player had tackled me. Everything hurt, from my freaking eyeballs to my toes.

I grimaced, focusing my attention on the wall of windows to distract myself from the throbbing pain in my muscles and joints. Last night they had been nothing but slates of black, but the focal point of the room—of the entire first floor, really—were the large windows starting from the floor and stretching all the way to the peaked ceiling that looked out onto the back yard and the forest beyond.

Morning rays streamed in through the panes of glass, soaking the room in golden light. Even in the winter, the view outside was breathtaking. Massive evergreens towered around the cabin adding lush, deep green to the mostly bare trees. The branches swayed in a soft breeze as birds flittered between them, their songs filtering inside. It struck me again the peacefulness of this place. It was quiet and serene. As much as I loved Cypress Falls and the community it brought, there was nothing like a cabin in the woods. I was tempted to walk out onto the back deck just to stand there and watch the sun continue to rise, but as I stood, I caught sight of him in the corner of my eye.

Dawson.

I remembered nothing after I'd fallen asleep, but he had kept his word and slept on the couch adjacent to mine. His long body was stretched over the couch that was too small for him, his ankles hanging off of the end. One arm was tucked behind his head, the other laid across his chest. His dark hair was a mess on the top of his head, but his face was almost...tranquil.

My legs screamed with each step as I made my way to Dawson's side. It had been a very long time since Dawson looked so at rest. There was no frown on his lips, no crease between his brows. An ache that had nothing to do with the car accident hit my chest. He looked like the Dawson I remembered before everything that happened with his mother...and his brother. Before he spent years of his life locked away.

The weeks that I had visited him would never leave my memory. I'd never missed one in all the time he was behind bars. It had been such a hard time. Whenever I came to see him, he looked worse.

As the lines around his face grew deeper, his eyes became so tired...not the kind of tired that could be mended with sleep...the kind of tired that came from your very soul. He had been so broken then. Things had gotten slightly better since he'd been out, but he wasn't the same.

My eyes narrowed at something on his forehead, distracting me from the sad past and bringing me back to the present. A small smudge of green paint was smeared above one of his eyebrows. A few more were on his hand and his clothes. The light green stood out against his perpetually dark attire. I grinned. He probably *was* painting a room upstairs. I didn't know why he had given me such a hard time about the "mysterious work" he was doing.

I was about to find something to feed Meatloaf, when a phone on the small table beside the couch lit up. It didn't make any noise, but a phone number flashed on the screen as an incoming call.

My stomach clenched. I recognized that number. One of the few that I had memorized. It didn't make sense she'd be calling Dawson, though.

I grabbed the phone before I thought about it and answered. "Ellie?"

There was a gasp on the other end of the line. "Faye?" She sounded panicked and out of breath. "Is that you?"

My heart quickened at utter fear in her voice. "Yeah, it's me. What's wrong? Are you okay? Is the baby okay?"

My sister was seven months pregnant with her first baby. The only thing that would make her sound this panicked was if something was very wrong.

"The baby's fine. I'm fine," she said, sounding on the verge of tears. "Are *you* okay? I've been trying to get ahold of you all morning. You weren't answering your phone, and we couldn't find you. I was terrified something happened and was calling Dawson to see if he knew where you were."

"I'm okay. Calm down." I pressed a hand against my heart, needing it to slow. Ellie was okay. "I had some car trouble and got stuck at Dawson's last night. Why are you freaking out?"

Her silence was long and heavy. "Faye, you really need to come back home."

Her voice shook on the last word, and I had to sit back on the couch as the dread in her voice leaked over to me.

"Why? What happened?"

Ellie paused again, too long. "You just need to come as soon as you can."

I wasn't about to let her off of the phone without telling me what was so urgent. "You know me better than anybody. It'll be worse if you leave me in the dark until I get there."

My sister drew in a deep breath, letting it out slowly. And then she said the words that had my entire world spinning.

"I don't know all the details, but it looks like someone broke into Southern Sunshine last night."

My eyes fluttered closed as my brain tried to process those words about my store. "How bad is it?"

"I think it's pretty bad. There's damage. You need to get there as soon as you can."

Chapter Nine

FAYE

WHATEVER I HAD IMAGINED during the drive down from the hills, it was worse.

I trembled as the cold air poured in through shattered windows. Glass littered the floor in sparkling shards that crunched beneath my toes with every step Dawson and I took through my boutique. A knot of dread and despair in my stomach tightened. It all was wrecked.

My tables and displays had been broken and torn off the walls. Clothes were strewn on the ground among the glass, making them impossible to sell. All the cash was stolen from the register, and the locked safe in the storage room had been drilled open, and all that money was gone, too.

My carefully curated life was destroyed.

I choked back my tears, my heart feeling as torn and broken as the shop. This place had taken hours—years of my blood and sweat and tears. It was mine...the one thing that I had nourished and grown from the ground up.

It wasn't only the boutique that had been broken into, either. It was also my home. The tidy, clean apartment above the shop wasn't in any better condition. My dining room table and chairs were in splinters. The curtains had been torn off the rods. Picture frames were smashed. My books—my precious books were ripped apart and thrown off my shelves. Anything that could be broken, was.

And my father was nowhere to be found.

"Have you checked the third floor?" I asked, the thought suddenly occurring to me. This building technically had three floors, but the very top hadn't been updated when I bought the building. I used the dilapidated space to store all my extra inventory in place of a warehouse.

Sergeant Atlas Ranes of the Cypress Falls Police Department nodded. "There doesn't seem to be much damage up there."

That was good. I tried to focus on any little piece of goodness in this situation.

Dawson's large hand encircled mine gently, minding the cuts under my bandages as we continued walking through my ruined apartment. My head spun as I fought with everything in me not to unleash the tears burning behind my eyes.

"So, you left this man—your father—here alone last night?" Atlas asked, his composed expression shifting with a flicker of pity.

Atlas wasn't just a police officer, he was also my Ellie's brother-in-law. He and her husband, Ty, were brothers. Though his presence brought little comfort, I knew he would do the best he could to get the answers we needed. He was also probably responsible for keeping Ellie away from this horrific scene, thankfully.

I nodded, barely able to breathe, let alone talk, through the huge lump in my throat.

"Do you think he had anything to do with this?" Dawson's voice rumbled in my ear, and I looked over at him. His face was hard, a muscle in his jaw popping as he stared at Atlas.

Atlas reached for a small plastic baggie I hadn't noticed was sitting on the counter beside him. "We did find something," Atlas hesitated before he extended it out to me. "This note was left here in the kitchen."

My pulse rushed in my ears as I took it, the plastic crinkling in my fingers. I didn't look at it long, just enough to take in the familiar handwriting and three simple words.

Good-bye, Sunshine.

I shoved the note back at Atlas as the sting of betrayal pricked my chest. "It's from my father," I muttered, avoiding Atlas's gaze.

"You're sure about that?" Atlas asked.

I nodded.

"And you don't have any security cameras?"

"No."

In this day and age it was a ridiculous decision not to have some kind of cameras in my boutique, but it was low on my to-do list. Cypress Falls was supposed to be safe. It had been years since a shop on Main Street was burglarized. The biggest thing that happened was a couple of kids getting caught shoplifting, and even those were few and far between.

"We will check the other shops around town and see if any security cameras in the area caught something. Until then, I don't have many answers," Atlas said, looking at me apologetically.

"But it doesn't look too good for him, does it? Especially if we can't find him?" Dawson's voice was deep with anger.

"It looks suspicious." Atlas conceded. "He's the only suspect we have to go on."

In my heart, I wanted to argue. I wanted to defend Marc—defend the man who I'd gotten to know the past half year. But the note made that almost impossible. This was such a mess. Everything was ruined, I couldn't believe I'd gotten myself into this.

I glanced down at the kitchen floor, and the phone I'd left with my father the night before was smashed into pieces across the tile.

A thought struck me. I gasped, heading toward the kitchen sink.

"What is it?" Dawson asked, concerned.

I didn't answer as I stared at the small jewelry dish shattered in pieces inside the sink. My heart constricted, tears welling. My eyes scanned every inch of the metal tub, but it wasn't there. A strainer sat over the drain, nothing had fallen down it.

"My ring," I whispered. "I left it here last night. It's gone."

"Was it insured?" Atlas said.

"No." I closed my eyes, taking in a deep breath. "It wasn't worth anything. It was...sentimental."

Forcing myself to turn back to Atlas, Dawson's hand touched my lower back, rubbing slow circles of comfort.

"Does your father have any kind of grudge against you? Something that would motivate him to do something like this?" Atlas asked.

I swallowed hard, forcing myself to get the words out. "No," I shook my head. "Not that I know of. He seemed genuinely happy to meet me."

"Or just happy to take advantage of you," Dawson said with disgust.

Tears brimmed my eyes, and I looked up at the ceiling, willing them to sink back into my head. I wasn't going to cry. Not here. Not now in front of Atlas.

Atlas shifted on his feet. "Why don't you find a safe place to stay for a little while until we can get some answers, Faye?"

"I can't stay here?" I wasn't sure why that fact hit me so hard. The state of my apartment definitely didn't seem livable, but it was my home. "When will I be able to come back?"

"Hopefully soon," Atlas said. "But for right now, we want to figure out what's going on. Until we have a few more answers we don't want you on the property."

"Okay," I said softly, feeling like it was anything but okay. *Where would I go?* I gripped Dawson's hand so tight it had to hurt, the cuts on my hands stinging.

"Maybe you can stay with Ellie and Ty?" Atlas offered. I must have looked as lost as I felt.

I nodded at his words, my brain fried. Visiting Ellie sounded like a good idea, though. "Can I get some clothes and things?"

Atlas pressed his lips together. "Of course." He turned and walked me to my bedroom door that was hanging wide open. "But be careful, it's...a mess."

That was an understatement. I blinked at the chaos that was my little bedroom. The bedding had been ripped off and strewn on the floor amid a mess of torn papers. My mattress and pillows had been slashed open, the insides pulled out and tossed around. I shivered at the thought of the knife that had to have been used to slice them open like that.

I cautiously stepped inside, paper crunching under my feet. My heart constricted as I realized where they had come from. I'd left a stack of my father's letters on my dresser, having gone through them to prepare myself to pick him up yesterday. Almost all our correspondence lay shredded on the ground like trash.

Hands clenching at my sides, I steeled myself. I needed to get out of this place. Quickly, I found a weekender bag and some clothes and shoes that miraculously hadn't been damaged. When I turned back toward the door, Dawson was leaning against the frame, his arms crossed over his chest. His face was set with anger, but his voice was calm when he spoke.

"Come on," he said, pushing off the door frame and reaching for my hand. "Let's get out of here. I can drive you over Ellie's."

I didn't fight him as he pulled me from the wreckage of my life. I didn't fight him as he walked me back to his Jeep and helped me into the passenger seat.

As he drove away from my little shop that sat in ruins, I let a few tears silently fall.

The man I'd wanted desperately to be my father, had turned out to be my nightmare.

Chapter Ten

DAWSON

I STOPPED THE JEEP after pulling into Ellie's long drive. I shifted into park, turning to Faye sitting in the passenger seat. She'd been quiet the whole drive, staring blankly out the windshield like she was lost and had no idea where to go.

"Check in with me, Faye," I said, making her jump.

She turned her head, those sapphire blue eyes wide. "What?"

One hand tightened around the steering wheel as I reached for her with the other. Her skin was cold beneath the bandages from the accident last night. She needed a good pair of gloves for a winter like this. It was the kind of chill that seeped down into your bones. The kind we didn't often get in Northern Alabama.

"What's going through your mind?"

Her chest rose with a deep breath, the whites of her eyes reddening with welling tears.

"I—I don't know," she confessed, her voice wavering on the edge of a sob.

I gripped her hand, wanting my warmth to transfer to her. She'd been just as cold as we walked through the mess that was her home and livelihood. I'd felt so helpless walking through there, pissed the only comfort I could offer was holding her damn hand. It wasn't enough, but I didn't know what else to do.

"It's a lot," I said. "But I need to know that you're going to be all right."

"I will be."

"You sure about that?"

She hesitated.

"Because it's okay if you're not."

She squeezed her eyes shut against her tears, somehow keeping them in. I didn't want her to fight it if she needed to let it out. I glanced at the windshield. Ellie's house was on a large plot of land in the country. The house could barely be seen from here at the end of the drive. We had time.

"Talk to me, Faye," I whispered, letting her hand go and tucking a strand of hair behind her ear.

Her eyes popped open wide, meeting and holding mine. I hadn't realized that I'd leaned forward, close enough that her rapid breaths ghosted my cheek.

"Dawson?" she whispered my name, sending goosebumps prickling along my skin. I stifled a shiver, clearing my throat and pulling back until I was firmly settled back in my seat. I had gotten too close to her.

"I don't understand why this happened," she said, voice flat.

My fingers itched to reach for her again, but I restrained myself. "It's not your fault."

Her expression hardened, her eyes cutting to mine. "No? How is it not?"

"Someone took advantage of you," I spat between clenched teeth. The thought had my blood boiling. I was willing to give that man the benefit of the doubt last night, for Faye's sake. The fact that he claimed her to be his daughter—his damned family—and then turned around and betrayed her had me wanting to hunt him down and make him pay for the pain he'd caused her. The pain that was stark on her face. I wished he'd never gotten the chance to step a foot out of that prison. He had been right where he belonged.

Faye shook her head. "He seemed so...genuine. I believed that he'd changed..."

"He's a conman. It's probably something he's spent his life perfecting...making people believe his bullshit. He needed money, and you were the easiest way to get it. It has nothing to do with you."

Her face crumpled, but still not a tear fell. "It feels like it has everything to do with me. What was done to my shop...to my home...that didn't feel like someone who was just looking to steal my money and run. That felt like—like anger. The things he did, that was rage."

I scrubbed a hand along my jaw. I couldn't argue with that. He'd done a number on that place, leaving it in pieces. Pieces that would take a long time to clean up.

"Maybe he was taking his anger out on you. Didn't you say that he and your mama didn't have a good relationship?"

"They didn't. My mama didn't have a good relationship with anyone." She pulled in a steadying breath. "It took me a long time to get her to confess that he truly was my father. She said he was an asshole..." She sniffed, looking down at her hands clasped tight in her lap. "I should have listened to her."

I scoffed. Her mama wasn't a good person, either. "Even liars tell the truth every once in a while. Doesn't mean you should believe them. You couldn't have known she was choosing this time to be truthful."

She shrugged, looking small and helpless and...scared.

"It's gonna be all right."

"You can't know that," she breathed.

"I can, and I do. You're strong, Faye. You're gonna get that shop back up and running in no time, and I'm going to help you however I can."

She glanced up from beneath her lashes. "I wish I had your confidence."

I cocked a brow. "I'm only confident when it comes to you."

Her teeth caught her lower lip, and she shifted her attention out the window toward the house. "I need to go talk with Ellie." She said it almost to herself rather than to me.

"Does she know about your father?"

She nodded, still not looking at me. "Yeah, I told her right away. She was really excited for me..."

"She's not going to blame you, either," I said.

"I know," she nodded. "I know she won't. I just..." She trailed off.

There was something she was holding back. "What is it?"

She nervously scratched at the base of her throat until it turned a delicate shade of pink. "I know that Ellie is going to insist that I stay with her until my apartment is safe again..."

She sounded so reluctant. I frowned. "You don't want to stay with her?"

"It's not that I don't want to." Her eyes darted to mine. "But I'm scared of what that might mean. She's pregnant, and I don't want to be a burden while she and Ty are getting ready to welcome their first baby. And mostly..." She shuddered. "I don't want anything like what happened to my home to happen here." Her voice broke, and this time, I didn't stop myself. I grabbed her hand gently, wanting to take away her pain.

"That's not going to happen," I assured her.

"How do you know? What if they can't find my father? We don't know where he is or what his plan is. What if he runs out of money and follows me home to *this* house." She flung her hand out toward the large, newly built home on acres of secluded land. "At this point I have no idea what he's capable of. He could break in here thinking he can find more money. If something ever happened to Ellie because of me..." For the first time a tear slipped from her lashes, cascading down her cheek and dripping off her chin.

It wasn't likely, but I couldn't tell her it wasn't a possibility. I wanted to tell her that the police were going to find that bastard and put him back behind bars where he belonged. But I couldn't.

"I don't think that anything bad will happen if you stay with your sister," I started, and she opened her mouth to argue, but I held up a hand. "But I understand where you're coming from. And I think I have a solution."

"Solution?"

I paused. This could be a huge mistake, but there weren't many options left, and I wasn't going to leave her high and dry. I was going to do everything I could to help her.

"You should stay with me."

Faye blinked. "What?"

"It's perfect." I shrugged, though my heart flitted against my ribs. "If you're afraid to stay with family, you can stay with me. It'd be almost impossible for someone to follow you all the way up the cabin without you noticing. It would be safe there."

"Safe?" she said, sounding almost mystified by the word.

"Yes, it would be safe. I have plenty of room and besides...Meatloaf would be more than happy to have you."

At the mention of the dog her eyes brightened. "You're serious?"

"I don't say anything unless I'm serious."

She paused again, like she was letting it all sink it. Then, she nodded. Something tight in my chest eased. "Okay," she said softly. "I'll stay with you, just for a little while."

"You can stay as long as you need."

"I do need to talk to my sister, though. I have a feeling she might take a little more convincing."

A grin tugged at my lip. I let her hand go and shifted the Jeep back into drive, making our way down the narrow path that led to the main house. "That will be all you, but I'm sure you can find a way to do it."

Chapter Eleven

FAYE

"No. There's no way."

Ellie shook her head so hard her dark braid almost smacked her in her face.

I winced. She wasn't exactly yelling, but her elevated voice made the ache twinge in my temple. A headache was lingering from last night, and the cut on my hand stung as I wrapped it around the hot mug of Earl Grey tea Ellie had prepared for me. We were sitting at her long farmhouse kitchen table, a plate of fresh muffins sitting between us. I hadn't touched them. My stomach was still in knots from the events of the day, but the tea was calming.

"I want to go, Ellie. I think it's the best option." I expected her to take the news like this, but I really, really didn't want to fight with my pregnant sister.

She hardened her stare. "Do you really want to drive up and down those godforsaken hills every day? He lives in the middle of nowhere, Faye. It'll take you forty minutes round trip to and from town."

True, but at least it was beautiful. The memory of the sunrise out the large windows of the cabin came to the forefront of my mind. I could get used to waking up to that view every day.

What I wasn't sure about, was Dawson.

We'd been friends for a long time, yes, but living together—even for a short time—was totally new territory. But I didn't want to be a burden to my sister, not when her life was about to change so much with the baby. I wasn't going to risk bringing any bit of trouble to her front door.

Dawson was right. It was safer to stay with him. The cabin was far away from town, away from Ellie and her growing family. The extra drive wasn't even an issue for me.

"It's not that far away. You're being dramatic," I said, rolling my eyes and taking a sip of tea. The warmth soothed the aches and pains lingering in my body. I still hadn't told Ellie about my little accident, and I didn't plan to at this point. She was already on edge, which couldn't be good for the baby.

Ellie pursed her lips, her ice-blue eyes narrowing. "Don't try to downplay this. This is a big deal, Faye. I know how much the boutique means to you. I'm not gonna let my own sister sleep in a shack in the woods when I have a perfectly fine house with plenty of room just minutes from downtown."

My fingers clenched around the mug. I'd removed the large bandages Dawson had put on them last night and replaced them with regular adhesive bandages, but I'd kept my sleeves down as far as I could to hide most of the cuts.

"Ellie, it's no trouble for me. You two have a lot going on, and I don't need to impose on y'all."

"Impose?" he scoffed. "Please. I *want* you here, Faye."

A shot of guilt hit me, but I couldn't let myself cave. Not about this. "Maybe..." I started, my voice barely more than a whisper. "Maybe I want to stay with Dawson."

It wasn't exactly true. I didn't have much of a choice, but she didn't know that.

Ellie blinked at me, her mouth falling open as she rubbed a hand absently on her round stomach. Even in the later months of pregnancy, my sister was absolutely gorgeous. She had always been pretty, but time had only done her favors. She was glowing, her face plump and radiant.

"Oh," she said, pressing her full lips together. "Okay, then."

I glanced away, staring around the open concept kitchen that had white and gray marble countertops and custom cabinets. The focal point was the large, white farmhouse sink situated in front of a wide window that looked out on the acres of land and wildflowers.

Her husband, Ty, had spared no expense in the building of the perfect house for their family. It was such a far cry from the small little trailer Ellie had lived in with her father. She'd grown up right here on this land. When her father passed away and the trailer was lost in a fire, Ellie and Ty had taken this place for their own. They were building not only a pretty house, but a beautiful life. A beautiful family. I wasn't going to put any of that in jeopardy.

"Are you two...dating?"

My gaze snapped back to hers. "No," I said, much too quickly, the thought sending a panicked jolt through my chest. "You know me better than that."

Ellie frowned. "I know that you have some convoluted fear of men, yeah."

I blinked at her, a little offended by her tone. "I don't fear them," I snapped.

"No?" she raised her brows. "You've never seriously dated anyone in your whole life, Faye."

"I'm perfectly fine by myself." I wrinkled my nose. "And Dawson and I are friends. I've missed him since he's moved out to the cabin, and I think it would be nice to spend some time with him."

Ellie continued to rub her belly with one hand, while the other started fiddling with the end of her braid. "Friends," she mused. Her eyes flicked toward the white mantel in the center of the living room to the right of the kitchen.

Hanging above the fireplace was a large, recent picture of Ellie and Ty. She wore a flowing blue dress that made her eyes pop as she turned toward Ty, hugging her baby bump. His arms were wrapped around her, their foreheads pressed together as his hand cradled her cheek. They looked so happy, so in love with each other.

"I know a thing or two about being 'friends' with someone you're in love with."

My eyes cut back to my sister. She gave me a knowing look, as if she could see right through me.

"I'm not in love with anyone. Not like that."

Ellie tilted her head to the side. "Be careful, Faye," she breathed.

"I'm always careful, El."

"Careful to keep things to yourself. It's not good to always be alone."

"I'm not totally alone," I said, defensive. "I have you. And Dawson."

"I just...I want you to be happy. I worry about you living by yourself, sometimes. What happened last night is one of my worst fears, and I'm so thankful you weren't there when it happened." She looked down at her belly, her face growing even more concerned. "I'm always here for you. I'll never not be looking out for you."

"I know." My mug of tea was starting to go cold. I'd suddenly lost my taste for it. "I'm here for you too. Always."

She was all I had. Neither of us talked to our mother, and our separate fathers weren't in the picture anymore. She had Ty and the baby, but she was all the family I had left.

I reached over and grabbed her hand, squeezing it as hard as I dared.

"I love you, El."

She blinked at me, her eyes suddenly brimming with tears. "I love you, too."

We stayed for a beat in silence, Ellie fighting tears until she sniffed, her dark lashes fluttering as she blinked them away.

"Ugh," she moaned, pulling her hand back to wipe her eyes. "You can't do this to me with all these hormones raging through my body." She shook her head. "Fine, you can stay with Dawson in the stupid cabin."

"Thank you. I'll come visit as often as I can."

"You promise?"

I smiled and nodded. "Us against the world, right?"

Ellie grinned at the old saying we used to tell each other as kids. "Us against the world."

Chapter Twelve

DAWSON

I GOT A TOW for Faye's vehicle. It wasn't an easy process and took a bit of work, but the local shop was able to get it out from between the trees. The good news was, they expected to repair it within the next couple of weeks. It wouldn't be much of a comfort considering what had happened today, but at least Faye hadn't lost her car, too.

I paid the quote for the repairs and requested they call me first if there was a balance remaining. Faye shouldn't have to worry about it, and there'd be no convincing her to let me pay for it if I didn't do it now.

After setting everything up with the auto shop, I swung by the hardware store to get some plywood and nails. I grabbed a hammer for good measure because I didn't have my tools on me at the moment.

As I loaded the plywood in the back of the Jeep, a familiar voice came from behind me.

"Need some help?"

I froze, my stomach dropping. Letting go of the board, I slowly straightened. Shaking my head in disbelief, I turned.

My brother pushed back his stupid cowboy hat, his shoulders hunched against the cold wind. Clouds had darkened the sky, hiding any warmth the sun brought.

"You've got to be kidding me," I muttered. "You stalking me now or something?"

Knox's expression hardened. "I'm mending a fence." He jerked his chin toward the small shop behind me. "It's a small town. Only one hardware store."

Being in town this often wasn't working out for me. Of course my brother was here at the same time I was. This day was actually the worst.

"Thanks for the offer," I said, bending to grab the last sheet of plywood from the cart. "but I'm perfectly capable of handling this."

I loaded the board in the back of the Jeep, hoping Knox would move on and leave me alone. He didn't. I snapped the rear door closed with a sigh.

"Have you considered our offer?" Knox asked, making me cringe.

Resting my hands on my hips, I faced him again. "I thought it was pretty clear that I wasn't interested in coming to your wedding."

He ran a finger over the brim of his hat. "Doesn't mean you can't change your mind."

"I have no plans to."

Knox glanced around the parking lot. It was empty besides the two of us, the last car driving away.

"I've already apologized to you, Dawson. What more do you want from me?" His voice held a hint of desperation and frustration.

That familiar anger lit in my chest. My teeth clenched. He didn't get to be frustrated with me. I stepped closer, pulling back my shoulders. "Why do you keep trying to fix something that can't be repaired?" I hissed.

Knox held his ground, collecting his face into a stony mask. "Because I have to keep trying. Mama would've wanted us to try."

I flinched at the mention of her. It still hurt when I thought of the way she died. Of the fact that I hadn't been there when she'd taken her last breath because I was in prison. She had been brutally attacked by someone we'd trusted on the ranch who ended up being deranged. Beaten and stabbed, she had fallen into a coma until she ultimately died from her injuries.

My hands trembled, and I curled them into fists at my sides. "Don't talk to me about her," I whispered. "Not you, of all people."

A crack appeared in Knox's mask, a shard of pity...and maybe guilt, too. "I know I was wrong, Dawson. What happened that night, I thought I saw something. It was so dark. You were holding that knife, and then you ran...you ran away, and I couldn't think of any other reason why except for your guilt."

I stumbled back from him at the mention of that night, retreating from him like a damn coward until my back hit the Jeep. I leaned against it for support as Knox's words instantly transported me back there; to the night my mother was attacked.

She'd gone out to the barn to check on the horses because of the brewing storm. Lightning flickered in the distance, the thunder nothing but a low rumble. Mama had only been gone a few minutes when I went to help her.

Instead, I'd found her body crumbled on the floor of the barn, lifeless.

I barely remembered going to her. But I was at her side, turning her over to try to assess what was wrong.

Everything was wrong.

There was so much blood. She'd been beaten badly, her face bloody and swollen. My mind went into shock, hardly able to function. Then, I saw the blood-coated knife lying beside her. I picked it up without a thought, staring at it as if it could tell me what had just happened. How this had happened.

I'd spent years wondering why I hadn't saved her. I had medical training, I could have done something. *Anything*. Instead I froze. I panicked.

Then Knox appeared in the barn, and I would never forget the sounds of his screams.

"What the hell did you do?"

Knox's eyes had been wild and scared, focused on the bloody knife in my hand.

I was trained to be a soldier. I was trained to heal people in the most stressful conditions.

But when my brother looked at me like that, screaming and trembling, I turned into a scared child. I wasn't brave. I wasn't a soldier.

I fucking ran.

I startled as present-day Knox shook my shoulders, fingers digging into my skin and snapping me out of my reverie.

"Dawson!" he said, his voice firm and loud like it hadn't been the first time he'd said it. "Are you okay?"

My chest was tight, my breaths shallow and rapid. I pushed my brother away. "Don't touch me," I gasped.

I spun around, desperate to get out of there; to get away from my brother and the memories of my failure.

"Just...just leave me alone," I spat, rounding my vehicle and getting in the driver's seat.

I glanced at my brother one last time in the rearview mirror, turning on the vehicle. His eyes met mine, making my heart constrict. I hated my brother. I had to. Holding onto the hate was the one thing that kept me from drowning in the truth.

As much as I hated Knox...I hated myself even more.

Chapter Thirteen

DAWSON

I DROVE UNTIL MY head cleared of the awful memory.

I drove until I hit water and couldn't drive anymore. My vehicle slowed to a stop near the bank of the Blue Cypress River. I threw the gear into park and jumped out, sucking in deep lungfuls of air.

The river was a cool gray...dull and missing its normal sparkling splendor with the absence of the sun. A harsh, bitter wind blew off the water, and I welcomed the sting of it on my skin. The burn of cold in my lungs.

I stood there, staring at the flowing river until my exposed skin was as numb as my heart. With every passing moment I forced the memories down, stuffing them deep down into a dark box and locking it tight.

My brother wasn't going to make me cower like that ever again. I wouldn't allow it to happen anymore.

I threw back my shoulders and straightened my spine. I compelled myself to calm and clear my mind.

When I was finally feeling better, I headed back toward the Jeep. My phone buzzed, making me halt. It was a text from Faye.

Ellie is leaving soon for her doctor's appointment.

I focused on her words. This day wasn't about me and my family drama. This was about her. I was supposed to be taking care of her.

Be there in ten.

FAYE WAS WAITING OUTSIDE on Ellie's front porch as I pulled up to the house. Her lips tipped up as her eyes met mine through the windshield and she rushed over to the Jeep.

The moment she opened the passenger side door and got a good look at my face, her smile vanished.

"Are you all right?" Faye asked as she climbed in and fastened her seatbelt.

I silently cursed myself. I hadn't done as good of a job wiping my emotion away as I thought.

"Nothing," I grumbled, heading away from Ellie's house and focusing on the road.

Faye was quiet for a beat, probably deciding if she wanted to press me.

"Why is there a bunch of plywood in the back?"

I let out a breath, glad she chose to leave it alone. That last thing she needed was me bitching about my brother.

"I figured we'd stop by your shop again before heading up to the cabin."

"Oh," she murmured.

I stole a glance at her, the sadness on her face visible. "I called Sargent Ranes before I picked up the plywood. The police are done with the building for the day."

She nodded, her teeth catching the side of her lip like they did when she was worried. "The plywood is for the windows."

She was sharp. "It's supposed to rain again tonight. You don't want any more water damage."

"Right," she said, but her voice sounded strangled.

My fingers tightened around the steering wheel, forcing them to stay in place. I longed to touch her. Both for her comfort and mine. But if she was going to stay at my cabin for any length of time, I couldn't be holding her hand all the time.

The sight of the dark and shattered windows of Southern Sunshine boutique had an ache building in my chest as we approached. It must be terrible for Faye seeing it like that.

She opened the Jeep door the moment I put it into park on the side of the street directly outside of the shop. I grabbed her elbow before she could jump out into the cold.

"I got it," I said. "You can stay in the warm vehicle."

She gave me a sharp frown. "I can help with the windows."

Of course she could, but she'd already been through enough today, and her hands were still healing. I didn't want her opening the wounds any more.

I stared at her. No matter what I said, she wasn't going to stay in this Jeep if I was out there working.

"Have you eaten yet?" I asked.

Her nose crinkled. "I haven't exactly been hungry."

Perfect. "Well, I'm starving. How about you run down to the deli and grab us some sandwiches. I'll get this done quick, and we can eat at the cabin together."

Her brow furrowed. "I can help you, Dawson."

"I know." I nodded. "And you'll help me the most by grabbing us some food. We really should eat."

Her mouth worried into a tight line as she considered. "Fine," she said, and relief hit me. "Do you want your usual?"

"Please." I grinned as she hopped out of the Jeep and headed down the sidewalk toward the deli.

Not wanting to waste time, I got out of the Jeep, hunching against a cold breeze as my boots hit the pavement. The wind cut right through to the bone as I unloaded the plywood.

The weather was calling for more storms tonight, and with this cold, I wondered if it would turn to ice up in the hills. This year had been an unseasonably rough winter. A few mornings already I'd woken up to a light dusting of snow. Cypress Falls was about as north as you could get for Alabama, and snow happened sometimes, but it wasn't common.

Taking out the hammer and the box of nails, I started securing the plywood over the front windows of the boutique. The work was actually helpful. The rhythmic motion of striking something over and over again helped me take out some of the pent-up energy and aggression that clung to me. It distracted my mind from wandering to places it shouldn't. Before I realized it, I was already finishing the last window.

I beat in the last nail, surprised that Faye hadn't returned yet, when a delivery truck pulled up behind my Jeep and stopped. I turned, frowning as a man climbed out of the truck.

He looked young, a few years younger than Faye and me. He was dressed in a delivery uniform with wavy brown hair that was a little too long. He didn't look happy as he approached me.

"What hell happened here?" He sounded distraught for a random stranger. "Is everything okay? Where's Faye?"

My hand clenched around the hammer. "Can I help you?"

The man ran both hands through his hair. "Did someone break in or something?"

I was about to ask who the hell he was when Faye's voice distracted me. "Julian?"

Both of our eyes snapped over to Faye, standing a few feet away on the sidewalk holding a brown paper bag. The man sighed in relief and immediately started toward her. I reflexively stepped closer to Faye, but she reached out to him, grabbing hold of his hand.

"What are you doing here?" she asked. Her fingers tightened around his, and I tried to ignore the sinking feeling in my stomach.

"I was working in town today and drove by the shop when I saw your windows being boarded up. What happened? Are you okay?"

She inhaled deeply. "It's...a long story. I can tell you about it later."

The man, Julian, scowled. "You can't leave me hanging like that, Faye."

She shifted on her feet. "Um, well, let's just say things didn't go well with the whole new father situation."

Every muscle in my body tensed. I had no idea who this guy was. I had never heard his name in my life, and yet Faye knew him well enough to talk to him about her father? Something she'd kept for me for six months? My back teeth ground together as I kept my irrational anger and frustration at bay. Faye could talk to whoever she wanted. I wasn't her only friend, and I had to be okay with that.

I *was* okay with that.

I must still be on edge from running into my brother earlier, that was all.

Julian's mouth dropped open. "I am so sorry, Faye." His gaze flicked back to the vandalized boutique. "Is there anything I can do? How can I help?"

Faye shook her head. "No, there's nothing you can do right now. I have a lot of things to figure out."

Juliann glanced at his delivery truck, and then back at Faye. "I wish I could stay, but I've got more deliveries. You'll call me when you need some help?"

"Of course I will, and don't worry about it. I wouldn't expect you to stay." Her eyes met mine for the first time. "I have some help already, anyway."

Juliann glanced at me, his eyes assessing me up and down. His face shifted from concern into a personable smile before held out his hand. "Hey," he said. "I'm Julian. I'm Faye's delivery guy, and her friend."

I stared at the guy's hand. There was no part of me that wanted to shake it or introduce myself, but I couldn't let my stupid testosterone fueled brain win.

"Dawson," I said stiffly, clasping his hand with mine and pulling away quickly. "I've known Faye since we were kids. She's staying with me for a little while until we can get this place cleaned up."

The change was subtle, but I saw it. The slight stiffening of his neck. The way his spine straightened and his jaw clenched. It shouldn't have brought me any kind of pleasure, but it did.

"Oh." His bright smile faltered briefly before he composed himself. "I'm glad she has you. If y'all need anything, Faye has my number."

I nodded. He turned back to Faye, and they said a brief goodbye before he returned to his delivery truck.

As soon as that Julian guy was gone, Faye glanced from me to the boarded windows. "You finished that really quickly," she said, frowning.

I shrugged, gathering up the extra nails and the hammer. "We should get back to the cabin before it starts raining."

I started toward the Jeep, but Faye grabbed my arm, stopping me. "What's wrong?" she asked again.

My jaw clenched as I fought the urge to tell her everything. She knew about the issues I had with my brother. She'd been there for me through that dark time. But she didn't know the full details. She didn't know how much of a coward I really was.

"You want to know what's wrong?" I said, voice low. My brows rose as I glanced at her from the corner of my eye.

She bit her lip, nodding. "Of course I do, Dawson."

I leaned toward her, and then I snatched the brown paper bag from her hands. "I'm starving," I said, faking a grin. "Let's get going so we can eat."

Definitely a coward.

She narrowed her eyes, but she didn't fight me as we got back into my vehicle.

We were quiet as we traveled up toward my cabin. With every passing minute, the sky grew darker, the clouds rolling in thick. When I built my cabin, it was to isolate myself. But Faye was the one person who I refused to let go of.

I glanced at Faye, studying her. As much as I tried to bury the dark memories that Knox stirred up in me today, they would never fully go away. They would always be a black scar on my soul.

The truth was, I was not good for Faye—I wasn't good. Period. She needed someone with a heart as pure as hers. She didn't need someone like me, with a broken, bitter heart and a reputation almost as bleak. Faye deserved more.

ABBEY EASTON

She deserved the damn world.

Chapter Fourteen

FAYE

Two weeks went by, and even with the heaviness of my situation, living with Dawson was actually quite...effortless.

We easily slipped into a day-to-day routine. I spent most of my days at the shop, and Dawson helped when he could. At night, I often made us dinner and we sat down together to eat. Having someone to come home to and rely on for help eased the stress of dealing with repairs on the boutique.

I purchased a new phone and a planner, and had been working diligently to strategize the best path forward.

Despite the police being on the lookout, there hadn't been any sign of my father. They speculated he was likely far away from Cypress Falls with the few thousand dollars in cash he'd stolen from me.

The thing I missed most, though, was my grandmother's ring. I hadn't realized how much it meant to me until it was gone. It was like a part of myself had been stolen, too.

Even with the pain and the loss, I needed to move ahead. So much work had to be done. Every piece of merchandise and damage was meticulously documented for the insurance company, who were dragging their feet. I took out a new line of credit in order to pay for repairs and supplies, praying to be reimbursed. When I purchased the building a couple years ago, I never imagined this would happen. It was a lot to do myself, even with help from friends, but I couldn't wait around. I had to get the shop back up and running because it was my life. My livelihood.

"They look perfect," I said, placing my hands on my hips and grinning up at the newly installed shelves. The craftsmanship was unmatched; thick and sturdy, they were made from full grain wood stained a rich dark brown. No one would be able to rip those babies from the wall anytime soon. "I'm really impressed. Where did you learn to make shelves like that?"

Julian hooked his thumbs into the tool belt hanging low on his hips, as he glanced at the shelves. His flannel shirt and faded blue jeans made him look so different. I was used to his usual delivery uniform.

"My dad was a woodworker," he said, still staring at the shelves. "I grew up working in his shop."

"Realy?" I said, intrigued. "He definitely taught you well."

"Thanks." His tone had my heart squeezing. He sounded so...sad. "He was a good teacher."

I put a hand on my chest, taking a step closer to him. "Are you okay?"

He shrugged one shoulder. "He passed right before I graduated high school..."

My stomach dropped. I reached him, gently wrapping my fingers around his forearm. His eyes zeroed in on my hand. "I'm so sorry for your loss."

He didn't reply, only staring at where my hand rested on his arm. We both startled as a loud *thump* sounded from upstairs. We both glanced at the ceiling, people had been filtering in and out of the shop all day, like usual. Some hired workers were currently up in my apartment repairing drywall. Julian pulled away, crossing his arms over his chest.

Concern creased my brow as my attention went back to him. "Do you want to talk about it?" I asked.

He swallowed hard. "It...was a while ago."

"Doesn't matter how long it's been, it still hurts."

Julian's eyes finally met mine, and I couldn't exactly read the emotions there. He just seemed so...upset. "I'm sorry," he said, his voice tight. "Working like this again makes me think about him..."

I waited because it seemed like he had more to say. He sighed, running a hand through his hair. "My dad struggled a long time with depression after my mom died when I was little. They weren't together at the time, but he never stopped loving her and eventually lost his battle."

My heart broke for him. I stepped closer, and warped my arms around him. His body tensed. "I'm so sorry you had to go through that," I whispered.

He cleared his throat. "Sorry," he murmured. "I don't mean to dump my trauma on you."

I let go of him, stepping back and shaking my head. "No, I'm glad you shared that with me. I'm always here if you ever need to talk. You know that right?" I asked, giving him an encouraging smile.

He blinked, shaking his head slightly. His face softened. "I know, thank you. I'm really fine. It's just..." He turned back to admire the shelves again. "It's hard sometimes when the memories come back so strong."

"I hope they were mostly good memories, though. The good times with your dad, I mean. Those shelves are too beautiful to be made with anything but happiness."

He glanced over his shoulder, his brow knitting. "Made with happiness?"

I grinned. "Well, yeah. If you're making something with your hands...I like to think that some of your energy gets put into whatever it is that you're making. A little piece of yourself."

Now that I said it out loud, it sounded a bit ridiculous. I didn't care, though. "I used to make my own clothes sometimes," I continued. "When you're spending hours of your time and skill into making something with your hands...you leave something behind."

"Don't worry," Julian said, and I appreciated that he didn't call me crazy. "Your shelves are happy."

He looked at them, pulling back his shoulders.

"I'm glad," I said, imagining just how beautiful some new glittering jewelry stands would look displayed on the shelves. I clearly envisioned the kinds of shoes that would look amazing displayed on the bottom ones. "What can I do to pay you for these?"

Julian made an exasperated noise. "You paid for the materials. We're good."

"I have to pay you for this."

"You're my friend, Faye. I'm happy to do it."

I scrunched up my nose. "Please? Is there anything I can do to pay you back?"

He turned to face me slowly. "Hmmm..." he said, pursing his lips. "I might know something you can do for me."

"Name it."

He paused, his eyes working down toward his shoes as he shifted on his feet. "How about you let me take you out to dinner?"

His statement sounded more like a question and hit me harder than I expected. "Dinner?" I repeated, sounding as stunned as I felt.

Julina kicked at the floor with the toe of his boot. "Yeah. I mean, only if you want to."

My mouth went bone dry. "As friends?"

I stared at Julian, and he finally glanced up at me, eyes half hooded. "Or as more than friends, if you'd be interested in that."

We stood in silence as I tried to process his words. Julian was asking me out...on a date. We'd become such good friends, even more than an average work friend, but I didn't feel anything like that for him. I enjoyed talking with him. He was so sweet and helpful and handsome. Any woman would be lucky to have him.

But that woman wasn't me.

"I, uh, I don't really date."

His brows rose "You don't date, or you don't want to date me?"

I sucked in a sharp breath. "I don't date, like, at all. I'm not really interested in the whole relationship thing."

The confused look on his face had my chest tightening. I'd gone out with guys before. I've done things with guys before, but Julian asking me out felt different. I only did casual and he seemed like the kind of guy who was looking for a relationship, not a simple fling.

He tilted his head to the side. "Is it that Dawson guy?"

My skin heated. "No, Dawson is my friend."

"A friend that you're living with."

I narrowed my eyes. "You know, that's really not your business, Julian. Dawson and I have been friends for a long time, and he's helping me out. Thank you for the offer, but I really am not looking for a relationship right now."

Julian raised his hands, palms out. "Hey, I'm sorry." His voice softened. "I was just trying to understand."

"Yeah, sure," I said flatly.

I wasn't sure why I suddenly felt so defensive. Julian wasn't the first person to assume things about Dawson and me.

"It's just..." Julian pulled in a deep breath. "I like you, Faye. But if we can only be friends, that's okay, too." He smiled the big, lopsided grin that had my heart softening.

I glanced back at the shelves, trying to orient myself. He had just done something kind for me, and I think I was being a bit too sensitive.

"Okay." I nodded. "I do appreciate everything that you've done for me."

"You don't need to thank me, but you're welcome." He smiled, though it still looked sad.

He gathered up his things and headed toward the door.

With my head still spinning from the unexpected request from Julian, I grabbed my planner and started looking over things. It was getting late, and as I finished up some lists and scheduling, the contractors finished upstairs and left. I didn't like to stay in the shop by myself after darkness fell.

I slipped on my winter coat, a long nude colored wool coat with lace details. The winters here hardly ever got cold enough to warrant a wool coat, but this year was different. A rare winter storm, or what passed as a winter storm in the South, was projected to hit in a couple days. They were calling for ice and some snow accumulation.

Where some places in the country scoffed at a couple inches of snow, it wasn't the same down here. We weren't equipped for it, we didn't have snowplows or salt trucks. Not to mention, no one knew how to drive on snow and ice. Things had to shut down, and

I'd moved things around in my planner just to accommodate for it.

I flipped off the lights, dowsing the shop in darkness. Plywood still covered the windows, and none of the light from the setting sun seeped in. As I opened the front door, icy wind licked my skin, and the hair on the back of my neck raised. I glanced back into the empty, dark shop, my eyes scanning the shadows.

For a moment, it felt as if someone was watching me...

I shook my head as I stepped outside, snapping the door shut. I was being paranoid. No one was in the shop. There was nothing left in there to want, anyway. My keys jingled on my key ring as I turned the deadbolt, locking the place up.

Taking a deep, steadying breath, I pushed past the wave of paranoia and turned toward Main Street. I'd gotten my car back a few days ago, and it was parked on the street out front, only a few steps away...

"Faye."

My stomach dropped, my blood running colder than the wind whipping through my hair. My heart skittered against my ribs as I turned toward the voice I'd recognize anywhere. The voice I hadn't heard in person for over thirteen years.

Mama leaned against the plywood covering my shop windows, her skinny fingers holding a lit cigarette.

I blinked a few times, thinking that I was hallucinating. She looked older than I remembered. Her skin was tanned too dark, giving it an almost leathery quality. Her hair was bleached a bright blonde and she was bundled up in a long red winter coat.

She tilted her head to the side, her glossed lips pursing. "What? You're not going to greet your own mother?"

"What are you doing here?" I hissed, my breath clouding in the cold air.

She arched a thin brow and took a slow drag on her cigarette before she nodded toward the shop behind her. "I heard you got yourself into some trouble with your daddy." She forced a frown. "I tried to warn you about him, honey."

The endearment grated on my nerves like broken glass. My mother had only come to Cypress Falls once, that I knew of, since she abandoned Ellie and me. It didn't make any sense that she'd show up now.

My hands curled into fists. "I have nothing for you."

Mama took one last drag on the cigarette before she threw in on the ground and smothered it with her high heeled pumps. "Obviously." She straightened, crossing her arms over her chest as she shivered. "Why is it so goddamn cold here all of a sudden? I don't remember it ever being so cold. It's awful."

"Then go back to where you came from."

Anger flashed in her eyes and I flinched. When I was younger, that same look came with a swift smack to the face. It was strange the way the body automatically reacted to old memories.

Mama didn't try to hit me this time. Her arms crossed tighter over her chest and her expression hardened. "You should speak kinder to your mama, hon." Her tone was as sharp as steel. "I only came to help you."

"Help me?"

Mama nodded. "You didn't trust me when I warned you about that man and now you got yourself into what looks like a right mess. I've just come to help clean it up a little."

I shook my head. None of that made sense. The one time she'd come back to Cypress Falls she was looking to get Ellie's land after her father had died. There's no way she came here to help me.

"How did you even know about this?"

She rolled her eyes. "I still have friends here, baby. You think word about this isn't spreading all around town like wildfire? People were popping into my messages asking about you and what your daddy did."

My stomach twisted in a nauseating knot. Anger and embarrassment surged through me, making my head pound. It still didn't make sense why she would come, even if she had heard about what happened. She had made it clear since almost the day Ellie and I were born that she didn't care about us. She only cared about how she could control us and what we could get her.

"Thanks for your concern," I said through clenched teeth. "But I have things handled. You can go back to wherever you came from."

"Actually, I think I might stay in town for a little while." She raised her brows.

"Why?" I said, panic surging through me. She couldn't be serious "Aren't you married now? Where's your husband?"

The anger and annoyance in her eyes dissipated as sadness replaced them. She looked away for the first time, smoothing back a piece of her wispy hair. "I just got divorced."

I couldn't stop myself from wondering how many times she'd been divorced, but I restrained myself from commenting. "Well, you don't need to stay on my account."

Mama cleared her throat. She pushed back her shoulders as her gaze met mine. "It's not just you. I also heard I have a grandbaby comin' soon."

My hands started shaking. I stepped closer to her, eyes widening. "You aren't going to see Ellie."

Mama stiffened, her nostrils flaring. "I can do what I want."

After everything, after all that had happened, now was when she suddenly decided to pretend to care? I stepped even closer, pinning her with the most angry glare I could muster. "I don't know what you're planning to do here, but if you try to hurt my sister again, I will make you regret ever coming back to Cypress Falls."

She swallowed, but that look of indignation flashed. She uncurled her arms from around herself and placed them on her hips. "You've changed, Faye." She cocked her head, and then a small, wicked smile curled her lips. "But you don't scare me, sweetie. I've already been through hell." She took a step back as she pulled a carton of cigarettes from her coat pocket and a lighter. "You just let me know when you want my help. I'll be around for a while, I think."

Then she turned and left, leaving me rooted to the spot as I watched the mother who ruined so much of me sauntered away.

Chapter Fifteen

DAWSON

I GLOWERED, CHECKING MY watch. It was too early for Faye to be home. She'd told me she wasn't going to leave the boutique tonight until dusk. But I had distinctly heard someone walk in and slam the front door closed.

I put down my paintbrush, wiping my hands clean on a rag before I headed out of the bedroom that was my studio. Everything looked clear in the hallway. The door to Faye's room down the hall was open, but the light was off.

The sound of a chair sliding over the kitchen floor made me tense. Someone was definitely in my house.

Silently, I made my way to the staircase, peering down into the first floor when a soft voice eased my nerves.

"Are you going to come down here and make me a cup of coffee or what?"

Fighting a smile, I descended the stairs. "You really shouldn't come into someone's home uninvited, you know. That's a good way to get shot in the South."

Annabelle, my little sister, tossed a long lock of red hair over her shoulder. "If you didn't want me coming in, you shouldn't have given me the code to your lock."

She was sitting at the kitchen island, her arms crossed over her chest. I padded over to the sink, turning on the water to wash what was left of the paint off my hands.

"That was supposed to be for emergencies," I grumbled.

"This is an emergency. I need coffee."

I held back an exaggerated eye roll as I dried my hands. "It's a little late for coffee."

One thing about my sister was that she was an extremely busy person. She oversaw operations of the family ranch, and she was going to school to be a vet tech on the side. I admired her work ethic, but there was no way in hell that she came all the way out here to drink a cup of coffee.

Glaring at her, I walked over to the coffee machine sitting on the counter and popped in a single serve coffee pod.

"Cream and sugar please," she added.

Normally, I would've told her I didn't keep such garbage in the house. Coffee was meant to be enjoyed one way, and that was as black as my wardrobe. But, I wasn't the only one living here these days, and there happened to be some kind of sugary, store-bought creamer in the fridge.

"There." I set the cup of offensively pale coffee in front of my sister. "Now tell me the real reason you're bothering me before I kick you out."

She was unfazed by my threat, taking a slow sip of her drink. "Mmmm," she said, smacking her lips. "That's delicious."

This time, I did roll my eyes. "Why are you here, Annabelle?"

Annabelle took another sip. The mug made a soft *clack* as she set it back down on the granite countertop.

"Knox invited you to his wedding a couple weeks ago." A flicker of pain flashed behind her eyes. "I think that you should go."

"Annabelle," I groaned. It didn't surprise me that she brought it up, but I wasn't in the mood to break my little sister's heart. Not tonight.

She held up a hand to silence me. "I know, you'd probably rather die than attend the wedding of the brother you apparently *loathe*."

"I wouldn't go that far." But pretty close.

She raised her brows. "Shiloh said you seemed pretty against it."

"True."

"I want you to reconsider."

I clenched my jaw. Ever since things between me and my brother had gone way off the rails, Annabelle was desperately trying to bring us back together. I understood, to an extent. Our family had been broken and battered. Annabelle wanted to repair what she could.

She was just trying to fix something that couldn't be mended.

"I don't see what that would accomplish," I said.

She reached for the horseshoe necklace around her neck. The sight of it had my gut twisting. Our mama had one just like it when she was alive.

"It would mean a lot to me..." Annabelle said quietly, gliding the horseshoe charm back and forth along the delicate chain. "And it's for a good cause. For the animal rescue, I mean. I'm helping to plan the whole event."

That didn't surprise me, either. Until recently, the ranch was a nonprofit equestrian rehabilitation center. Now, the place was self-sustaining, but before that, my mama and Annabelle would plan a yearly fundraiser gala for the ranch. She was a seasoned event planner at this point.

"They're lucky to have you."

"They'd be luckier to have you show up."

I scoffed. "I highly doubt that."

Annabelle looked down at her coffee. "You could at least try, Dawon. Knox has...grown a lot since he did what he did to you. I...I think he just wants forgiveness. He was only doing what he thought was right at the time. He's sorry for what happened to you."

I straightened my spine, clenching my hands. Pent-up emotion vibrated through me. Not only the familiar anger...but also pain. There were too many bad memories, too much hurt. Hating him was easier than facing that pain.

"If he's sorry then he'd leave me the hell alone and let me live my life." I spat.

Annabelle flinched. I looked away.

My brother might've been doing what he thought was right at the time, but he also hadn't believed me when I told him the truth. I hadn't hurt my mother like he had first thought, and he chose to convict me for it.

"Okay," Annabelle breathed. "If you can't come for him...come for me. Come for Paws and Pastures." I glanced back at her, her eyes were wide and pleading. "This is a big event I'm trying to plan. It would mean the world to me if you not only came, but I could really use your help with the preparation."

I pushed a hand through my hair, grabbing a clump of it in my fist. "So, not only do you want me to come to the wedding, but you want me to help out with it?"

"The *event*," she said, accentuating the last word. "I'm going to need all the help I can get. Especially when it comes to donations.

I'm short on items for the silent auction in particular, so if you can think of any local businesses who'd want to donate, I need to know ASAP."

I rested my hands on my hips. It didn't escape me that she was speaking as if I'd already agreed to this.

"I'm not exactly friendly with local businesses," I muttered.

"No, but you're living with someone who very much is."

Faye.

I shook my head in disbelief. I had to hand it to her, the woman knew what she was doing. "I can ask her when she gets home, but I'm not going to push it. She's had enough going on."

Annabelle nodded. "Fair." She took another sip of her coffee, looking more like her confident self.

"I still haven't agreed to come."

"I understand." She paused, the mug halfway to her mouth. "But promise me you'll think about it. Not for Knox, but for me."

I ground my back teeth together. "I'll take it into consideration."

"Thank you, Dawson," she said, her eyes softening. "I appreciate it."

My sister made quick work of her coffee after that. Moving the conversation to lighter topics, like how the horses were doing, and telling me the latest stories going around the ranch. Apparently our father, a very prominent business man, had actually started to learn how to horseback ride.

I didn't see that one coming. Our father was as straightlaced and stuck up as it came. Always working to grow and maintain the family fortune. He'd had an accident about a year ago that had changed him, though.

"Well," Annabelle said, leaving her empty mug on the counter-top and sauntering over to the front door. "I should probably get back home. Colton's cooking tonight, and I wouldn't dare want to be late." She grinned this happy, love-drunk grin at the mention of her husband.

I walked her to the front door, opening it for her. "You definitely don't want to make him wait."

When my baby sister first got married, it was a shock to all of us. It'd been totally out of the blue, but I'd grown to like Colton more than I expected. He was a local cop and a good guy.

Annabelle pushed up on her toes, planting a soft kiss on my cheek. "You gonna cook for your lady?" she asked, wiggling her brows.

"She's not my lady. She's my friend."

Annabelle pressed her lips together like she was physically holding something back. "Right. I was kidding."

"Goodbye, little sister," I said, taking her by the shoulders and gently turning her around and shuffling her out the door.

She threw me a look over her shoulder, and I couldn't tell if it was more exasperation or concern. "Take care of yourself," she said.

"I always do."

She gave me a wave and then finally headed off to her vehicle.

I watched until she hopped in and drove away. A shiver from the winter air rattled down my spine, and I stepped back inside, closing the door.

The heat from the woodburner warmed my skin, but my heart felt cold and hard. I leaned against the closed door, going over the conversation with Annabelle about my participation in this upcoming "event."

Knox's wedding.

I hated disappointing my sister. I hated that it hurt her when Knox and I didn't get along. It was just the reality of the situation.

I scrubbed a hand over my face. I needed to shave; it had been days, and it was getting long.

Annabelle was right, I had to stop thinking about it as a wedding or anything for my brother. I was going to do something, it was going to be for her. And for Axel. His animal rescue could benefit a lot from a successful event filled with lots of people and lots of donations.

I could at least help him.

Thinking of Axel reminded me of Meatloaf who'd I'd left upstairs. I quickly went to retrieve him, and he hadn't moved a muscle from his designated corner in my studio, tail wagging frantically. I brought him downstairs and out the back to go to the restroom.

Meatloaf took his time finding a good place to do his business.

I blew warm air into my cupped hands, rubbing the cold from them. He always seemed to take the longest when it was dark and freezing. Meatloaf finally finished up and trotted up the deck steps to join me, a big doggy grin on his face.

"Took ya long enough," I mumbled, turning to let us both back into the warm cabin.

The front door opened as I closed the back one, and I froze as Faye came barreling inside, her cheeks red and blotchy from the cold. She slammed the door behind her, her sapphire eyes lacking their usual happy sparkle.

Faye paused as she caught sight of me, her mouth set and jaw rigid. She looked...pissed.

She barely looked down at Meatloaf as he excitedly greeted her.

"What's wrong?" I walked across the space to her.

Faye told Meatloaf to go lie down as she met my gaze. "Nothing."

She was lying. Faye wasn't a good lair. It was one of the many things I found endearing about her.

"Want to try again?"

Her brow furrowed, and she turned away, shrugging off her thick coat and hanging it up on the coat rack.

"Dawson," she said, voice sharp and exhausted. "I—I don't know if I can talk about it."

She tried to walk around me toward the stairs, but I caught her arm. "Whatever it is that made you so upset, I'm here for you."

Faye stared down at my hand wrapped around her elbow. I wasn't holding on hard, but she didn't try to pull away. Her shoulders sagged as she let out a long breath. "Yeah?"

I touched her chin with my other hand, tilting her face up to meet my eyes. "You can talk to me. I'm not going to judge."

Her brow furrowed, her mouth opened slightly before she clapped it shut again. My stomach dropped. "Keeping it inside isn't going to solve anything," I said softly.

She shook her head. "I don't even know how to process."

I let out a frustrated sigh. If she wasn't going to talk to me about it, then I had to find another way to make her feel better. She'd been holding it together these past couple of weeks, being so strong through everything that had happened with her father and the boutique. Whatever it was that finally broke her resolve, I wouldn't let it consume her.

"Fine," I said. I let her chin go, but I held on to her arm. "Follow me."

I walked her toward the staircase.

"Where are we going?"

"I have something to show you."

She didn't reply, but she didn't fight me as I took her up to the second floor. I didn't bring her to her bedroom.

I brought her to the door of the studio.

Chapter Sixteen

FAYE

I stared at the door Dawson had asked me not to enter since the day I started staying here. These past two weeks I'd been too busy to push him about his "secret work," but my heart raced as he gripped the door handle. Despite what had just happened with my mother, I welcomed this distraction.

"I finally get to see the room?"

Something sparked in his eyes. "It's time."

He opened the door and pulled me into the room. My breath caught in my lungs.

The space was filled with...art.

My mouth opened, gaping at the sheer beauty and overwhelming chaos of the scene before me. Blank canvases of various sizes and shapes were stacked and lined up in cupboards on the far wall. Multiple wooden tables lined the adjacent wall, laden with paints and brushes and cups and pieces of stray papers. Writing utensils were randomly strewn in the mix with paint splattered rags and palettes of various colors. Easels were set up in multiple places, sitting on top of paint-speckled drop cloths that looked like their own form of mosaic portraits.

My eyes were wide as they connected with Dawson's. Everything I knew about him coming into clearer focus.

"Dawson," I breathed. "You *have* been keeping secrets from me."

A range of emotions built up within me, in awe of this room, but also confused. This was...amazing, but how long had he kept this from me and why?

Dawson gave a shrug. "It's not really a big deal."

My eyes felt like they were going to bulge out of my skull. "Not a big deal?" I gestured around the room. "This looks like the exact opposite of that. This looks..." I trailed off as I caught a better glimpse of one of the paintings in the corner. Before I realized it, I walked toward it, drawn in by something I couldn't quite place.

All the paintings were beautiful. They had this unique texture to them, as if he was building the paint out of the canvas, giving it a depth of dimension. Exactly like the painting I loved hanging downstairs in the living room.

I sucked in a breath as I got closer to the painting in the corner. It was a forest scene, a recurring motif in most of the art in this room. It was all lush greenery in various hues of subtle greens. The colors were so deep and complex, capturing the stunning details of the forest so accurately.

Though, that wasn't what caught my eye. What drew me to this piece was the girl. She looked like she was dancing in the brush surrounded by tall, thick trees, her long blonde hair trailing in the wind behind her. Her arms were raised over her head, reaching for the glowing rays of sunlight streaming in through the gaps in the canopy of leaves above.

The paint was built upon itself until the dancing girl looked like she was stepping right out off the canvas. She almost looked real, like if I reached for her, I'd feel the warmth of her skin...

"It's a commissioned piece. I don't paint people much, but the concept of this just...resonated with me."

I blinked, glancing at Dawson. "Commission? You sell your paintings?"

He shrugged again. "It kind of just happened. I found myself getting more and more into painting, and I didn't know what to do with it all. I started a social media page to share what I was doing and...people liked it. They started buying."

My brows raised. "You're on social media?"

"Not as me, no." He shook his head. "I've never shared this part of myself with people I actually know. I interact with my following and customers through the online persona and pseudonym I created."

My eyes widened. "Why don't you want people to know about what you do?"

He glanced around at the paintings on the easels. "I don't know. It seemed so easy at the time. I started to post to just...be someone else. No one knew who I was or knew my past. It was like a clean slate."

I wrapped my arms around my chest. "You didn't even want to tell me?"

"I'm telling you now."

My gaze snapped back to the dancing girl. My heart panged. I was so happy for Dawson. This was all amazing for him, but it stung that he'd been keeping this from me. This huge part of his life.

"Do you not trust me?" I asked, my voice giving away the hurt cutting through the awe.

"Of course I trust you." He sounded almost offended.

My attention went back to him. He tilted his head to the side, his forehead wrinkling in confusion.

I lifted my shoulders in a slow shrug. "A secret this big seems like something best friends share with each other."

His expression cleared as he stuffed his hands in his pockets. "We don't tell each other everything, Faye."

"Obviously not."

He let out a heavy, frustrated breath. "Look, I didn't bring you here to piss you off more. And I wasn't keeping this from you because I don't trust you or because I think of you any less." He stepped closer to me, the warmth of his body and the smoky, spicy scent of him enveloped me.

"When I first started painting it was to...help me process what I'd been through after—after my mother was attacked. It gave me a way to express what I couldn't even admit to myself or put into words. It was a private thing. A dark thing that somehow brought light. I never intended to make this into a career."

I bit my lip. "I get that. I do. It just seems strange that you share your art with strangers online, but not with me?"

He swallowed, his throat bobbing. "Because they *are* strangers. My art is something that was just mine for a long time. It was...intimate."

His hand flinched, and I thought he was going to reach for me, but he didn't. "Then...why are you telling me now?"

"Because it was time. And because you deserve to know. It's time I start treading outside my comfort zone."

He turned, and the absence of his warmth had a shiver running through me. He pulled out a medium sized white canvas from the cupboard and brought it over, replacing the gorgeous painting of the dancing forest girl with the blank canvas.

He gestured to the canvas. "And I think you should, too."

ABBEY EASTON

I stared at the canvas, frowning. "What?"

"This is for you."

"For me?"

He nodded, and then he grabbed a nearby rolling cart that was chock full of paints and brushes. "Paint. If you're pissed at me, fine." He plucked up a brush and held it out to me. "Take it out on the canvas. It'll help."

My eyes darted between the brush, the canvas, and his face. "I don't know how to paint."

"I can show you."

I wasn't sure what he was trying to accomplish, but his face was calm, almost encouraging. Cautiously, I reached for the brush. "Fine."

A ghost of a smile touched his lips. He grabbed a palette from the cart and squeezed small beads of various different colors on it. He looked in his element, working smoothly and efficiently like the process was second nature.

"Here," Dawson said, holding out the prepared palette.

I shifted on my feet, clenching the paintbrush in my fist.

When I didn't take the palette from him, recognition flashed in his eyes. "It's not hard, Faye. There's no rules."

But rules were what I lived on. Rules made things easier.

I glanced back at the canvas. Part of my job was designing. I wasn't completely inept at creative work, but designing clothes and painting like this were entirely different. And being surrounded by Dawson's breathtaking art was intimidating.

I was about to hand him back the paintbrush because this was a stupid idea, but Dawson wrapped his hand around mine. The air caught in my throat as he came up close behind me, pressing his body against mine as he gently coaxed the hand holding the paintbrush.

"You just have to begin," he whispered in my ear, sending waves of tingles across my skin.

I let out the breath I was holding. For a moment I held still, my body tense and unrelenting. It wasn't in my nature to give up control. Dawson chuckled soft in my ear, making my heart react in that way it shouldn't.

"You need to relax," he whispered.

I bit my lip. "It's hard."

"Mmm," his chest vibrated against my back with the sound. "Do you trust me?"

I hesitated. The fact that he'd hid this from me for so long stung, but I wasn't entitled to him. He wasn't mine. He was my friend, my best friend, and at least he was sharing it with me now.

I straightened my spine and nodded. "Of course I do."

"Then trust me with this." He tightened his fingers around my hand in a gentle squeeze. "Let go."

We both stood there, my heart pounding against my ribs for no good reason. Gradually, I forced my muscles to relax, and I relented to Dawson.

"Thank you," he murmured in my ear. A pent-up breath escaped my lungs, both proud and scared that I was letting this happen.

With his hand over mine, he dipped the paintbrush in the paint. His arms wrapped around me from behind as he worked—as *we* worked. I could hardly focus as he mixed paints together, his hand moving mine, and making an entirely different color that hadn't been there before. Seeming satisfied, he scooped a good portion up on the brush, and his hand guided mine over to the canvas.

Highly aware of how much of his body touched mine, my skin heated. It felt like a fire had kindled in the pit of my belly and was roaring through my veins.

He moved with fluid, sure motions. I wasn't sure what we were painting, but I let him move me how he pleased...watching in fascination the ways he spread the paint over the canvas and the colors he used.

"What are we making?" I finally asked, my voice faint and fluttering with the beats of my heart.

He stilled, the brush stopping mid stroke. His breath caressed the shell of my ear, making goosebumps rise on my skin.

"I don't know," he said, his voice low and husky. "Sometimes you have to let your hands wander and see where they take you..."

"Oh," was all I managed to utter.

He started moving again, mixing colors and running the brush over the canvas like he knew exactly what he was doing. I watched in awe, every part of me wound tight as I tried to control the fire burning inside me.

"Remember to stay relaxed," Dawson whispered. "This is supposed to make you feel better. You don't have to be so tense."

I cleared my throat, trying to let loose some of my locked muscles.

"Right," I murmured.

Dawson somehow stepped even closer, pressing every part of his body flush against mine.

I focused on the end of the brush and the way Dawson used it to push the paint over the surface as my thoughts swirled in my brain. Everything started bubbling to the surface: the utter betrayal from my father, the jarring appearance from my mother, how Dawson hiding things from me bothered me more than it probably should, and the way his damn body felt so good against mine.

Why did being close to Dawson like this feel so much different?

It was all so much. A flare of anger erupted from inside me, anger for my mama, for showing up the way she did and for myself, too, for letting it all overwhelm me. I latched on to that anger, letting it distract me from the heat of desire I felt for the man behind me who was nothing more than my friend.

I took over the movement of the brush before I even thought about it. Dawson let me, not caring that I was ruining the beauty of the painting. I just wanted to move, to do *something*.

"Talk to me, Faye," Dawson breathed into my ear.

"It's just..." I shook my head, the words stubborn and getting lost in translation from my brain to my mouth. "This whole couple of weeks have just been..." I pulled back the paintbrush. "Bullshit." I brought the brush back down so hard that it slipped right out of my hands and clattered to the floor.

It didn't matter to me though. Not right now. I tore my hand away from Dawson's, using my bare fingers to smear the paint around the canvas. This wasn't like me at all, but I let the anger, the fear, the hurt, flow through my hands as I used both of them to push paint round the canvas, turning whatever beautiful thing we'd been making together into total chaos. The paint gathered between my fingers, making them glide smoothly over the canvas. It was raw and tactile and cathartic.

"I hate being so...so stupid and shameful and ignorant and so damn gullible," I spat, speaking to the canvas and to myself. I let the emotion seep right through me as the wet paint mixed and swirled together creating new colors and a whole new...thing.

As much as I hated my Mama, she was right. She had warned me about Marc, but I hadn't listened. I had wanted to believe he was good. I wanted so badly to have a parent to love, and who loved me, too.

I felt so stupid. No matter how much I wanted to hate my father, I didn't. I mourned him. I mourned the relationship I thought I had and the father I had wanted so desperately.

I didn't realize until something caught a hold of my wrist, holding it steady, that there were tears in my eyes.

I blinked rapidly, trying to make the blur of tears go away as I came back to my senses.

Dawson grabbed my hip with his other hand and gently pulled me back a few steps from the mess of a painting I'd ruined. He turned me around to face him, but I couldn't meet his eyes. I didn't know what had come over me, but my heart was racing, my breaths heavy. Dawson still held on to my wrist, my hands covered in paint.

He hooked a finger under my chin, and I didn't fight too hard as he tilted my face up to meet his.

"Faye," he said my name in a deep, low rasp that I felt in my very core. It sounded like more than my name. It sounded like a plea. "You are anything but stupid."

I closed my eyes, my face heating. "If I was smart, none of this would've happened. I wouldn't be picking my life up, piece by piece, every day."

"That's not true."

My eyes popped open again, and a tear dripped from my lashes and down my cheek. Dawson wiped it away with the back of a finger. His lips pressed together in a firm line as his eyes roamed my face, like he was looking for something he'd lost a long time ago.

"It is true. And now I'm here crying like a fool because my damn mother showed up at my destroyed boutique and reminded me that if I wasn't so gullible—"

He pressed his thumb over my lips, silencing me. "Wait, your mama is in town?"

The shocked look on his face quickly melted into rage as I nodded.

"No." He shook his head, his jaw hardening. "She doesn't get to define you anymore, Faye. I won't stand here and listen to you hate the best things about you."

The best things about me?

A crease formed between his brows like he was trying to make a decision.

Then his eyes flicked down to my mouth and stayed there. The thumb he still had pressed to my lips moved, slowly brushing back and forth along my lower lip.

The blood rushed in my ears as I forgot everything we were talking about. That heat ignited in my core, coursing through my body in hot scalding waves.

"So what if you're a little gullible, Faye," he breathed. He leaned forward, pressing his forehead against mine, making my heart swell until it almost burst. "You just choose to see the best in people. You believe in people, even when they don't deserve it, and I don't think that's a weakness...I think it's a strength."

He let go of my wrist, and my arm fell limp at my side. He took his hand and ran it through my hair. "You were the one who believed in me when no one else did. For that, I will always be grateful."

My lips parted as his thumb trailed lazily across my jaw. He was so close I could almost taste him. His breaths were hot against my over-sensitized skin.

I took in his words slowly, letting them sink into my heart like warm honey. It drew me to him, and I got even closer, pressing myself against his chest. The tips of our noses touched as our heavy breaths mingled. Every nerve in my body wanted to close the minuscule gap between our lips. I wanted to wrap my arms around him and pull him closer than he'd ever been.

A heavy silence hung between us, and his eyes closed briefly as he swallowed hard. "We should—we should get some space." His words sounded strangled, but he pulled back a half step, his heat suddenly replaced by cold nothingness.

I blinked, rocking back on my heels before realizing I'd been standing on them to get close to him...to his mouth.

Damn him. Damn him and his perfect smell and beautiful face.

"Yeah," I said, my voice sounding as raspy as his. "You're right."

I didn't move away though. I was planted to the spot, that ache of wanting coursing through me. My eyes bounced to his lips, wondering what would happen if I just...tasted them. Just once. I bit my lip.

Dawson made a strange noise between a sigh and groan as he took another half step back.

I tore my eyes away from his mouth, shaking those stupid thoughts from my brain. "I, uh...I should go clean up." My paint-coated hands fisted at my sides.

He nodded, his breaths still heavy. "Yeah, right. You should."

With an embarrassing amount of effort, I turned from him and headed toward the door, feeling as if I was walking against a gravity pulling me back toward Dawson. Once I was in the hallway, my chest eased, but not much as I went to the guest room that had been mine for the past two weeks.

I slammed the bedroom door closed behind me, leaning against it as my heart pounded so hard my ribs ached. That was too intense for my liking. Yes, Dawson was attractive, but he was my friend. I didn't do anything but friendship.

I held my paint-coated hand out in front of me, my eyes focusing on my ring finger and the bareness of it. It was times like now when I ached for my grandmother's ring. It had brought me so much comfort when I was lost. I wasn't sure if I'd ever get used to not having it.

Clenching my filthy, bare hands into fists, I headed to the attached bathroom and turned on the tap, not waiting for it to get warm before I stuck my hands under the water. The paint ran off my skin as I scrubbed them together, tinting the water with color.

The paint swirled and twisted hypnotically in the water before disappearing down the drain.

I wished my conflicted feelings could be washed away just as easily.

Chapter Seventeen

DAWSON

I WAS A DAMN coward.

Last night with Faye was too much.

The frigid air burned in my lungs as I pushed my legs down the last incline of the trail. A jolt of electricity shot through me as I remembered how close her mouth had been to mine. Having Faye stay here was becoming more complicated than I anticipated. I had to be more careful.

I broke out of the forest and into my backyard, I glanced up at the sky. The dark gray was ominous, and I hoped the predicted winter storm that was supposed to hit tonight would pass us over.

It didn't seem likely.

We hadn't talked more about the sudden appearance of her mama, but I knew it wasn't a good thing that she was here. That woman has been nothing but heartache and trouble for Faye. Seeing how torn up Faye was last night about seeing her had rage coursing through me.

I slowed as I approached the back deck of the cabin, trying to control my heaving breaths. Running had become more difficult with the wild winter weather this year, but I had needed it this morning. I was too high-strung with the memory of how close Faye and I had been. Too close for friends, that's for sure.

Meatloaf was waiting for me inside, spinning in a quick circle as his tail wagged. I gave him an ear scratch before I headed to get some water. My skin started thawing, painfully stinging as I filled a glass and chugged it.

My gaze caught on Meatloaf who had settled by the front door. He had stationed himself there since Faye had left early this morning. He tilted his head to the side, staring at me like he knew exactly what had happened between Faye and me last night. I think his eyes even narrowed a little.

"Don't look at me like that," I grumbled, setting my glass down onto the countertop too hard.

I ran my hands through my sweaty, damp hair. I needed a shower. Turning away from my judgmental dog who was patiently waiting for his girl to come back home, I threw some logs into the wood burner. The pile was getting low, even though I'd chopped more yesterday. The temperature outside had dipped below anything I'd had to deal with up here ahead of this storm coming.

Meatloaf whined softly as I headed to my room to shower. "She'll be back soon, bud," I assured him.

It was Saturday, and she usually spent the day with Meatloaf, spoiling him by taking him for long walks in town and buying him gourmet treats from the pet store.

This morning she'd snuck out the door with barely a goodbye to the two of us.

Meatloaf huffed as if scolding me for chasing her away. I hadn't, though. Right?

141

I shook my head. He was probably feeding off my crappy mood. I dragged myself to the shower to hopefully wash away the lingering memory of my lips so close to Faye's.

The shower didn't make me feel better. I was clean, but the uncertainty and frustration lingered in my gut.

The cabin was quiet when I walked out into the main room. It had gotten darker outside, the clouds thick and angry as the wind kicked up with a high-pitched whisper. I flicked on the lights. Meatloaf's ears perked up from his spot by the door. He hadn't moved.

I let out a sigh. "Come on, Meatloaf," I called to him. "Go lie down on your bed."

He stared at me whining again and pacing nervously before the front door.

Great.

I was about to assure the poor creature that his most favorite human would be home soon, when a flash of headlights hit the front windows.

Meatloaf let out a sharp bark, something he didn't normally do.

I shushed him, relieved that she was home.

The door swung open, and Faye stepped into the cabin, her arm cradling a large box in one hand and a coffee in the other. She kicked the door closed, stumbling slightly and I rushed over.

"Where have you been?" I asked, making sure she was steady.

She blinked at me over the box, her cheeks pink from the cold. Her eyes darted to my mouth for a fraction of a second before she cleared her throat. "I, uh, needed some me time." She shoved the box toward me, forcing it into my hands. "I got my hair done and stopped by the coffee shop, and I picked up the mail while I was in town. You had a package."

My eyes bounced from the package back to her. Her hair did seem fuller than normal, bouncy and shiny and maybe a tad bit shorter than it was before, just skimming the tops of her shoulders.

With the box out of her hands, she smiled and stooped down to greet Meatloaf as his whole body wiggled in an attempt to restrain himself from attacking her with love.

"Hello, sweet boy," she said, giving him a good rub before straightening her spine and brushing off the dog hair.

I brought the package to the kitchen island, inspecting it. Normally I was the one sending out packages, not receiving them. I hadn't ordered anything, and I carefully popped open the tape and lifted the flaps.

A small note was nestled on top of a mess of white tissue paper. I plucked it up, recognizing the small, neat script.

Dawson,

I put together this album as a wedding gift for Knox, but I thought that you might want a copy too. These are some of the best memories I have.

Love,

Annabelle

P.S.

Daddy helped, too.

I swallowed hard, putting down the note from my sister and pulling out the crinkly tissue paper.

"What's that?" Faye's voice close to my ear made me tense, but I didn't look at her. My gaze was trained on the album I'd uncovered. The picture on the front was one of the last family photos we'd ever taken.

The five of us were standing in front of the small pond on the ranch. Our father had his arms wrapped around Mama, her face bright and radiant as she grinned at the camera. Her red hair, so much like my sister's, was pulled up in her signature ponytail.

Knox and I were in high school and towered over Annabelle standing between us. Her head was leaning against my shoulder, and we all were grinning, smiling like everything in the world was fine. Totally oblivious to the tragedy that would ruin us some day.

My chest tightened as I lifted the album out and sat in on the counter. In my peripheral, Faye picked up the note from Annabelle, but she didn't say anything as I started to flip through the pages of my past.

With each page, my hands began to tremble. It started when we were little, Knox no older than five and Annabelle a little toddler. It was memories of the ranch, where we spent so much of our childhood.

And with Mama.

"Who's that?" Faye asked, breaking her silence as she pointed to a picture of me and a little black puppy.

A pang seared my heart as I looked into the dark eyes of the kid who was so damned happy to have his own dog. A dog that had grown up by my side and became one of my best friends. A dog who I'd let get trampled by a spooked horse when I accidentally left a stall open.

"It's me and Bo," I said, my voice thick.

"I didn't know you had a dog. He's cute."

"He died." The words came out colder than intended. There was so much guilt there even after all these years.

Her body tensed beside me. "I'm sorry."

"Me too."

I kept flipping through pages even though I could hardly breathe. It had been years since I'd seen our mama, since I'd looked at her face even in a picture.

When I turned one of the last pages, I froze.

There was only a singular photo big enough to cover the whole page. It was Mama, standing in front of the stall barn. She had a cowboy hat on, her hands on her hips as she stared out into the distance at the pastures filled with her horses.

She was beautiful, and my heart ached for her. A wave of grief washed over me, almost bringing me to my knees. I stumbled back from the album, from the memories that haunted me and the regret it brought.

"Hey," Faye said, her voice soft as she reached for my arm. "It's okay, Dawson."

My eyes met hers, and I shook my head. It wasn't okay. I glanced back at the album lying open on the picture of my mother. The picture of her standing right in front of the place where I'd found her broken and bleeding.

Tears burned in my eyes.

"Dawson," Faye said my name again, pressing her palm against the side of my face and gently turning my stare away from the album. "Look at me."

I did. I stared into her sad, beautiful blue eyes and wanted to drown myself in them. The image of my mother's body was burned into my brain, and I just wanted it to go away.

Something wet touched my cheek. I was completely losing it. I turned away from her, dragging in deep ragged breaths.

Faye stepped around me, but I turned my face away. "Don't hide from me," she said.

My jaw clenched, half embarrassed and overwhelmed that I'd let a few simple pictures undo me. When I stayed silent, she stepped closer. Her scent washed over me. It wasn't a perfume, because Faye didn't wear any, but it was intoxicating. She smelled like sunshine after a rainstorm, fresh and warm and perfect.

145

"You're scaring me," she whispered.

My eyes collided with hers as she pinned me with her stare. "It's nothing," I rasped.

Her mouth fell into a sharp frown. Her eyes flicked to my cheeks, where my tears betrayed me. Slowly, she lifted onto the tips of her toes. The air around me thinned, like I couldn't get enough oxygen and she pressed her lips against my cheek before pulling away.

"I've known you for a long time, Dawson," she said, her voice low and intense. "Your tears don't mean nothing. You can tell me how you're feeling."

My jaw hardened. She shouldn't be this close. She shouldn't be putting that perfect mouth so close to mine. "I just..." I stuttered, sounding choked. "I haven't seen her face in a long time."

Faye's expression pinched. "I'm so sorry." She bit her lip, her hands tightening around my face. "I know it probably doesn't make you feel better, but if she was here, she'd be so proud of you."

It was as if she'd reached right into my chest and tore out my heart. I shook my head. "No, she wouldn't be." How the hell could she? I had left her on that barn floor to die. I had run away.

It didn't matter what I accomplished, it wouldn't make up for my sins. I left a black stain on everything I freaking touched.

"Stop," Faye snapped, her nails biting into my skin. "You always act like you aren't worth a damn, and I'm tired of it. Your worth isn't in what people think of you. It doesn't matter what your reputation is or if people think you're a bad person. I know the truth. I know *you*. You are generous and brave and talented, and regardless of what you let others think, you care about people. You will go to the ends of the earth to help anyone...you are *good*. And your mama would be proud of you."

Her words hit me hard. I tried to let them sink in, I could only focus on her, on the pain in her expression—pain she was feeling for me. I had cared for this woman most of my life, and she was so very close.

My eyes burned as a lump formed in my throat. I was so incredibly stupid. I sucked in a deep breath, my last ounce of self-control snapping like a twig. "You're—you're too close, Faye," I choked out.

Her eyes darkened. "I don't care."

I made a noise deep in my throat. "If you stay this close to me I'm going to kiss you."

She tensed, the breaths hitching in her chest. I scanned her face, looking for any sign of repulsion or fear. There wasn't any.

Her throat bobbed as she swallowed. "Maybe that wouldn't be so bad."

"We can't cross that line," I said, but my entire body wanted to fling myself over it and take her in my arms. My brain was clouded, desperate to lose the wave of grief in anything—even my best friend.

She looked at me from beneath her dark lashes. "How about we draw a new one?"

My brows furrowed. Where was she going with this?

She craned her neck, her lips a breath away from mine, our heavy, hot breaths mingling. "We can be friends who also kiss, Dawson." But even as she said the words, they were full of doubt. "I'm not looking for you to be more, but it's okay to kiss me. We can try it, just once. It doesn't have to mean more than it is."

I glanced at her slightly parted lips, wanting and waiting, and I didn't care that it could be a horrible idea. All I cared about was that I needed her. I wanted her.

Before I let my brain decide better, my body moved. My hands cupped her face as my lips crashed against hers.

It was unlike anything I'd experienced in my whole damn life. The closest thing to describe kissing Faye was like we were literal fireworks, bursting with heat and sparks of color. She tasted like the sweetest golden honey, and I drank her in, devouring her soft, plump lips like I was famished.

She sighed softly, melting into my body and making my blood roar in my ears. My hands moved from her face and tangled in her hair, pulling her closer.

I wanted all of her.

Her mouth opened, and our tongues met in an intricate dance that had my core winding so tight I was sure I'd burst. My skin was electrified by her touch as she wrapped her arms around my neck.

Everything in me wanted to lose myself in her and this moment. I wanted to kiss every square inch of her and make her mine...but she wasn't mine. The thought nagged at the back of my brain, making its way forward. This was exactly what I needed—-getting lost in a frenzy of sensations. But if I kept going, I wouldn't be able to stop.

I pulled myself back with an aching amount of difficulty. Pressing my forehead to hers, I tried to catch my breath.

She stiffened in my arms. "Dawson?" she whispered.

"You said...one kiss," I gasped, my voice ragged. "If I keep going, it's gonna turn into more than just one kiss."

Her lips twisted up into a small smile. "Well, it was a good kiss."

"Yeah." My gaze met hers. "Thanks."

"You're thanking me for kissing you?" Her eyes twinkled.

I shrugged one shoulder. "I feel better."

"Good." She bit the corner of her lip, almost undoing all my resolve. "You can still talk to me, you know. If you need to. I'm good at kissing, but I'm a better listener."

I swallowed down the urge to kiss her again. It took all the strength I had, but I stepped back. The absence of her heat made me shiver. "I'm fine, Faye."

She wrapped her arms around herself, rubbing her arms like she was fending off a chill. I chastised myself for not chopping more firewood. If there was going to be a winter storm, we'd need the heat, but the rain had already started falling outside, spattering against the windows.

Faye chewed on her lip. Slowly she raised her pinky finger out toward me. I stared at it for a moment, confused.

"We need to update our promise," she explained. "Since we're redrawing lines."

I cocked an eyebrow. "What am I promising, exactly?"

"Promise me that no matter how much you kiss me, no matter how far we go physically, that our hearts are not on the table."

My stomach clenched. I stared at her little finger reaching for me. A warning went off in my mind, but I ignored it. "My heart is already made of ice, Faye. It's not in any kind of shape to be given away."

She shifted on her feet, seeming unsure for a fraction of a second, but she held her pinky out closer. "You promise?"

I sighed, reaching out and hooking my pinky finger around hers. "I promise."

Chapter Eighteen

FAYE

I DIDN'T REMEMBER FALLING asleep, but suddenly my sore eyes opened to soft sunlight drifting in through my bedroom window.

The taste of Dawson still tingled on my lips.

My heart fluttered as I touched my mouth. I'd been kissed before, but not like that. It never felt like a man had literally stolen my breaths and left me dizzy in the best way. Last night, after our mind-blowing kiss, Dawson had put away the album, and he'd spent the rest of the night up in his studio while I watched movies with Meatloaf. I'd spent most the night wide awake, highly aware that Dawson was in this very house only steps away. My skin flush at the thought of the way his hands had tangled in my hair.

It might have been an impulsive decision, letting Dawson kiss me, but I couldn't bring myself to regret it. The tension building between the two of us these last weeks was becoming too much. Maybe it was good for us to get it out of our system.

I listened closely for any sounds of movement in the house, any sign that Dawson was awake. I hadn't seen him last night before I got in bed, and I worried about him. I'd never seen him react like he had to the photo album of his family. The lost, agonized look on his face would be seared into my memory for a long time.

Everything in the cabin seemed quiet, it was almost deafening. I rolled over, untangling myself from my crisp, white sheets and grabbed my phone from the nightstand to check the time.

It was late morning, closer to afternoon. Dawson had to be awake. He was an early riser.

I quickly got dressed and ran a brush through my hair. It still was soft from the salon and smoothed out quicker than it normally would. I didn't even have to run the straightener through it.

After putting on a cardigan to stave off the winter chill that had seeped through the bones of the cabin, I left my bedroom and padded downstairs with Meatloaf close behind me. He must have had to use the restroom badly. I'd slept in much later than normal.

Dawson wasn't on the main floor at first glance. Unease squirmed in the pit of my stomach. The kitchen was clean and tidy, no pan sitting in the sink as a tell-tale sign he'd made himself his usual breakfast of eggs and bacon. There was no smell of coffee in the air.

I turned toward the living room, heading to the back of the cabin to let out Meatloaf, when I froze.

My mouth dropped open at the scene set outside the windows looking out on the back yard.

Everything was covered in fluffy, pure snow. I blinked a few times, the bright white making my eyes sting. There weren't more than a few inches, but I had never seen so much snow in my entire life. It didn't seem real. It blanketed everything. Barren tree branches were covered in white. Heaps of downy snow were nestled on top of the dark green pines. The ground looked like a sea of sparkling clouds.

It was a whole different world.

Meatloaf's nails clicked on the floor as he spun in a circle and whined, breaking me out of my awe at the snow-covered wonderland.

"Sorry," I muttered, continuing on to the back door.

I slipped on a pair of shoes I kept next to the threshold and opened it, shivering as a gust of icy wind glided over my skin. I inhaled the fresh, sharp scent of snow and pine. Meatloaf sprinted out into the snowfall after taking a few suspicious sniffs, bounding off the back deck and into the yard to do his business. Everything was quieter with the snow, like the world was muffled and calm.

A soft, rhythmic cracking sound distracted me. I frowned, my eyes scanning the area for the source of the sound.

Then I saw him.

Dawson stood at the far east end of the property near the fire pit as he chopped some logs. He wore his worn, dark leather jacket that wasn't warm enough for a winter this cold.

I huddled down into my thick cardigan, wrapping it tighter around me. If Dawson was going to live up in the hills, he'd need a real winter coat. I had to find something nice for him soon.

I watched as he positioned a section of log on the wide stump he used as a cutting pedestal. When the wood was in place, he widened his stance. Taking the splitting ax in both hands, he lined up his aim before raising the ax above his head. His muscles coiled as he brought it down swift and hard, splitting the thick log right in two.

He cut the log down to manageable firewood. Meatloaf had gone off sniffing in the woods like he did sometimes, and all my attention zeroed in on Dawson. He worked quickly and efficiently.

There was about watching a man chopping firewood....it *did* things to me. I bit down hard on my lip.

Dawson swung the ax again, splitting the wood and embedding the blade into the stump. Then, he froze. Eventually, he let the ax drop, running a hand through his hair. His chest expanded with a deep breath before he turned his head back and his eyes locked on me.

My heart ricocheted against my ribs. Though he was a good distance away I saw a glint in his expression...his face was red and chapped from the cold like he'd been out there for a long time. By the amount of chopping wood piling up around him, he'd probably been at it for a while.

My brows narrowed as he stood there staring without making a move.

I took in a deep breath, my lungs burning as I walked down the steps of the back deck. The snow was up to my ankles as I trekked forward, feeling clumsy and inelegant, but I didn't remove my eyes from his.

My breaths were heavy by the time I reached him, clouding in the air as I stopped a few yards away. My feet were wet from the snow, my limbs numb.

Dawson's eyes were bright, like they were on fire as the sunlight reflected off the amber specks in brown eyes.

I opened my mouth, but before I could say a word, Meatloaf's frantic barks pierced the air.

I whirled around as the dog bolted out of the tree line on the far end of the property. He'd never barked like that, and the loud echoing pop that followed was even more confusing. Before I could comprehend what was, something heavy hit me from behind, knocking me face first into the snow as another loud *pop* rang through the air.

Dawson's hand covered my head, pushing me down further as he cursed in my ear.

Another pop, and I finally realized what was happening.

We were being shot at.

Chapter Nineteen

FAYE

"Dawson!" I yelled in a panic, my voice getting lost in the snow.

"Stay down," he ordered low in my ear.

His whole body was on top of me, a human shield protecting me.

Meatloaf barked again, closer this time and my already hammering heart raced with another spike of fear.

"Meatloaf!" I called as Dawson cursed.

"Come here, you damn dog," Dawson hissed. Meatloaf growled, his bark sharp and deep, rattling my bones. He didn't bark much, but when he did, it was menacing.

I lifted my head, peeking up as much as I could with Dawson's hand on the top of my head. Meatloaf was a few feet away, his gaze homed in on the tree line as the hair on the back of his neck stood on end.

"Meatloaf!" I cried out. "Come now!"

The dog spared a glance back at me and I held a hand. "Come here," I cried, desperate, the anticipation of another pop, another bullet, made my brain spin with panic. Meatloaf let out another bark, sending another stare toward the forest. Then, almost begrudgingly, he came to us. Relief washed over me as Dawson pulled all fifty pounds of him onto the ground beside us. He didn't resist as I wrapped an arm around his neck, pulling him close.

We waited.

The silence that settled around us was stifling. Anxiety soared as the silence stretched on. A bird called in the distance, making me flinch. Dawson tightened his grip on me, but he didn't say anything. His heavy breaths on the back of my neck were the only sign that he wasn't as calm as he appeared.

I wasn't sure how long we lay there, the snow melting and soaking through my clothes. Meatloaf whined and licked my cheek. I kissed him on the snout.

"We need to get inside," Dawson finally said.

"What's going on?" I asked, my voice breaking with fear.

Dawson's voice was a low, frustrated growl in my ear. "I don't know."

I turned my head as she shifted onto his side, yielding his protective shield on top of me while still keeping close.

"But we can't just sit out here," he continued. "We're too exposed."

Nodding, I tried to get up, but he held me down. I frowned as he leaned in close, his eyes sharp, but something like terror shifted behind them. "Be quick. On the count of three I want you to run back to the cabin. I'll be close behind. If you hear another shot, drop immediately."

My pulse thumped in my ears. "Okay," I said, breathlessly.

His jaw clenched. "Ready?"

156

I wasn't, but I dipped my chin once in a small nod. "Ready."

"One," he said, his eyes flicking to the cabin before they returned to me. "Two..."

I pushed up on my hands, getting my knees up under me. My eyes focused on the back door of the cabin, the one I had accidentally left wide open. That was probably good, I wouldn't have to take the time to open it.

"Three!"

I launched up to my feet, almost slipping on the melted snow beneath us. Dawson grabbed me by the elbows and pushed me up.

I ran faster than I'd ever run in my entire life. The snow was like running through water, but I forced myself to go faster, my legs burning and breaths gasping. Meatloaf stayed right at my side, even though he could've been at the house by now.

Heart in my throat, I leapt up the stairs of the back deck. My feet thumped on the wood beneath the snow, and then I raced through the door, skidding to a halt in the living room. I turned as Dawson barreled in behind me, slamming the door closed and locking it.

He turned and grabbed my hand. "We need to stay away from the windows."

I glanced at the freaking floor to ceiling wall of them right behind us, eyes widening. "How?"

Dawson didn't answer. He walked swiftly, pulling me behind him as he headed for his bedroom. He flung open the door and rushed us inside, Meatloaf slipping in behind us.

Dawson locked that door, too. And then he turned to me, his eyes assessing me up and down.

"Are you all right?"

I stared at him, trying to get my brain to form the right words. Was I all right? My legs were trembling so bad I could barely stand up. My head throbbed. My skin was numb and burning and soaking wet...but I wasn't injured.

"I think so," I gasped.

Dawson sagged against the door, letting out a relieved breath. His forehead glistened with sweat. "What the hell is going on?" he murmured, almost to himself.

My eyes brimmed with tears for no other reason than from overwhelm and shock. "Did someone...did someone just try to shoot us?"

A muscle feathered in Dawson's jaw. "I think someone was trying to shoot *you*."

"Me?" A hand flew to my chest. "Why would someone try to shoot me?"

That didn't make any sense in my brain. Dawson pushed back his thick, dark hair. "I don't know...why would someone rob the store and destroy it in the process?"

Shock speared through my chest, making me wince. "Wait...you think—do you think my father could have something to do with this?"

Robbing me was one thing, but trying to hurt me? Kill me? I shook my head. That was too much. There was no way.

"You said it yourself, Faye. Whoever tore up your shop was angry. I can't say that I disagree with you. Maybe he's just a bad guy that wants to hurt people." He grimaced and grabbed his left arm, bracing it against his body. "Maybe you were a loose end."

A loose end?

I wanted to tell Dawson that he was crazy and wrong. But...maybe he wasn't. There hadn't been any sign of Marc since the night I left him alone in my apartment, but that didn't mean he wasn't being looked for. I'd been checking in with the police. They'd taken statements from me. I wasn't letting them forget, because despite everything that he'd done, I wanted him found. I wanted to look him in the face and ask him *why*.

I wiped at my eyes, smearing away the tears that swam in my vision. "I don't know what to think," I said, defeated.

"I'm sorry, Faye," Dawson's expression pinched with pain. "But maybe I'm wrong...maybe—maybe it was just a hunter or something, and this is all an accident."

My brow creased. "Have you ever had hunters up here near the cabin before?"

He shook his head, and his face paled. "No."

My frown deepened as I looked closer at him. He was slumped against the door, his breathing heavy and erratic even though we'd been still for a while.

"Dawson?"

It took him longer than it should've to answer. "What?"

I didn't like the way he held his arm, cradling it against his side. A new rush of adrenaline washed over me as I focused fully on this left hand. It was streaked with blood.

"Oh my God!" I squeaked, rushing to him. He shrank away from me, trying to hide his hand, but I wouldn't let him. "You're hurt."

Nausea roiled in my stomach.

"It's fine, Faye," he muttered between clenched teeth.

Pure and utter panic bubbled inside me. "No, it's anything but fine. Dawson, you're shot!"

He made a noise deep in his throat, somewhere between a grunt and growl. "Calm down. I said it'll be fine."

My head spun, and it felt like a tight rubber band was restricting my lungs. I couldn't get enough air. "I have to call 911," I said, almost not believing this was the first time either of us were considering calling for help.

I pulled out my phone—it was wet from being inside the pocket of my cardigan, but it worked. I held the phone to my ear, but there was nothing but silence as the phone tried to connect the call, and failed. I tried again, but got nothing.

"Yeah, I would've tried that sooner, but my phone hasn't been able to get reception all morning. I'm assuming yours is the same. The winter storm must've messed with the cell tower."

My arm fell limp at my side, my phone suddenly nothing but a useless brick. "Then I have to drive you to the hospital."

I tried to reach for the door, but he stopped me, grabbing hold of my wrist. "We don't know if it's safe out there yet. And we can't go anywhere in the vehicles anyway. That drive is nothing but ice under the snow, and I expect the road down into town is just the same."

I stared at him, wild eyed. "So what are you saying?"

"I'm saying that we're stuck here until the ice melts."

"No." I shook my head. "You need a doctor."

The panic sounded like it was strangling me. I was helpless if we were stuck here. Dawson let go of my wrist, his face softening as he brushed a lock of hair behind my ear. "Faye," he said, his voice dropping to a low, soothing tone. "Everything is going to be okay."

My teeth caught my trembling lower lip. Tears welled and fell from my lashes in silent steady streams. Dawson cupped my chin in his hand, tilting my face up to his. "Shhh," he whispered. He pressed his lips against my forehead. "Calm down."

But I couldn't calm down. Nothing about his situation warranted being calm. "I'm so sorry," I said, my voice thick. "This is all my fault."

I was standing on a precipice of despair, my toes curling around the edge, primed to launch over and fall. If what Dawson suspected was true, and it had been my own father who shot at me, this was all my fault. Dawson was shot because of me.

"Baby," the endearment sounded like a prayer on Dawson's lips as he pulled me closer. "Stop. It isn't your fault. Don't take that burden." His lips brushed over my cheek, kissing away the tears. "This isn't on you. It's whoever the hell pulled that trigger."

A sob escaped me. "But if it wasn't for me—"

He cut me off by covering my mouth with his.

Heat rose from my core, dousing the terror and fear and guilt. His lips were soft as they moved against mine in achingly slow movements. He smelled like evergreens and wind and wood, and tasted like the fresh snow. Our skin was still chilled from outside and our mingling breaths felt like fire, stoking the heat flooding through my veins.

This kiss was slow and soft. But it ended all too soon.

Dawson pulled back a fraction. My lips buzzed with the electric sensation of his touch.

"Now," he gasped, his words almost trembling. "I need you to hear me when I tell you that I am going to be fine."

My mind swam with all the conflicting emotions raging inside. "How do you know?"

"Because," he said, his mouth pulling up at the corner. "You forget that I know a few things about treating wounds." He straightened, widening the gap between our mouths, helping me clear my mind a little. "I'm pretty sure the bullet just grazed me, but I'm going to need your help, okay? Can you do that and remain calm, Faye?"

It took a few moments for his words to sink in. *The bullet only grazed him? He's going to be okay?*

I pulled in a deep breath, pushing aside the part of me that wanted to fall apart at the mess I'd made. I needed to focus.

161

"Yes. I can help."

His grin turned into a full-blown smile. "That's my girl."

Despite everything, I blushed at that. "What do you need me to do?"

Chapter Twenty

DAWSON

FAYE HARDENED HER STARE, her tears drying. Pride swelled in my chest at the determination replacing her panic.

The feeling was short-lived, though, as I pushed myself off the door and straightened my spine, wincing at the searing pain radiating from my left upper arm. The adrenaline was tapering off, and now it felt like someone had dragged a red hot poker over my skin. It fucking *hurt*.

I glanced at the far wall of the dim room. The doorway to the closet was surrounded by my floor to ceiling bookshelves. Only one small window was in this room, by design, and the shades were drawn over it. It wasn't that I didn't like the sunlight, but my bedroom was for sleeping. This was supposed to be a safe place.

"My medical bag is over there in the closet. Can you go get it?" I gestured toward the door, glad I hadn't returned the bag upstairs where I usually kept it.

Faye nodded, immediately heading across the room. Her head swiveled as she walked, taking everything in. She had never been in my room before. The pain didn't stop my stomach from tightening at the thought of her spending more time here.

My room was nothing exceptional. I had a large king-size bed at the center against the wall. The furniture was minimal, a couple of dark wood nightstands and a high-backed leather chair sitting by the bookshelves. The only decoration was the painting leaning against the wall, obviously out of place. Last night, I'd taken it down from where it normally hung in the living room. It was one of my favorite pieces I'd ever painted of the hills.

The space was simple and warm and cozy. My favorite, though, was the fireplace sitting opposite the bed. Embers were still glowing in the hearth.

As Faye entered the walk-in closet, I turned the opposite way and toward the attached bathroom. Every small movement caused a lick of stinging pain to vibrate up and down my arm. A bit down the inside of my cheek, keeping myself from crying out. Despite what I had assured Faye earlier, I was nervous to get a good look at the wound.

I glanced in the mirror above the double vanity. My skin was pale, making my eyes darker than usual. I looked like shit.

Pulling in a deep breath, I mustered up the nerve to shrug my uninjured arm out of my jacket sleeve. I clenched my teeth, looking down at my injured arm braced at my side. The black leather was torn open near the middle of my upper arm, closer to my shoulder. There was blood, but it was hard to see against the dark material.

Faye stumbled into the bathroom, and our eyes met through the mirror. She had the large medical bag in her hands, and she set it down as her eyes widened.

"Here, let me help you," she said, hurrying to me.

I braced myself as she carefully pulled the rest of my jacket off. The soft movement of the leather against the wound made every muscle in my body clench.

Faye let the jacket fall to the white marbled tile floor. I grimaced, wondering vaguely if the jacket was still salvageable. It was my favorite, a gift from my mama when I was in high school. "What a waste of a nice jacket," I grumbled.

Faye winced. "I think the jacket is the least of your problems. I can get you a new one."

I didn't have the energy to argue with her as I glanced down at my injured arm, stifling a groan at the fact that I also wore a long sleeve shirt. I needed everything to be removed so I could get a good look at the wound.

"I need my shirt off, too."

Faye blinked, her face flushing the slightest as she nodded. "Of course."

Her fingers tentatively gripped the bottom hem of my shirt. Her eyes locked on mine, and I nodded encouragingly. This wasn't quite the way I had envisioned her removing my shirt for the first time.

Her throat bobbed as she carefully pulled up the dark cotton of my long sleeve shirt. Her skin flushed a deeper shade of crimson as she exposed my abdomen and then chest. I focused on that, on the lovely shade of her skin to distract myself from the pain as I first pulled my uninjured arm out, and she lifted the shirt over my head before carefully inching it steadily over the injury.

She couldn't hold back her gasp as she exposed the bullet wound.

My stomach churned as I forced myself to examine it.

We both sat in a long silence as I studied my arm. I'd seen different kinds of bullet wounds in my short time in training in the army. Bullet grazes looked gnarly, but were superficial. Though the bullet had only kissed my skin, it left a good fourth of an inch thick open laceration, the edges jagged and an angry red.

I glanced back at Faye—she had gone ghostly pale, her eyes filling with tears again.

"It looks worse than it is," I assured her.

She pressed her lips together. "It looks so painful," she said, her voice quivering.

She wasn't wrong about that. It burned and throbbed with pain, but that was something that I could handle.

"It's a flesh wound. I told you, I'm gonna be just fine." Before she could start spiraling into another pit of guilt, I gave her instructions. "Bring the bag over here and open it. I need some supplies."

Faye pulled in a deep breath and then shook her head as if clearing it. She grabbed the bag and hauled it up onto the counter. She unzipped it, looking at me expectantly.

"I need the saline wound wash, as many sterile gauze pads as you can find, antibiotic ointment, and the self-adhesive wrap."

Faye helped me thoroughly clean and bandage up the wound. It hurt like absolute hell, but I was happy to have her to get me through it.

"Is that too tight?" she asked, as she wrapped the self-adhesive wrap around my arm, securing the gauze pads in place.

I shook my head. Her eyes flicked up to mine, and I smiled. "If there's any consolation in getting shot, it's the fact that I have such a pretty nurse to help take care of me."

"You must be feeling all right if you have the energy to flirt."

She cut the end of the wrap and began cleaning up the mess of wrappers and bloody gauze on the counter. The lidocaine spray in my bag, mixed with the over-the-counter painkillers I took, helped with the pain. It would be a rough few days, but if this is all I had to deal with in order to keep her safe, then I'd take the bullet any day.

As Faye cleaned up, I pulled my phone from my back pocket, clenching my jaw at the fact that I still had no service. The internet was out, too. There was no way to call for help.

"What's wrong?" Faye asked.

I glanced up, meeting her eyes in the mirror again. I stuffed my phone back into my pocket. "Nothing."

"Liar."

I pinched the bridge of my nose. "I'm trying to figure out what our next steps should be."

"Next steps?"

She looked so innocent standing there, her eyes wide and scared. She shouldn't be scared. I didn't want her to be scared. I was, however, pissed at myself for not having better security. If there was someone out there trying to hurt her, we were going to have a hard time keeping them out. The first thing I was going to do the minute we had access to the outside world again was get a security company up here.

"We need to protect ourselves until we know what's going on."

I turned and left the bathroom, crossing the bedroom in long strides. Meatloaf glanced up at me curiously from his dog bed by the hearth. He obviously hadn't been too worried about me.

Entering the closet, I walked to the very back where a tall, metal gun safe was. I wasn't much of a gun person, but when my grandfather was alive he'd taken me and Knox hunting. Knox never had the stomach for it, but I didn't mind. Although I didn't hunt anymore, I'd kept my guns for protection if I needed them up here at the cabin.

I retrieved a long rifle from the safe and a box of ammunition. Faye was standing near Meatloaf's bed when I walked back into the room, tensing when she saw the rifle.

"Do you think you'll need that?"

"I hope to God not, but we need to be prepared. We should stay in here for the night at least. We'll keep the only window in here covered. Out there, we're basically on display for anyone to see. Hopefully tomorrow things will start to thaw out."

Faye focused on the gun in hand. "And what if it doesn't?"

I placed the rifle and ammo on the bed and crossed the space to her. I grabbed her hand, and placed it on my chest, above my heart. "No matter what happens, Faye, I'm going to protect you."

She glanced at my wrapped shoulder, her forehead furrowing. "Maybe that's what I'm afraid of."

I didn't like the tone of her voice. "What are you talking about?"

She stepped away, just out of my reach. She wrapped her arms around her chest. "Nothing." She shook her head and looked away.

I opened my mouth to push her on it, but she changed the subject before I got the words out.

"Why is the painting of the hills in here?"

I frowned, confused until I followed her line of sight. She was staring at the painting I'd removed from the living room last night.

"I'm getting rid of it."

Her head snapped to me. "What? Why? It's gorgeous."

"I'm donating it to the auction for Paws and Pastures."

"Oh," she blinked and then glanced back at the painting. "Well, I guess it's going to a good cause." She tucked a lock of hair behind her ear. "Isn't the auction part of your brother's wedding?"

I tensed at the mention of my brother. "It is."

"Are you planning on going to the wedding?"

We hadn't talked much about Knox's wedding, but it wasn't a secret. "It seems my sister won't let me off the hook about it, so...perhaps." I didn't want to go. Especially with the feelings the photo album had stirred up in me, I didn't want to be around Knox. But I didn't want to hurt my sister, either. And I wanted to support Axel and the animal rescue.

A gleam flashed in her blue eyes. "Annabelle is a force to be reckoned with."

I huffed out a heavy breath. "That she is."

She paused. "So, how do you feel about going to Knox's wedding?"

"I'm not going for him, I'm going for Annabelle...and Axel."

She nodded. "I get that." She pursed her lips. "But...if Knox invited you to his wedding, don't you think he might want to, I don't know...fix things?"

I sucked in a deep, slow breath, fighting the anger that raged whenever I talked about my relationship with my brother. An anger I needed to embrace to keep me from drowning in the guilt, otherwise. My arm twinged with pain, but I welcomed the distraction, embraced it.

"I know that he does."

Faye stepped closer again. "I know how you feel about him, but everyone deserves a second chance, Dawson. You should understand that better than anyone."

"You think too much of me."

She took another step. This time, she reached for me and pressed a hand against my chest. "And you don't think enough of you." She paused, and my heart beat so hard against my ribs I was sure she could feel it. "Just think about it, okay? Not just for Knox, but for you. For your heart."

For my heart?

Every muscle in my body wanted to step closer to her. I wanted to wrap her in my arms and get lost in her, no matter how much it might hurt. Bullet wound or not.

It took all I had to step back. As much as I wanted her, this conversation was reminding me of how bad I was for her. My heart was too far gone to forgive my brother. It was bitter and cold and set in its ways.

"I'll think about it," I mumbled.

I turned away from her, I tried to fight the voice in the back of my mind that told me I was making a mistake with Faye. It reminded me that Faye deserved more. She needed someone softer, someone who wouldn't get her stranded in the middle of nowhere while someone was trying to possibly kill her.

I'd made a promise, and her heart wasn't on the table anyway.

Chapter Twenty-One

FAYE

WE SPENT THE REST of the day holed up in Dawson's bedroom. I'd never been in Dawson's room before this, and it was both strange and exciting. The room was quaint, but cozy. He didn't have many decorations or excess things. The basics. Very much Dawson's vibe.

He'd gone out into the main area of the cabin a few times to get some food and water, but he hadn't lingered. There'd been no other signs of danger or distant sounds of gunfire, and I wanted to believe so badly that it had all been some kind of hunting accident.

But Dawson wasn't convinced.

We'd spent the time trying to decompress from the traumatic morning. Dawson's injury worried me, no matter how many times he assured me he was fine. The bullet wound on his arm looked awful.

Time passed slowly. We talked on and off and read books from Dawson's bookshelves. He always liked to read, but I hadn't realized quite how much until I saw his massive collection.

I looked up from a beautiful vintage copy of *Pride and Prejudice* as Dawson put another log on the fire smoldering in the fireplace. The sun had started to set, the already dim room getting darker as the glow of sunlight around the drawn curtain dissipated. The room was warm and cozy and smelled like firewood and books and...Dawson.

"How's your arm feeling?" I asked, setting the open book down on the small table beside the reading chair to keep my place.

Dawson brushed the palm off his good hand on his jeans, eyes trained on the flames he'd reawakened in the hearth.

"It's...fine," he said, but I heard the strain in his voice.

"When was the last time you took some pain medicine?"

Dawson glanced at his watch and grimaced. "Probably too long."

I hopped up off the chair and went to the restroom where the bottles of medicine were. We'd been switching between ibuprofen and acetaminophen, but Dawson wasn't good at staying on top of it; he let the time get away from him.

I shook a couple pills into my hand and brought them to him.

"Thank you," he said, as I dropped the medicine into his palm. My skin brushed across his as he closed his fingers around the pills. I pulled back quickly, the faint touch making my heart react.

"You're welcome," I said softly, returning quickly to my chair.

I picked up my book and pretended to start reading again, sensing that his eyes were still on me.

I peeked over the top of the book, confirming my suspicion when my eyes collided with his dark ones.

"What?" I said, fidgeting under his lingering stare.

He was still standing by my fire, his face lit up with an orange glow on one side. "It's...getting late," he said.

I took out my phone and checked the time. It was after nine. Not exactly late, but not early.

"Okay..."

He shifted on his feet. "We're going to have to sleep in here."

I tilted my head to the side. I thought that had already been established. "And?"

He ran a hand through his hair. "Uh...I mean, you're more than welcome to the bed. I just need to know where you're planning on sleeping because...I'm getting tired."

My eyes widened. I jumped up from the chair. "Oh, right," I stuttered, glancing at the bed, then at Dawson. "If I take the bed, where are you going to sleep?"

"I can take the floor."

I stared down at the cold, hardwood floor. "What are you talking about?" I grimaced. "You're not sleeping on the floor, Dawson. You're injured."

"I'm not making you sleep on the floor, either."

My sigh was long and loud as I rolled my eyes. "Don't be ridiculous. That bed is huge. It's big enough for the both of us."

His entire body stilled. I wasn't sure if he was even breathing. "You want to share the bed?"

My face heated with the increase in my heart rate. "If you're okay with it. I promise I don't have cooties or anything."

That coaxed a small, half grin from him.

"I would still share with you, even if you did."

I returned the smile, wishing my face didn't turn beet red every time he said something vaguely flirtatious. "Anyway, we should probably go to bed. It's been a crazy day." I looked over at Meatloaf on his dog bed, wishing we could let him out for the night. We'd decided it was too dangerous and he'd had to use the puppy pads we had on hand.

"You'll be our guard dog through the night, won't you Loafy?" I cooed to him in the voice I only reserved for good doggies. His tail wagged, and he rolled over in his bed, exposing his tummy. "Oh, goodness." I chuckled going to him to give him a belly rub.

Meatloaf was some kind of mutt, maybe somewhere between a boxer and a lab. Either way, he'd been so brave this morning. He hadn't been scared at all, and I had no doubt that if the person who was shooting at us had shown his face, Meatloaf would've done anything he could to protect us.

"His bark is pretty menacing," Dawson remarked.

I nodded. "I'm thankful we have him around." I straightened and turned to Dawson. He was standing closer, the flames from the fireplace flickering in his eyes.

"So am I."

I cleared my throat and stepped back, trying to figure out if it was the heat from the fire or just Dawson's closeness that had my skin tingling. "Well, I'm going to go get ready...for bed."

There was a slight pause before he nodded. "Right, yeah. There's extra toothbrushes in the bottom drawer, feel free."

"Oh, thank God." I hadn't wanted to risk Dawson running upstairs to get mine, and I definitely didn't want to get in bed with a man without having a clean mouth.

Jeeze. I couldn't believe I was about to get in a freaking bed with Dawson Evans. He had been my friend for so long, and still was, just with a bit extra.

I tried to hurry in the bathroom. I'd taken a shower earlier and was currently dressed in another pair of Dawson's clothes. The oversized t-shirt and sweats weren't the most attractive, but maybe that was a good thing. There wasn't much the two of us should be doing in that bed other than sleeping. Dawson needed his rest. He needed to heal.

But as I brushed my teeth and washed my face, heat pooled low in my stomach. I felt almost jittery, making it hard to focus on the mundane tasks of getting ready for bed.

When I came out of the bathroom, Dawson had turned off the light by the reading chair and one of the bedside lamps. The only light was a small lamp on one of the nightstands and the flames in the fireplace.

Dawson sauntered toward me, nodding toward the bed. "Take whatever side you want. I'll only be a few minutes."

He walked past me and entered the bathroom, closing the door behind him.

I shifted on my feet as the bed loomed before me. It seemed both huge and not big enough. Chewing on the corner of my lip, I took a few nervous steps toward the bed, as if it was about to jump up and bite me.

My heart raced as if I was about to jump off the edge of a cliff. And maybe I was, in a way. Jumping into bed with someone I'd been best friends with most of my life felt a lot like that.

I shook my head, trying to clear it and focus. There was nothing to be nervous about. I couldn't think about anything involving kissing Dawson tonight. Tonight had to be for rest, nothing else.

Padding to the side of the bed, I grabbed an extra decorative pillow. There weren't many, only a few square gray ones, but they were better than nothing. I pulled back the soft cotton comforter to the dark gray sheets underneath and climbed in. Then, I carefully lined the pillows up vertically down the very middle of the bed, creating a small barrier between the two sides.

When I was satisfied with my pillow divider, I sat down on my side, pulling the covers up to my waist.

I jumped when the door to the bathroom opened. Dawson stepped out of the bathroom, and I forgot how to breathe. He'd taken his shirt off, wearing only his sweats low on his hips. My stomach clenched, face heating. I'd seen Dawson without a shirt, but it was always a shock at how muscled he was. His chest was sculpted and abs chiseled and defined. I forced my eyes not to follow those ridges that formed that signature V at his hips.

Dawson froze as his eyes caught on the bed. He cocked his head to the side, his lips fighting against a smile.

"Really?" he asked, eyeing my arrangement of pillows.

I pressed my lips together, focusing on anything but his bare chest as I pulled the covers up to my chin. "What? I thought it was a good idea to set a boundary. You stay on your side, and I'll stay on mine."

He didn't look convinced as he crossed over to his side of the bed. The mattress shifted as he got in and peeked at me over my pillow barrier. "Ready for lights out?"

No, I was not ready in the slightest, but I nodded anyway.

When he clicked off the last lamp, the only light was the flicker of flames. I fisted the covers tightly, my skin prickling as Dawson's proximity.

I stared straight up at the ceiling, not an inkling of sleep in me. Normally, I would enjoy the ambience of the fire and the cozy warmth, but they were nothing more than background noise amongst the noise inside my brain.

Moments passed, and I tried to think of something—any-thing—other than Dawson being in the same bed as me, recovering from a bullet wound that was meant for me. At one point, I was considering getting up and trying to read by the firelight, but when I turned over in bed, Dawson's voice drifted to me in a soft whisper.

"Restless?" he asked.

I hugged the covers tighter. "A little. You should sleep, though. You need the rest."

A few seconds later the bed shook as he moved. He plucked up the first pillow, the one closest to our faces and tossed it away to the floor.

"Hey," I frowned, rolling over onto my side. "You're ruining my barrier."

He propped himself up on an elbow. "I can't sleep if you can't sleep."

"Why? I was being quiet."

"Too quiet. And still. I've seen you sleeping before, and I know for a fact that you snore."

"I do not snore!" I hissed.

His lips twitched. "You definitely do."

I wrinkled my nose and muttered under my breath, "Whatever."

"Do you want to talk about it?"

"Talk about what?"

"Whatever it is that's keeping you awake."

"We've literally had all day to talk," I said. "You need to rest, now."

He paused, his eyes searching my face for something. "You've been...very patient with me," he said gently. "A lot happened today."

His voice sounded so...sad. My eyes went to his arm, at the thick bandage wrapped around it. "The last couple days have been a lot." I sighed. "This whole month has been a lot. But you're hurt, Dawson. Rest."

The creases around his mouth deepened. A nervousness flashed in his eyes.

"About our updated promise..." he started. My stomach pitched. "Are you sure about it?"

I nodded before thinking. I couldn't think too much about it. All I knew was that I liked kissing Dawson. "Why? Are you not sure?"

He looked down at one of the pillows, he ran one finger along the soft edge, back and forth. The firewood crackled in the fireplace, filling the silence.

"Faye," Dawson finally said, and his eyes shot up to mine. "You hold a significant place in my life. I love my family, but your family, too. Perhaps even more so. You've always been there for me, even in my darkest moments."

I let his words sink in. His breaths quickened, his perfectly sculpted chest rising and falling rapidly.

"What is the problem then?"

"The problem is," he said, his face scrunched with pain as he carefully moved his arm—his injured arm—and gently cupped the side of my face. "That I don't want to lose you."

My heart felt like it stopped beating before it launched into overdrive. "Lose me?" I shook my head. "Why would you lose me?"

He swallowed hard. "I don't know... Maybe I'm afraid you'll regret it. I know we promised our hearts are off the table, but—"

I shook my head, cutting him off as I understood where he was coming from. Dawson has lost more than most. When his mother died, the whole town, including his own brother, blamed him for it. He'd lost his whole life, and I was the one constant thing that he'd held on to through the years.

My heart broke for him—for the young man who'd lost everything and still hadn't managed to heal from it.

I reached for him, putting my hand on his chest. His skin heated beneath my palm. "Dawson, you're not going to lose me. It doesn't matter what happens between us, I'll always be your best friend." I drew nearer, our noses touching the sweet and spicy scent of him invaded all of my senses. "But I don't want anything more than this. My heart is guarded well. Not even you could break though."

"You're my best friend." There was sadness in his expression, but there was also something else. Something like...longing.

"I have been your best friend since we were thirteen years old," I breathed, my lips so close to his they almost touched. "I will *always* be your best friend."

His eyes sparked as his chest heaved. His stare held mine for a beat. Then, two. In the next breath, his lips were on mine. This kiss was different from earlier. This was...hungry. Wanting. It was like he was trying to consume me as his mouth moved over mine. My lips parted, and our tongues met in a frenzied dance that had my core tightening. His good arm snaked under me, and before I could comprehend it, he tugged me against him, rolling onto his back at the same time until I was on top of him.

I gasped, bracing a hand on his bare chest and pulling away. "Dawson," I hissed. "Your arm. You're going to hurt yourself."

His good hand moved slowly up the side on my thigh, over my hip. His smile turned devilish as I shivered under his touch. He continued to leisurely run his fingertips up my arm and shoulder and finally, he gripped the back of my neck. "You'd be shocked to know the things I can do with only one hand."

The comment left me breathless as he pulled me to him, kissing me like I had never been kissed in my entire life. Our hands roamed, his skin was soft and smooth as my fingers drifted up his chest and tangled in his hair.

Something deep in my core tightened, a sweet ache building beneath my skin. Dawson's hand went to my hip, his fingers slipping under the hem of my shirt. I shivered against his touch. With a lot of effort I managed to pull myself back, my chest heaving as

I stared down at him, my legs on each side of his hips. His eyes were smoldering like embers, setting my skin on fire.

I bit my lip, and grabbed the edge of the baggy shirt and lifted it swiftly over my head, tossing it to the side. Dawson groaned low in the back of his throat.

"God, you're beautiful, Faye." Our eyes met again, and my heart pounded in my ears. "Are you sure that you want to do this? We—we can go back to bed, if you want."

I frowned at him. "Dawson, I just took my shirt off. I have no plans on going to sleep any time soon."

That was all the confirmation Dawson needed. He claimed my lips with his own, kissing and sucking and setting my body in a whirl of sensations.

Even with his injury, he had no issue getting rid of the rest of our clothes. It was nothing like I'd ever known, he had my brain spinning with desire and pleasure until I trembled to my very core.

"God, Faye," Dawson's breaths echoed in my ear.

His words almost sent me over the edge. I kissed him deeply, as our bodies found a rhythm.

But even as I became lost in ecstasy, in the very back of my mind, an inkling of uncertainty sparked. What we were doing could alter our friendship forever, but I couldn't let myself believe that. The potential regret wasn't enough to stop me. I hadn't realized how much I wanted him, and I was going to take everything he was willing to give me.

Those tall, hard walls around my heart started to shake, but I was going to do my damndest to not let them fall.

Chapter Twenty-Two

DAWSON

The next week flew by in a haze of bliss and uncertainty.

Being with Faye was everything I'd imagined and more. But there was still a part of me that way waiting for something to fall apart. What we were doing was changing things, no matter how much both of us wanted to deny it. I just didn't know if they were good changes or bad. All I knew was that I needed her.

The day after the shooting, it warmed up enough for the roads to thaw enough that I was comfortable making the drive down the hill. We'd made a full report to the police, and they'd come to look around the property. They didn't find much but a few spent bullets in the yard. Since all the snow had already melted by the time they got here, there weren't even any footprints.

I worried about what role Faye's mama had to play in all of this, too. She was still lingering in town, from what I'd heard. It seemed strange that the day after she had a confrontation with Faye, she was shot at.

In the end, whoever was responsible wasn't getting anywhere near the cabin anymore. I hired a security company to come to secure the house and the property. No one could step within the property lines without tripping off an alert sent right to my phone. I'd had all the windows tinted, a full alarm system inside and out, and motion sensor lights installed on all sides of the house. Faye thought I'd done too much, but there wasn't such a thing when it came to making sure she was safe.

I wasn't going to let anyone hurt her. And it pissed me off that someone had gotten so close.

My arm was healing well, like I expected it to. Faye had forced me to go to the doctor, but the only thing she did was give me some antibiotics to ward off infection. It had finally started to scab over, and I had almost full use of my arm.

It was a sunny day in the middle of the week as I worked to catch up on some paintings I'd gotten behind. Faye had gone to visit her sister, and it was me and Meatloaf alone around the cabin for most of the day.

I was cleaning off some brushes before I took a break for lunch when my phone started ringing.

Annabelle's name came up on the screen.

I hesitated before answering. We had only talked once since she'd stopped by last time. She'd called me in near hysterics when word about the shooting had gotten to her. I'd been able to calm her down, but it hadn't been easy, and I wasn't looking forward to another conversation like that.

Begrudgingly, I answered the phone.

"Hello?"

"Hey, big brother, what are you up to today?"

My eyes narrowed. Her voice sounded much too sweet. "What do you want?"

"What makes you think I want something?" she asked, feigning innocence.

I set the brushes on a towel and walked out of my studio, Meatloaf trotting behind me. "I've only known you your entire life. I can tell when you want something."

"How's your arm?"

I walked down the steps, my eyes flicking toward the back wall of windows and scanning the yard outside. Paranoia was prevalent these days even with the new security measures, but everything looked normal.

"It's healing well."

"Do you have any, like, movement restrictions?"

I paused on my way to the couch. "Why you wanna know?"

She sighed. "Okay, here's the deal. I really need a big strong man to help pick up the wedding pergola in Sherrodsville and bring it over to the ranch. Colton is working all week, and I just found someone selling it for an amazing deal and if I wait on this, someone else will for sure snag it up."

I put my hand on my hip, swallowing a groan. "What the hell is a wedding pergola?"

"Does it matter? All you need to know is that it's heavy and I need help. I wouldn't be asking you if I had other options."

There was a hint of desperation in her tone that stirred up my guilt. "I don't know, Annabelle."

I'd relented to donating and helping with the fundraiser, but this felt like...too much.

"Please, Dawson?"

I cursed under my breath at the way her freaking begging tugged at whatever heartstrings I had left.

"Fine."

Annabelle literally squealed with happiness. "Thank you! I'll pick you up in a half hour with the truck."

I hung up the phone before she talked me into anything else. After stuffing the phone in my pocket, I carefully ran a hand over the spot where the bullet had grazed my skin. It had been incredibly sensitive and painful the first few days, but it barely hurt when I lightly touched it now. I rotated my shoulder a few times, making sure the movement didn't hurt. It didn't. Part of me wished I could use the injury as an excuse not to help.

I grabbed a quick sandwich and chugged a glass of water. I let Meatloaf out back, and when I was finished and he was snuggled up in my room on his dog bed, I set the alarm and walked out onto the porch to wait for Annabelle. The quicker I got this over with, the better.

I didn't wait long before the truck roared up the path and inched toward the cabin. As I watched, a sinking feeling settled in my gut. I squinted at the truck. It looked like whoever was driving was much taller than my sister.

My feelings were validated as the truck neared, finally parking in front of the porch, and I glared at the man sitting in the driver's seat.

This was not what I signed up for.

I stomped down the porch steps and yanked open the passenger side door. My brother looked over at me, damn cowboy hat and all, looking infuriatingly calm.

"What the hell is going on?" I demanded.

Knox shrugged, his calm demeanor only further fueling my frustration.

"Annabelle had an emergency with the florist, or something like that. She sent me instead."

Forget the fact that I had no idea how someone had a florist emergency, but the timing of this "emergency" was more than a little suspicious.

"Convenient timing, don't you think?" I muttered.

"You don't have to come." The sharpness in Knox's tone surprised me. He didn't often let his emotions come through. "Annabelle seemed to think it would require two people, but I can find a way to manage on my own."

My fingers gripped the edge of the door. Every part of me was screaming to retreat back to the cabin and ignore my brother. He was probably right, he'd manage without me one way or another. But I'd told Annabelle I would help. Sure, she went ahead and changed the rules, but I'd made a commitment.

So, despite my better judgment, I gritted my teeth and climbed into the truck. The moment I snapped the door closed, a sense of entrapment settled around me, stifling like the heat pouring out of the vents.

Knox stared at me a beat, and then he turned forward, shifting the truck into reverse. "Okay, then."

Knox turned around, heading back down the narrow winding road toward Cypress Falls. The tension between us was as thick as our silence. We didn't speak a word to each other as we made it into town and drove along Main Street. We kept going though, heading out toward the large bridge that stretched over the Blue Cypress River.

The sun shone bright in the sky, sparkling off the dark blue water as we hit the bridge. It was beautiful, but the turmoil in my mind made it hard to enjoy the sight. That sharp bitter anger burned in my chest whenever I looked at my brother. An anger that was really something else...hurt.

The agonizing silence stretched on as we drove, broken only by the monotonous hum of the engine. Finally, we turned into a subdivision and pulled up to a quaint house with a discarded wood pile sitting out front by the curb.

"Well, that looks like a right mess," Knox grumbled. I glanced at him, raising a brow. He nodded toward the pile of wood. "That's the pergola."

I did a double-take at the wood pile. "I don't see how that's supposed to be anything."

"Annabelle said it'd be on the curb. I guess the homeowners decided to deconstruct the one in their backyard and offered it for free."

I scoffed, shaking my head. "Of course they did."

Frustration mixed with all the other emotions raging inside of me as I stared at the mangled pile of wood. It barely seemed worth the zero dollars we were paying for it.

"Come on," Knox said, opening the truck door.

I rolled my eyes, but for once, I didn't argue. I wanted to get this done and get away from Knox and stay a good distance from my family for a while after this stunt Annabelle pulled today.

Knox and I had a hell of a time trying to load all the pieces into the truck bed. It was far from what I envisioned when I agreed to pick up the thing. Annabelle had told the truth about one thing; it was all pretty damn heavy.

We were both sweaty and dirty by the time we picked up the last piece. The weather was still cold, but the sunshine made it feel warmer, and I had to take off my sweater. I turned on the air conditioning when we got back in the truck and headed toward the ranch.

"Let Annabelle know we're on our way," Knox said.

My gaze shifted to him as I pulled out my phone. Despite all the years of contempt for each other, working together wasn't horrible. Knox wasn't much of a talker. Neither of us were. He was also a hard worker, something the both of us learned while growing up on the ranch. Sometimes, people assumed that since our family had money, we were a bunch of spoiled brats, but that was far from the truth.

Our father came from money, a businessman through and through, but our mama was the opposite. She'd been rough and wild and made sure all of us kids were firmly grounded as we grew up. We learned how to work and how to be efficient in our ranch chores and running the business side of things too.

I'd forgotten how familiar family could be and how...comforting that was. When I didn't let the memories of death cloud me.

As Knox crossed the bridge and entered back into Cypress Falls, it struck me that any emotion other than anger could emerge in relation to my brother, but maybe things were changing.

Everyone deserves a second chance, Dawson, Faye's voice replayed in my mind.

I shook my head. I didn't know if I was ready to let go, yet.

I sent a quick text to Annabelle, letting her know we'd be at the ranch soon and also giving her a hint of how pissed I was at her shenanigans today.

She replied almost immediately.

"She wants us to meet her at the pond."

A faint crease formed between Knox's brows, but he nodded.

When we pulled into the entrance to Willow Hope Ranch, a strange sensation washed over me. The first time I'd come back to the ranch after the death of my mother, I'd been angry. Angry and scared.

Those feelings still existed in me, but as the truck rumbled up the long path, and the sights of the horses grazing in the pasture and the big barn towering in the distance, I felt a small sense of...peace. I didn't know what had changed that in me. Maybe it was Faye, her words of encouragement these past week as I tried to put myself back together after falling apart over the family album.

That feeling didn't last long, though, as we made it to the glimmering pond and my sister. She was sitting in one of the ranch's ATVs, and the moment we parked the truck she sprinted toward us.

Knox rolled down his window, and Annabelle stuck her head through, her eyes wide and slightly wild looking...the sight of her reminding me starkly of my mother. A pang shot through my chest, and I rubbed a palm over my sternum, trying to chase away the sudden ache.

"Oh my God, I am so sorry to do this to y'all, you wouldn't believe what I've been having to deal with today."

Knox jerked a thumb over his shoulder. "What do you want us to do with all this?"

Annabelle glanced at the mismatched pieces of wood filling the truck bed. Her lips pulled back from her teeth in an awkward grimace. "About that..." she started, and I had a feeling I wasn't going to like what she was about to say. "I was hoping you two could put it together."

We both stared at her.

"Put it together?" I said, incredulously.

Annabelle had the decency to look a bit ashamed. "I know, it's a lot. But it needs to be put back together. I can send you a picture of what it's supposed to look like. It couldn't be that hard to do."

Knox and shared a glance. He looked as stunned as I was.

I clenched my jaw as my eyes shot back to Annabelle. "I agreed to pick up a pergola. That's all."

Annabelle opened her mouth, but Knox cut her off.

"I can put it together by myself. It's fine."

At least it made sense for Knox to do it. He'd basically built the home he lived in. I, however, had little experience with building things.

Annabelle shook her head. "No, you can't. You'll need help. I need this done today, and it's going to be dark soon. Tomorrow I'll have to paint and decorate it. I have the photographer coming in two days to take some pictures to display at the wedding."

Knox slumped back in his seat. "I'm sure I can figure it out alone."

Annabelle gave him a doubtful look. "Maybe, but I don't have the time to gamble with." She widened her eyes, looking at me from beneath her lashes as she pulled out her lip in a pathetic pout. She was freaking worse than Meatloaf and his puppy-dog stares. I was getting tired of everyone trying to manipulate me.

"Please, Dawson. I know you've already gone above and beyond what I've asked of you, but I need this one last thing."

"One last thing?" I muttered, doubting it.

"I'm sure it won't take you too much time if you work together."

A humorless laugh escaped me. "Have you seen the pile of crap back there? It looks nothing like a pergola, whatever the hell that is."

But then, her baby blue eyes brimmed with tears. My stomach dropped as her nose turned red and she pulled in a shaky breath. "Dawson, please, I promise this is the last thing I'll ask you to do. It's been a stressful day and I really need this to get done."

She pressed her lips together as if stifling a sob.

"Jeeze," I muttered, scrubbing the back of my neck. "You don't have to cry. I'll do it."

It was the last thing I wanted to do, but I wasn't going to make my sister cry. She never cried. Especially not in front of people.

Annabelle blinked in shock. "Really?"

I crossed my arms over my chest, nodding once.

Her lips curled up into a wide smile. "Thank you," she said, swiping at her eyes. "I owe you one."

"You owe me more than that."

She ignored my quip and pulled out her phone. "I'm sending you both the picture now. Knox, I have all your tools in the ATV so y'all can get started right away. Call me if you need anything else."

And with that, Knox and I got out of the truck and helped unload the tools, both seeming a little dazed by our sister's antics. As soon as the tools were out, Annabelle hopped back in the ATV and drove off, leaving us very alone with a plethora of very sharp, dangerous tools.

Chapter Twenty-Three

DAWSON

"WE SHOULD LAY OUT all the pieces and try to organize them so I can see what we all have," Knox instructed.

I nodded, and we both headed back to the truck.

With muscles screaming, we unloaded all the damn wood we'd just loaded up. At least I was getting a good workout for all this trouble.

My brother and I laid every rugged board out on the grass by the pond. As we did so, it became easier to differentiate between the pieces. With the picture Annabelle had sent us, I started to recognize what pieces went where from the seemingly irreparable mess of wood.

Knox stood, adjusting his cowboy hat after we laid down that last board in its appropriate space. He put his hands on his hips as he examined it all.

"It's not as complicated as it seemed," he mused.

I shrugged. "Let's get started actually putting it back together again before you make any assumptions."

Knox's eyebrows rose. "Fine. Let's get to it, then."

We started with post bases, setting them up in the approximate area Annebelle had indicated where the ground was most level. The main posts came first, and I held them up straight as Knox secured them firmly to the bases.

We worked quietly, the sun gradually lowering in the sky. The physical work combined with the last of the warm rays had me rolling up the sleeves of my tee shirt.

Knox's gaze caught on the bandage on my upper arm before flitting back to the level resting on the cross beam.

I raised my brows as the heavy beam dug into my shoulder. "Well?" I grunted.

Knox cleared his throat. "A little lower."

I adjusted, and he began securing the beam to the post. "Are you sure you're good to do all this?" he asked as he finished.

I wanted to roll my eyes. I doubted he cared about my little injury. I ducked out from under the beam. As I backed away, thinking of something snarky to say to my brother, my foot caught one of the stray pieces of wood. I stumbled, trying to keep my balance and losing miserably. I was about to faceplant right into the ground, but Knox caught my arm, pulling me back up straight.

I faced my little brother, his expression stoic but for the slight furrow in his brow.

A beat passed, and neither of us spoke. His hand was still on my arm, and he let go, patting me on the shoulder before he turned away.

"Annabelle told me about the shooting," he continued, as if nothing had happened. He stooped down, picking up one side of the beam that I'd tripped over. "Did the police find anything?"

I paused before cautiously picking up the other side of the beam, helping him lift it. "No, they didn't."

"That's frustrating. How's Faye handling it?"

"She's fine."

"Shiloh's been worried about her. She has a lot going on."

I didn't reply as we hauled the beam up, preparing to secure it to the posts. Knox didn't pry, continuing to work as if we hadn't been speaking. I didn't want to talk about Faye with Knox. I didn't want to talk about the shooting. I wanted to get this done and get out of here.

At least, that's what I thought I wanted. As my brother and I put the pergola together beam by beam, screw by screw, I found that somewhere deep inside of myself—I'd actually missed him.

The realization hit me so hard I almost doubled over.

I rubbed a palm over my chest, taking in a deep breath. Knox finished drilling in a screw and shot me a concerned look.

"You okay?" he asked.

I clenched my jaw. "Fine."

"You don't look fine."

"I'm not one for small talk, little brother. Can we get back to work and get this day over with?" I snapped, immediately regretting the sharpness of my tone.

That was the last straw for Knox. While my brother usually remained composed and level-headed, this time his demeanor shifted. His face grew rigid, his eyes homing in on me with a sharp glare. He threw the drill down on the grass. "You know, Dawson, why don't you just get the hell out of here if you're so unwilling to stay?" he spat, his arms outstretched in exasperation. "I don't understand what you want from me. I don't know how you want me to act, but I've been doing my best not to step on your toes all day."

I flinched at the harshness in his tone, shame sinking to the pit of my stomach like heavy stone.

"You can't finish by yourself," I said, crossing my arms over my chest.

"I've had to do a lot of things alone in my life, Dawson. I can manage."

I looked away, glancing at the structure that was over half done. He was probably right. He could figure out how to do it without me. But the beams were heavy, and it would be easier if he had help.

"Let's just finish what we started."

Knox made a noise deep in his throat, somewhere between a sigh and a snarl. He ran a finger over the brim of his hat, and I expected him to pull it down over his eyes, but he didn't. Instead, he gritted his teeth.

"I don't know why I ever decided to try with you. I made a mistake. You paid deeply for it. I'm sorry. How many times do I have to apologize?"

My hands fisted at my sides. My brother's eyes were full of pain making my heart twist. I looked away, not wanting to face it. I tried to grab a hold of that familiar anger that had been my life preserver for so long, keeping my head above the sea of grief and guilt.

"You shouldn't have to apologize," I said, more to myself than him. When I forced my gaze back, his eyes were round with surprise.

"What?"

A whirlwind churned inside me, rebelling against the words, but I knew that I needed to say them. "It wasn't your fault. I wanted it to be, because it was easier that way, but—" My voice splintered. I closed my eyes, the memory of our mother's blood on my hands flashed in my mind. "It was my fault."

"Dawson, what are you talking about?"

I shook my head, opening my eyes and taking in the confused expression on his face. "I wasn't the one who killed our mother, but I didn't save her, either."

A beat of silence passed as he processed that. He stepped toward me, and I tensed, bracing myself. Knox's hand clenched, the muscles in his arms flexing from wrist to shoulder.

I flinched as he grabbed on to my shoulders, his fingers digging in. "It wasn't your fault, Dawson."

My heart felt like it was cracking as I shook my head. "Who's to say I couldn't have saved her?" I held out my hands, the same hands that had been covered in her blood. "I was trained to save people, Knox. I should've known what to do. Instead, I fucking ran away. She died because I'm a coward."

My hands started to tremble as Knox's face drained of color. He shook his head, his mouth opening, but no words came out. Instead, he pulled me to him. He wrapped his arms around me, squeezing tight until I couldn't breathe.

My eyes screwed shut against the welling tears. We'd never embraced like this before, but it soothed a deep, agonizing wound that I'd neglected for too long.

"I didn't know you've been carrying that around," he said, finally pulling away, but keeping a hand on my shoulder.

I didn't know what to say. I felt empty, numb, like my insides had been pulled out.

"Hey," Knox said, shaking me slightly. "Listen to me, even if you could've saved her, and I don't think you could've, it wasn't your fault. You weren't the one who attacked her, and I'm so sorry I ever thought that you were. She was your mama, Dawson. She was our mama, and we loved her. It doesn't matter how much training you had, nothing could've prepared you for what we saw in that barn. Nothing."

His words hung there between us, but I didn't know if I dared to believe them.

My brother reached up and pulled off his cowboy hat. I blinked, not remembering the last time I'd seen him without it.

"I don't know what you need now, Dawson, but I want you to know this," Those gray eyes bore into mine. "I forgive you. I don't think you need it, but maybe you need to hear it. You're forgiven, and you need to forgive yourself, too."

My chest eased, and I leaned forward. His words released something in me, something I hadn't realized needed to be set free, causing my bitter heart to soften. The ice was beginning to thaw.

After all these years, I felt a glimmer of hope. Maybe I could be redeemed after all.

I reached for my brother, landing a hand on his arm and squeezing. "We've both lived through enough hurt." I nodded. "It might be a long road for me, but you were right about needing to move on."

His eyes misted over, and he laid a hand over mine. "Thank you," he breathed, his voice brimming with relief.

I used to believe I could thrive on my own, that I didn't need family anymore. I thought I could live alone and create art and be fulfilled. I was wrong. In the end, it's not selfishness that satisfies. It's selflessness. It's family. It's love.

I'd gotten a taste of all those things in the past month, and it was becoming very clear what truly mattered in this world.

Knox patted my hand and smiled. It had been a hell of a long time since he'd smiled at me, the hope shining out of him.

"Well," he said, stepping back and gazing at the project we'd started. "The only thing that will make Annabelle more happy than us not hating each other, is getting this pergola finished."

I laughed, actually laughed. It felt like a soothing ointment over an old wound. "Let's get it done."

And so, we got to work. As we pieced together the rough beams that had looked like a pile of trash a few hours ago, we talked. I still wasn't good at small talk, and neither was he, but we managed a slow and steady conversation with each beam we secured.

When the pergola was finished, the sun was barely hovering over the horizon. My brother snapped a picture before darkness made it impossible and sent it to Annabelle. The thing looked better than I'd imagined.

Annabelle confirmed it looked exactly how she wanted, and we climbed back into the truck. Our muscles were sore and tired, but at least the tension that had covered us like a lead blanket was gone.

Knox turned the key in the ignition, and the truck's engine roared to life. I slipped out my phone and texted Faye, letting her know I was on my way home.

We were leaving the ranch property when I received an answering text from her that had my blood running cold.

I'm at the hospital, please come.

Chapter Twenty-Four

FAYE

"So how's your tall dark and handsome boy toy today?"

I gaped at my sister as she folded a gigantic pile of laundry consisting of more baby clothes than any one child could ever wear.

"Stop, he's not...I mean—don't call him that," I sputtered, shifting uncomfortably as we sat cross-legged on the living room floor. I'd left Dawson at the cabin not long ago because I needed some sister time. We talked every day, but it had been a while since I'd seen her in person, and since Mama had showed up in town, I wanted to make sure she really was doing alright.

Ellie had hunkered down in her home the last week, trying and gratefully succeeding at avoiding our mother. Luckily, she hadn't grown the balls to come to Ellie's house. At least not yet.

Ellie's lips fought against a knowing smile. She added the onesie she'd folded to the neat stack on her left and shrugged. "I want to make sure that Dawson's being nice to you is all. I know how grumpy he can be."

"Yes, he's being nice." I bit my lip as the memories of how *nice* he was to me flashed through my mind. I shook my head to clear it.

It seemed like ages since I'd visited my sister, and I was thankful to have the time to do so today. I'd missed her. Cleaning the shop and trying to figure out finances kept me busy, but Ty was out of town for some kind of fitness conference, so it was the perfect time to give her some company.

Ellie ran a hand over her noticeably bigger belly. She winced and arched her back. "Ugh, come on kid, please stop kicking my bladder."

She'd already been to the bathroom several times in the hour I'd been here.

"Why don't I finish this laundry, and you can go lie down?" I offered.

That apparently was the wrong thing to say because Ellie looked at me like I had insulted her.

"I'm going to be uncomfortable no matter where I am. I might as well be doing something productive." She picked up another piece of baby clothing and went back to folding. "Anyway, I'm glad you and Dawson have finally seemed to drag yourselves out of the friend zone after all these years."

I cleared my throat and grabbed a piece of baby laundry, avoiding her gaze. I'd given Ellie some details, but I hadn't exactly explained the whole situation.

I felt Ellie's eyes on me as I folded the clothes.

"What?" she asked.

I shook my head. "Nothing."

"Faye, what aren't you telling me?"

I peeked over at her, my nose wrinkling at the flash of suspicion in her eyes.

"Dawson and I aren't really out of the friend zone, exactly."

Her mouth opened as her brows furrowed. "What do you mean? You aren't dating?"

"No, we aren't."

She set her jaw, tossing the onesie in her hands at my face. "Faye Marie Liles, you have got to be kidding me. Why the hell would you be sleeping with Dawson and still demanding that he only be your friend? News flash, it doesn't work that way."

I gritted my teeth. "Says who?"

Ellie rolled her eyes. "If you think that you aren't in love with that man, then you're lying to yourself."

My chest burned, my heart skittering. "I don't love him."

I wasn't looking for that kind of love from him. I couldn't. My heart had to stay fully walled off. Protected. This was all physical, not romance.

I had to believe that.

She opened her mouth, but then winced, her expression contorting with discomfort. Inhaling sharply, she adjusted herself on the floor.

"You okay?" I asked, my agitation melting into concern.

She held up a finger, closing her eyes as she pulled in another breath. Anxiety crept up the back of my neck as I waited for her to say something. It seemed like a whole minute passed before she finally relaxed, her eyes popping back open.

"What the heck was that about?"

Ellie grimaced. "It's nothing. I've been having contractions, but I'm pretty sure they're the Braxton ones or whatever."

I sat up straighter. "Contractions? Isn't it early?"

She waved a hand, like it was no big deal. "I have a few weeks before my due date. I'm not in labor. It happens sometimes this far in pregnancy. They're random and irregular so don't worry about it."

Easier said than done. "You sure you're okay?"

"Yes." Ellie rubbed her stomach. "Now, let's get back to our conversation."

I stared at her, nervous now that she could be on the brink of labor. Ty wasn't supposed to be home until tomorrow night.

"You can deny that you don't love Dawson, but it doesn't change the truth."

I looked away from her, my face heating. "I don't want to love him."

"Why?"

I shook my head. "Love doesn't last."

She paused, and then she let out a sad sigh. "Faye," she said, and she reached across the pile of laundry and grabbed my hand. I stiffened at her touch. "I know the way we were raised was...not good. I get it. Mama left us with scars, but that doesn't mean we can't heal. I was terrified when I let Ty into my life as more than just my friend, but it has been the best decision of my life."

My eyes burned, and I focused on her hand over mine. "And I'm happy for you," I said, my voice thick. "I'm glad you found Ty, but I don't want that."

I didn't want to risk the pain that came when love wasn't enough.

"Faye—" Ellie started, but didn't finish the sentence as her mouth pressed into a thin line and her brow furrowed. She grabbed her belly.

My anxiety returned as she remained quiet during what I assumed was a contraction.

It didn't last as long as the previous, though. About thirty seconds later she let out a long breath.

"Another one?"

Ellie shook her head. "It's fine. Sometimes they come in a few close spurts but then they slow down and stop. Anyway, what I wanted to say was that you deserve to be happy, Faye."

"I am happy."

She tilted her head to the side. "Are you sure?"

I stared at her. It had been a hard month and a half, but things were looking up. Of course I was happy, wasn't I?

I opened my mouth to reply when a sharp, explosive crack echoed through the house. The sound was unmistakably shattering glass, and I sprang to my feet as Ellie yelped in shock.

"What the hell was that?" she hissed, struggling to stand.

My heart was in my throat. "Stay right there. Call 911."

She gave me a confused look. "What? Why?"

"Do it," I said shortly, heading toward the noise.

My brain immediately jumped to the worst conclusions and calling the police wouldn't hurt. Something in my bones was warning me.

The hair on the back of my neck rose with every step toward the back of the house. Ellie's voice drifted from the living room as she was on the phone with a dispatcher. That was good.

Off the kitchen was a door where the mudroom and the laundry were. The heavy black door was open, swaying in a noticeable breeze. My pulse spiked, the blood roaring in my ears.

It wasn't wise to inspect alone, but my pregnant sister was in the next room. If someone had broken in, they would have to get through me before they would ever land a hand on her. My eyes darted around the kitchen, looking for anything to use as a weapon.

I zeroed in on the block of knives on the counter. I grabbed the biggest one, gripping the hilt so hard my knuckles hurt. Fighting down the fear clawing its way up my throat, I stepped closer to the mudroom door. Icy cold air slipped through, sending a shiver skittering down my spine. I pulled in a breath, holding it as I placed my hand on the door handle and pulled. The door flew open, slamming back into the wall as every muscle in my body coiled tight, ready to strike at a moment's notice.

I stood there, frozen in place.

A large window near the back door in the room was shattered. Shards of glass littered the tile floors like a sparkling mosaic of chaos. Amidst the jagged fragments glinting in the sunlight, sitting on the floor right in front of me, was my grandmother's ring. The same ring I hadn't seen since the night I picked up my father from prison.

My stare locked onto the ring, hardly able to believe it. Dread snaked up the back of my spine and curled around my aching heart.

"Faye?" Ellie's voice said from behind me as she touched my shoulder, making me jump.

"Oh my God," Her big eyes bulged as she took in the knife and the shattered window. "What the hell is going on?"

I tried to speak, but a lump in my throat blocked my words. I glanced back at the floor, and the ring, to make sure it was still real.

There was something else among the broken glass, too. A small, folded piece of paper.

I didn't think about it before heading toward it, glass crunching beneath my shoes. Ellie hissed for me to stay out of the room, but only one thing was on my mind. I snatched up the piece of paper and opened it.

Written on the paper were six words typed out in black ink.

Next time, I won't miss.

Bile burned the back of my throat as I reread the note. The threat clearly from the person who had shot at Dawson and me. My skin broke out in a cold sweat as my breath picked up. I had wanted to believe it had been some kind of hunting accident, no matter how improbable it seemed.

"Faye?" Ellie snapped to get my attention. My panicked eyes flicked to her. "What's going on?"

This was all my fault. I couldn't believe I had brought this danger to her front door. I glanced at the window again, paranoia surging inside of me. "We should probably get away from the windows," I said, backing out of the mudroom.

When Ellie didn't respond or move, I grabbed ahold of her arm.

"I—I have to pee," she said, and then she was half sprinting, half waddling away down the hall toward the half bath.

I blinked after her, but I didn't have time to think about it. I had to act. I hurried back into the main space of the house and started pulling down blinds and curtains over any windows that had them. Unfortunately, my sister lived on a secluded piece of land with few neighbors, so window coverings weren't on all of them.

Some of the panic started to wane when I heard the sirens. Help was coming.

As I pulled closed the last set of curtains, Ellie came out of the bathroom. She slowly walked into the kitchen where I stood, her face whiter than I'd ever seen it before.

"Faye?" she squeaked, sounding terrified.

"The police are coming, I heard the sirens." But those words didn't comfort her. She pulled on the end of her long braid, her eyes filling with tears.

"I think my water just broke."

Chapter Twenty-Five

FAYE

"I CAN'T DO THIS." Ellie thrashed her head back and forth as the contraction subsided.

"Yes you can, El. You were literally made to do this." I messaged her lower back as she swayed back and forth on the fuchsia pink birthing ball. We'd been at the hospital for a couple hours, and the contractions were getting closer together.

"Ty is supposed to be here," she cried, voice cracking. "It isn't supposed to happen like this."

My fingers stilled on her back, my heart breaking. Ty was trying to get a plane back home, but the way things were progressing, it didn't look good for him to make it in time.

Guilt festered in my chest. I had no idea if Ellie went into labor early because of the shattered window, but it didn't seem like a coincidence. The doctor assured us that, though it was three weeks early, the baby was technically term and should be fine.

I shoved down the panic and fear as I rounded the birth ball and looked my sister directly in the eye.

"I know he should be here, El, but he's not." I grabbed her hand tightly. She looked at me with exhaustion and defeat, but I wouldn't let her give up. I held up our clasped hands between us, grasping on to her with all my might, as if I could force some of my strength to seep into her. "But I'm here and we're going to do this together. Us against the world, Ellie, remember?"

She sucked in her bottom lip, her stare piercing through me. It seemed like she was going to give up, but then her hand clenched around mine. Her face hardened as she jerked her chin down in a nod.

"Us against the world."

Whether this was my fault or not, I would get her through it.

The freshly kindled determination fizzled as she groaned. Her face dropped, head tilting back with a low moan—a contraction. Swiftly, I took my place behind her, massaging her back through the wave.

Then, a new beep started. Ellie had been fitted with multiple monitors, tracking her contractions and the baby's heartbeat. The various machines had intermittently emitted beeps, but this noise was distinct. It was a high-pitched, frantic beep, more like an alarm more than anything else.

My anxiety escalated by the multiple nurses that blew inside Ellie's hospital room, followed by the doctor herself.

"What's wrong?" Ellie snapped as her contraction waned.

The doctor went to the monitor making the incessant beeping noise, and one of the nurses checked the monitor strapped to Ellie's belly.

"Let's see what's going on here," the nurse said.

"Is something wrong?" Ellie repeated.

The nurse glanced at the doctor who looked up from inspecting the machine. "The baby's heart rate started to have some decelerations during the contractions."

I gripped Ellie's shoulders as her body tensed. "Is the baby okay?"

The doctor brows knit together. "I'm going to be honest with you, Ellie. For a first-time mom, your labor is going pretty quickly. It seems to be causing some distress to the baby."

Ellie's hand reached up to cover mine. "Distress?"

The doctor pressed her lips together. "If it's okay with you, I'd like to have the anesthesiologist come up and give you the epidural. It might help slow things down. In the event you need a cesarean, you'll be prepped for that."

"Are you sure that's necessary?" I asked, hurting for my baby sister. She was terrified of needles and was hoping to do this without the epidural.

The doctor nodded. "It's what I advise, but it's ultimately Ellie's choice. I'm going to continue to keep an eye on the heart rate through the next few contractions, and we'll see how the baby handles it. I'd be very concerned if it drops lower than this last one."

Ellie was silent for a long moment. Her voice trembled when she spoke. "We'll see how the next contraction goes, but if we can avoid the epidural, I want to. But the health of my baby comes first."

"I'm going to keep you and your baby safe, Ellie." The doctor nodded. "Let me take care of something quickly, and I'll be right back in to check on you."

As the doctor left, Ellie's fingernails dug into the back of my hand. She started shaking slightly. "Us against the world," she whispered under her breath.

Us against the world.

I SAT IN THE labor and delivery waiting room, staring blankly at the wall as I tried to get my bearings.

My brain was trying to reset and understand what just happened. It hadn't been long after the doctor left Ellie's labor room before there was another intense contraction. Ellie made a guttural noise that I'd never heard a human make, and before either of us could process it, the room was filled with a whole team of people, including the doctor. I didn't have time to think before Ellie was on the bed and I was holding her hand, doing my best to keep her calm and be her strength.

Barely any time passed before that tiny baby was born. Her little, but strong cry filled the room easing all of our fears. It was the single most terrifying and amazing thing I had ever witnessed.

After making sure that Ellie was okay and the baby was healthy and snuggled up on her chest, I needed a few moments to catch my breath. That sweet baby had come into this world like a hurricane, fast and strong.

I swallowed hard. Despite my brain knowing that both mom and baby were healthy, the guilt lingered. I covered my mouth as my lips quivered. The sting of tears touched my eyes as everything that happened today came crashing down on me: the shattered window, the threatening note, putting my sister and her baby in danger. Ellie was going to pull through and so was her baby, but this wasn't the birth that she had planned. Ty had missed the birth of his first child.

The double doors that led to labor delivery opened as someone buzzed in. I looked up, my eyes widening as Dawson rushed in. I'd forgotten I'd texted him shortly before the baby was born. The moment our eyes locked, I felt both relieved and utterly guilty. Ellie hadn't been the only one hurt because of me. Dawson had taken a bullet for me. I had no idea why the hell my father was trying to kill me, but I put everyone around me in danger.

I launched myself from the chair, running until I flung myself into Dawson's embrace. I wrapped my arms around his neck, pressing my face into his chest. He held me tight with so much strength, and I let myself break down. The tears flowed freely as the sobs crawled up my throat.

Dawson pressed his lips against my temple, and he whispered fervently into my ear. "Are you okay? What happened?"

Another sob ripped from my chest as I told him what happened. I told him about the incident at Ellie's house. About the note and the ring.

Dawon cursed. "Are you okay?" He repeated. He wasn't asking if I was physically okay.

Shook my head. "I don't know. I should be. Ellie and the baby are okay, but..." A fresh wave of tears fell from lashes and soaked into the cotton of Dawson's shirt. "I'm scared."

"I am so sorry, Faye," he said between clenched teeth. "This whole thing is bullshit. Did the police say anything? Why the hell haven't they caught this guy already if he's still in the area?"

I tried to get ahold of myself, and I pulled my face back from his hard chest. My eyes flicked up to his, his beautiful face blurred by my tears. "They were at Ellie's house before we left the hospital. I gave them my statement. They said they were going to continue the investigation. Ellie has security cameras, so they're hoping to get some information off of that."

The sharp line of his jaw hardened as his eyes flared with anger. "You'd think they could do more. Somebody must've seen your father somewhere around here. His mug shot is circulating all over the place."

I shrugged, feeling too overwhelmed and exhausted to be angry that my father hadn't been caught yet.

Dawson's hand cupped my chin, his thumb caressing my tear-stained cheek. His eyes darted over my face, his expression softening with concern.

"Can I bring you home?"

Bit my lip, the emotion surging again. "I don't know if that's a good idea," I mumbled.

Dawson frowned. "What do you mean?"

My arm unwound from around his neck, my hands running over his shoulders and down until they were pressed against his chest. I fisted the cotton fabric that was drenched in my tears. "I don't know if it's a good idea to go back home with you. Being with me right now is just a bad idea."

As he comprehended what I had said, he scoffed. "I've had a lot of bad ideas in my lifetime, Faye. You are not one of them."

My eyes welled with more tears. "It's not safe for you."

"I'll take a bullet for you every damn day if I have to. If someone wants to hurt you, they're going to have to come through me first."

I pushed my fists against his chest, hanging my head. "Don't you see? That's the problem, Dawson. It's my own stupidity that got me into this mess. My own willingness to let a complete stranger into my life. I can't go back to that cabin knowing, for sure, that someone is after me. Someone who has no qualms about hurting the people I'm close to."

I was drowning in guilt and worry, my breaths short and shallow. Dawson grabbed my face in both of his, forcing my eyes to his.

"None of this is on you," he said, voice vibrating with certainty. "Do you so easily forget the extra security at the cabin? I have basically built you a fortress. It's safe."

I shook my head. It didn't matter, no matter how much security he had, we couldn't be protected all the time. What about when we left? Another soft sob escaped me as my heart fractured.

Dawson tightened his grip on my face, creating just enough resistance that I had to stop shaking my head.

"Faye," he said, his voice low and firm. "I think it's time we both stop blaming ourselves for things out of our control."

"I don't know how" My teeth sunk into my lip. "And I would never be able to live with myself if something happened to you."

"I could die in a car accident tomorrow. We can't live in fear anymore. *I* can't live in fear anymore. When I was in my lowest place, you never left me." He placed a hand on his chest. "Because of you, I am finally starting to rip out the dead tissue festering and rotting inside my heart. It's on the path to healing. If I'm not giving up on myself, I sure as hell am not going to give up on you when you need me most."

My stupid heart ached. "Dawson—" I said, my voice shaking.

He put a thumb over my lips to silence me. "I am not going to let you go, Faye. I've spent too many years letting my cowardice win. I'm done holding you at arm's length."

The way he was looking at me had my insides turning to mush. His eyes glowed with heat. Those words didn't sound like someone who only wanted to be my friend. Something had changed.

"We made a promise," I reminded him.

"I know," he said, and he tucked a strand of hair behind my ear.

I closed my eyes, taking in a shaking breath. "I can't give you my heart, Dawson."

He stilled. "That's okay."

It didn't feel okay. Nothing about this felt okay. The tears streamed down my face as I tried and failed to control my sobs. "I just—I don't know if I can do this."

He pulled me against him, and I tucked my head against his chest. His lips pressed on the top of my head.

"You can't end what we have here when it hasn't even begun."

I sniffed. What did we have? Everything was suddenly all messed up, blurring together. "What do you want from me, Dawson?" I asked, exhausted to my core.

There was a long pause. "I want you to let me take you out on a date."

I pulled away. "Date?" I asked, almost flinching at the word.

Dawson nodded slowly. "Just one date. I want to redraw the line. If you don't like it, we can reevaluate."

Redrawing the line. "What kind of date?"

"I want you to be my date to my brother's wedding."

I tensed. "You want to take me to Knox's wedding?" I had never heard him call it that before. He always referred to the wedding as "the event." "When did you decide to go?"

Dawson's face started to change color. A very soft blush kissed the tops of his sharp cheekbones. He looked almost sheepish. "My sister's meddling might have finally paid off."

"Annabelle?" It finally started to sink in. "Oh my God, did you...did you make up with Knox?"

Dawson pressed his lips together. "I think," he said softly. "We might be on the road to healing."

I opened my mouth to ask how all of this had happened, when the large double doors opened again.

We turned, and I gaped as Ty Ranes ran up to us, his face pale and panicked. Sweat glistened on his brow as he pushed back his wild, curly hair.

"Faye, thank God, where is she? Is she okay?"

"Ty?" I was completely shocked to see him. "How—how did you get here so quickly? I thought you couldn't find a flight."

"Turns out if you throw enough money at something, you can make anything happen." A deep crease formed between his brows. "I haven't heard from Ellie in a while. Is she okay? Did I miss it?"

A pang shot through my chest. I reached for his arm. "She's fine. Come on, I'll bring you to her room."

If he didn't know the baby was born, I wasn't the one to tell him. I shared a brief glance with Dawson.

"I'll wait here," he said.

Nodding, I headed toward the labor and delivery rooms.

I knocked softly on the extra wide door. "Come in," Ellie soft, exhausted voice called.

I opened the door, sticking my head in first. She was lying propped up in the hospital bed, her baby lying on her chest. Ellie smiled when she saw me, and though she had been through something traumatic, she was absolutely glowing with happiness.

"I have a surprise for you," I said softly.

She raised her brows. "Oh?"

I grinned and walked into the room, Ty following right behind. The moment she saw him, she gasped. And then she started to cry. Fat, glistening tears welled and fell down her cheeks.

"Ty," she rasped, one hand securing the baby against her chest as she reached out to him with the other.

Ty was at her side in an instant. "Shh, baby, I'm here." He wrapped both his hands around hers, bringing it to his mouth and kissing the back of her hand. "I'm so, so sorry I'm late."

Ellie shook her head, a smile pulling at her mouth despite her tears. "It doesn't matter. You made it."

Ty leaned down and pressed his lips to the top of her head. "I shouldn't have left so close to your due date."

"Stop it," Ellie scolded, her eyes fluttering to get rid of her tears. "We had no idea I'd go into labor early. There's no fault here."

I winced. No fault except for mine.

Ty shook his head. "You're amazing, you know that right?"

Ellie grinned. Then, she glanced down at the tiny baby against her. "Are you ready to meet your daughter?"

Ty's eyes bounced to the bundle on her chest. An expression of shock and awe crossed his face before he smiled from ear to ear. He sucked in a deep breath, his eyes misting over. "God, El, she's absolutely beautiful."

He was right about that. Baby girl had a full head of dark curly hair that she got from her daddy. She had her mama's full lips and the sweetest chubby cheeks. She was literally perfect.

"Take off your shirt," Ellie said, making Ty give her a double-take.

"Wait, what?" He asked, eyes widening.

Ellie sat up, carefully shifting the baby off of her chest and into her arms. "It's recommended to do skin to skin with Mom and Dad."

Ty still didn't look convinced, but he reached for the buttons of his shirt and started undoing them.

"I'll just give you guys some privacy," I said, turning to duck out of the room. Ty was a handsome guy and all, but I didn't need to see his naked chest.

"Wait," Ellie said. "Don't go yet."

I halted, turning back to her. She glanced down at the baby in her arms, and then back at me. "Do you want to know her name?"

Excitement sparked in my chest. "You have a name? Of course I want to know."

Ty and Ellie's eyes met for a fraction of a second. She ran one finger over her baby girl's round cheek and smiled. "This is Amelia Faye Ranes," she said, her voice breaking with emotion.

I stared at her, stunned, thinking there was no way I'd heard her correctly. *She'd named her baby after me?*

And then, I completely burst into tears. I ran over to my sister, wrapping my arms around her neck and pulling her close.

We both started bawling, and she wrapped one arm around my waist, the other holding the baby, and the three of us were pressed against each other in a tight knot. My heart was so full and so happy that I soaked it in because I never knew how long it would last.

"I love you," Ellie whispered.

I gave her one last squeeze, and reluctantly let her go. I touched baby Amelia's head. "I love you both." Then I stepped away, giving space for Ty to properly meet his daughter. "I should give you some privacy," I said, heading to the door.

This time no one stopped me.

As I reached for the door handle, I glanced back at them. Ellie had scooched over, and Ty was sitting next to her on the bed. He'd unbutton his shirt, and Ellie beamed at him as she handed baby Amelia into his arms.

His eyes glazed over as he stared at the little baby, as if he couldn't believe she was real. He pressed his daughter to his chest and kissed the top of her head. Ellie wrapped her arm around them both, leaning her head on Ty's shoulder as she gazed at the two of them.

They looked so insanely happy. More happy than I'd ever felt in my whole life. I'd always believed that romance didn't last, and maybe it didn't. This was something more than that. Maybe this was what real love looked like...a deep, enveloping, beautiful thing that I could feel radiating from them.

I had closed myself off so hard for so long, because I was afraid of this? I knew what love looked like when it was wrong, but I hadn't known what it looked like when it was truly right. When it was whole.

Something broke inside me. I crack that reverberated through my bones. I pressed a hand on my chest. Those walls of defenses I'd built up so strong and so tall around my heart were crumbling into dust.

I turned away from Ellie and Ty as tears filled my eyes and slipped quietly out into the hall, needing some air. The door to their room had just snicked closed when a mass of bleach blonde hair turned around the corner, headed in my direction.

My body stiffened, and I wiped away the remnants of tears in my eyes as my mama came strutting toward me, her heels clicking on the hospital floor. I planted myself in front of Ellie's door holding my arms out.

"What do you think you're doing here?" I spat.

Mama blinked at me, her pink lipstick cracking as she grinned. "I'm going to see my grandbaby."

I bristled. That was the last thing she was going to do if I could help it. "How did you even know she was here?"

Mama shook her head. "You two are my daughters, Faye. Of course I know where you are. And Mirium's husband has a police scanner. The moment that 911 call came in from Ellie she called me right up."

I gritted my teeth. Miriam was her old high school friend and the local salon owner. It seemed she needed to keep her mouth closed more often.

I shook my head. It didn't matter how she found out Ellie was here. She wasn't about to go into that room and ruin the perfect moment Ellie and Ty were having with their baby.

"You need to go. *Now*."

Mama hoisted her fake designer purse higher up on her arm. Her brows shot up, almost getting lost in her bangs. "And what exactly are you going to do to stop me?"

Visions of me tackling her on the spot flashed through my mind, but I was already so exhausted. I didn't have the energy for any of it. "Why can't you just leave us alone?" I said, almost begging her.

Her lips pulled back from her teeth. "I am your mother, Faye."

"And as our mother you were supposed to look out for us." My voice was a low hiss as I tried not to yell. My hands started to shake. "All you ever did was look out for yourself."

"I think it's time for you to leave this hospital."

Mama and I jumped at the deep voice. She whirled around, her eyes widening as she took in the sight of Dawson standing behind her.

He looked utterly threatening, the look of anger stark in his dark eyes as he stood tall with his shoulders back, dwarfing my mother.

"Who are you?" She snapped. Then she paused, her eyes narrowing. "Wait, are you that Evans boy?"

I was surprised she remembered him. He was around a lot when I was younger but I didn't know she paid that much attention.

Dawson's gaze flicked to me briefly before it returned to her. "I will gladly get hospital security. Do I need to do that?" He raised a brow.

Mama seized him up again, and I wondered if she was considering challenging Dawson.

But after a long moment, she said tightly, "That won't be necessary." She glanced back at me. "Tell Ellie I'll want to see my grandbaby at some point. She can't avoid me forever."

Oh, how I wished she could.

Mama turned back down the hall, stomping away.

I stared after her until Dawson's hand brushed my shoulder. My eyes met his. Everything in me felt absolutely drained.

Dawson tucked a lock of hair behind my ear as he whispered, "Let me take you home."

Chapter Twenty-Six

DAWSON

THE CABIN SMELLED LIKE smoked embers and pine, a smell that had always comforted me. I inhaled it deep into my lungs as I took Faye inside. She had stumbled back into the waiting room in a daze, and she still didn't seem like herself. Her eyes were missing that bright spark, and her skin was pale. Too pale.

When we were safe inside with the alarm system engaged, I turned to her. "What do you need?"

She paused before she answered. "A shower."

I nodded and took her hand again. She followed me to my room, where Meatloaf greeted us with a wiggly body and wagging tail. Faye smiled at him, calling him a good boy, but she didn't reach town to pet him. That concerned me.

Meatloaf whined with disappointment as we continued into the bathroom.

I didn't let her hand go as I flipped on the lights and pulled her toward the shower. Reaching in through the glass door, I turned on the rain shower head mounted to the ceiling. Water cascaded down, crashing onto the tiled floor. The sound was one of my favorite parts, soothing and calming, like literally standing under a waterfall.

I redirected my attention to Faye and released her hand. She stood there, eyes fixed on the shower as if in some kind of trance. Gently, I lifted her chin, meeting her gaze.

"I need to go let Meatloaf out, but I'll be back to check on you, okay?"

She stared for a moment longer, then nodded.

Reluctantly, I stepped away.

I went as quick as I could, giving Meatloaf his nightly meal and letting him outside. It was only about ten minutes, but it seemed far too long.

When I made it back to my bedroom, I listened at the bathroom door. Nothing but the sound of the shower came through. I hesitated, but needed to make sure that she was doing okay. I knocked on the door. When there was no reply, I knocked again. On the third knock I tried turning the doorknob and it opened. She hadn't locked it. I inched open the door, saying her name as I peeked in.

She stood in the same place I left her, staring blankly, arms limp at her sides. I stepped inside, worry twisting my gut. Wispy steam filled the room, fogging over the mirror. Her hair clung to her skin from the moisture as I brushed a lock out of her face.

"Faye, baby, tell me what's wrong." I wanted her to let it go, to know what was going through that mind of hers. She'd been through so much.

Her eyes met mine, but it didn't seem like she was truly focusing on me. It was as if she was miles away, lost somewhere in the tresses of her mind.

Her teeth caught that lower lip. "I'm...just so tired," she breathed. The exhaustion was poignant in every word.

I wished she'd tell me how I could be of use. My jaw tightened and released as I wracked my brain for any damn thing that might bring her some solace.

My gaze darted toward the shower and then back at her. She'd been fixated on the water when I entered, as if she longed to step in, but lacked the energy. My lips pressed into a line as I contemplated my next move.

If she wanted a shower, I wasn't going to let her skip it because she was too tired. I could help her.

Slowly, my hands drifted to the hem of her shirt. It was a soft, smooth fabric that was like butter against my skin.

"Arms up," I instructed.

Her eyes held mine for a beat, but then she complied, lifting her slender arms above her head.

I lifted the shirt an inch, exposing the delicate skin of her lower stomach. My core tightened, my nerves prickling at the proximity of her body. Steam continued to fill the space around us as I inhaled the musky scent of her damp skin.

Before I went any further, I made absolutely certain this was the right thing to do. I leaned close, my lips pressing against the sensitive skin below her ear.

"Is this okay?" I whispered, pulling back to watch her expression.

She swallowed, a bead of sweat rolled down her neck and into the hollow between her collar bones. Her eyes widened, but there wasn't hesitation in them. "Yes."

I nodded, and pulled her shirt all the way up and over her head. I tossed it to the floor beside her as her arms fell. My hands dropped onto her thin shoulders. My fingertips drifted up and down her arms in long, lazy strokes all the way down to her hands. Goosebumps raised on her skin, and I suppressed a smile.

As my hands ran over the backs of hers, I dipped my head, pressing a small kiss against her collarbone, and then her shoulder. Her skin tasted sweet and salty, and a shiver rocked through me as I brushed the waistband of her pants.

I pressed small quick kisses along her neck and jaw as I unbuttoned her jeans, trying not to let myself out of control. My body heated to the very core, aching and wanting for her, but this wasn't about me. This was about Faye and what she needed.

I eased her jeans down her legs, slow and steady. My head tipped up to look at her as I knelt before her. Her breaths were rapid as she stood, completely bare and sucking hard on her bottom lip. I dragged my nails up the side of her calves, the backs of her knees, and up her thighs. She shuddered. My hands made it to her hips, and I stilled here.

"You are absolutely gorgeous," I murmured. "So much more than I deserve."

My lips brushed against her stomach. Her muscles clenched. I would never tire of her kissing her.

Except this wasn't supposed to be about kissing. This was supposed to be about her.

I stood. A soft groan of disappointment escaped her, and I tried to ignore the surge of heat coursing through my veins.

I kissed her forehead, using every ounce of my willpower not to ravage her where she stood. She was the most beautiful thing I had ever seen—but her soul was even more exquisite. It was her soul that I loved more than the stunning body it was wrapped in.

I took her hand and led her gently to the shower, snagging a washcloth from the drawer on my way. I opened the glass door and stepped inside, clothes and all, pulling her in behind me. The hot water soaked into the fabric of my clothing, and Faye frowned slightly. Beneath the cascading water, we stood silent. I grabbed the bottle of shampoo and lathered it in my hands.

I had never washed anyone else's hair before, but it felt natural as I threaded my fingers through Faye's. I wanted her to understand that when she was tired, I'd be there to support her. When she was sick, I'd take care of her.

My fingertips massaged her scalp. She closed her eyes, letting out a low moan that set my blood on fire. The white, sudsy bubbles contrasted with her dark hair, dripping down to her shoulders and sliding down her body. Her hair was like silk between my fingers, soft and delicate.

When I was satisfied her hair was clean, I rinsed it out and went back with some conditioner on the ends, though it was already soft enough without it. I grabbed the washcloth and applied some body wash.

I met Faye's gaze. Her lips parted slightly, and I wanted to taste them, but I had a task to do. Carefully, I turned her around. Starting with her neck, I gently rubbed the washcloth up and down her skin. I was thorough, but not too invasive, washing her shoulders and back and down each leg. Straightening, I drew nearer to her, making our bodies flush as I reached around and dragged the washcloth over her stomach and hips. Every soft curve of her body fit perfectly against mine, as if we were made for each other.

Faye leaned her head back on my shoulder. She let out a soft sigh as my hand drew lazy circles over her stomach, enjoying the feel of her skin against mine.

After a while I let the washcloth drop to the floor, and we stood under the water as it washed away the soap. The heat sank deep into our bones.

I kissed her cheek, holding her tight against me. Another small sigh escaped her, and then she turned around, looping her arms around my neck as she faced me.

"I need to tell you something," she said, her eyes looking sad and tired.

"What is it?"

She pressed her lips together. "I think I'm broken, Dawson. I thought I knew what I was doing, but now—" She stopped and shook her head, looking so helpless.

My chest ached. I put my hands on each side of her face, looking deep into her eyes. "We're all a little broken."

Her mouth trembled. "I don't want to lose you."

God, I didn't want to lose her either, but I was too far gone, now. "If I have the choice, I'll stay by your side until the end of the world, Faye."

"I want to believe that, Dawson. I really do."

I leaned in, my forehead resting against hers. "Then believe it, Faye. Lean on me when you're scared. Let me be your strength. You're not alone in this journey anymore."

A choked sob escaped her. Her tears were lost among the water cascading down her face. She didn't answer. She didn't have to.

"You might not want to hear this," I said, running a thumb over her cheek. "But I need to say it anyway." I pulled in a shaky breath. "I love you, Faye. I love you so fucking much that it terrifies me. I know I made a promise to you, and I'm sorry, but I'm done lying to myself. I'm done lying to you."

She stared at me, her eyes searching my face as the silence stretched on. She didn't say it back, and I didn't expect her to. But then, her hands slowly traveled up the back of my neck and into my hair. She pushed up on her toes and closed the miniscule gap between our mouths. Her lips were wet and soft and supple. I pulled her in closer, needing the taste of her to envelope me.

All too soon, she broke away, leaving me breathless and wanting.

"It's your turn," she said. I frowned, but she reached for my soaked shirt, tugging the hem up.

I didn't hesitate. I raised my arms, and she pulled the shirt off and dropped it to the floor with a heavy splash. Her hand splayed out on my heaving chest, as if she was feeling the beats of my frantic heart. With an aching slowness, she slid that hand down over every hard plane and ridge of muscle until she stopped at my waistband. One flick of her finger and she undid the button, almost undoing me in the process. Suddenly, my pants were nothing but another pile of soaked clothing on the floor.

Every touch of her hand across my skin sent pleasant shocks along my nerves. When she stood, she grabbed the shampoo, rubbing some between her hands. She raised a brow, waiting for permission. I dipped my chin in a nod, and she reached for me, fingers weaving into my hair. Her long nails brushing against my scalp had my eyes rolling to the back of my head.

I wrapped an arm around her, my head dropping onto her shoulder as she continued running her hands through my hair.

"Oh my God," I groaned against her skin. "You're fucking amazing, Faye."

"Mmmhmmm," she murmured, her hands moving down my neck and then to my shoulders, massaging and scratching. Drawing noises from me I'd never made in my life.

Her hands stilled at my waist, and she placed a kiss on the crook of my neck.

Lifting my head, I gave her a questioning look.

I wasn't prepared for the fire in her expression, the neediness. "Dawson," she said, the sound of my name on her lips almost ending me. "I want you."

Those three words were all I needed.

My mouth was on hers in the next breath, my lips desperate and hungry. My hands locked onto her hips, and I took a step forward, pressing my body against hers until her back met the shower wall. Her arms wrapped around me, her nails digging into my back.

We lost ourselves in the heat, in the sounds of the crashing water and the beats of our hearts. I kissed my way down her neck and to her chest, licking and nipping until she arched her neck back and let out a sweet noise that had me on the brink of losing it.

"Dawson," she panted. "Please."

I lifted my head and met her mouth again, parting her lips and meeting her tongue with mine. My arm hooked around her waist, pulling her in close, our bodies fitting together as if we were made for each other.

As we reveled in each sensation in rhythm with the thrum of our hearts, it was very clear to me that this was more than our bodies meeting. It was our very souls melding, entwining together until I didn't know where I ended and she began. Each caress was a prayer, each kiss a promise. I was giving myself to her for the rest of my existence.

My heart was no longer bitter and cold. It was hers.

Chapter Twenty-Seven

FAYE

I DIDN'T KNOW WHAT I was doing, but when everything else in my life was chaos, I turned to my planner and anything that could keep me busy. During the following two weeks, both Dawson and I had started helping with the wedding and fundraiser. Ellie was safe with Ty, staying away from town and my lurking mother while I networked with the other businesses in town to get donations for the silent auction. Together, we'd been able to curate an assortment of items that would bring in some good money. It was good for me to work and get my mind off of everything.

Thankfully my mama hadn't tried to come "help me" or whatever she'd come to town for. It didn't hurt that Dawson was often at my side, never leaving me alone to be ambushed by her alone again.

The police upped their search for my father, who fit the same build as the masked intruder who'd been caught on Ellie's security camera. They posted fliers around the town of his mugshot, asking for information on anyone who'd seen him or had any information of his suspected crimes.

No one had come forward. A cloud of anxiety of the unknown hung low over my head.

But I had to keep going, and for the first time in maybe my whole life, I leaned on something that wasn't my own strength. I let Dawson be there for me in ways no one else had. I was taking baby steps, but even though I was still very much broken, Dawson hadn't run away. Yet.

The little shop of mine had also come a long way. I breathed in deep; the space smelled like fresh paint and endless possibilities as I hung the painting on the wall behind the counter, a focal point to bring the whole room together.

I stepped back, my chest filling with happiness and pride as I inspected the painting—the green hues of trees and plants with pops of bright, luscious flowers brought a sense of peace to me. Dawson had created it specifically for the shop.

The thing that had changed most in the last two weeks, though, was Dawson.

His talent and skill with painting was no longer a secret, and I was so proud of him. Ever since he'd started making up with his brother, he was different. In good ways. He'd purchased a small space around the corner from my shop to be his gallery. He hadn't set the place up yet, since we were putting all of our extra time into getting the boutique ready to reopen, but Dawson reached out to the local paper, and they'd done a whole article about his social media fame and his new business venture of opening a gallery in Cypress Falls.

To say the town was shocked was an understatement. People were stopping by Southern Sunshine whenever they noticed I was here working, trying to ask me questions about the estranged Evans child and his artistic notoriety.

Most people were warming up to him, finally. With working at the boutique, and starting the gallery, he was in town much more often. He actually talked to people with a smile on his face. Something I never thought I'd see again.

The freshly fitted front door of the shop swung open, and the bell above chimed with a joyful ring that resonated throughout the nearly completed space.

"I have a delivery," a familiar voice called.

I turned, a wide grin spreading across my face. "Julian!" I said, more happy to see him in his work uniform than I ever had been before.

The two of us hadn't spoken as much lately, but he'd been stopping by when he could to help with repairs. He'd remade my checkout counter, and it was stunning.

I almost bounced over to him as he ushered in the dolly loaded with new inventory. I'd almost had a breakdown when I finally was ready to order new merchandise. It felt like a part of me had been put right back into place.

Julian tipped back his hat and winked at me. "My last delivery of the day, and I'm glad it's to you."

He put the dolly down and glanced around at the shop. "Wow," he said, his head swiveling all around. "It looks better than it did before."

My heart swelled with pride. "Thank you. And thank you for dropping this off on a Saturday. I wasn't expecting it until Monday."

He shrugged one shoulder. "Eh, I was excited to get it to you, let's just say that."

I nudged him on the arm. "You better not be working late because of me."

He rolled his eyes. "Does this go in the back room like usual?"

I pursed my lips, instantly feeling guilty. "Actually, the back isn't quite ready for merchandise yet. I'm so sorry. You're going to hate me, but can you help me get these up to the third floor storage?"

He gave me a slow blink, tilting his head up toward the ceiling. "The third floor, huh?" he said, not sounding excited at all.

"Or I can have Dawson do it sometime." I shrugged, but he shook his head.

"No, I got you." He took a deep breath and tilted back the dolly. "Lead the way."

I guided him up the two flights of stairs, apologizing the entire way. When we made it to the third floor landing, he was sweating, and I said sorry for the hundredth time as I opened the door.

"Stop, Faye. I'm doing my job. You don't have to be sorry," he said, his breaths heavier than normal as he followed me into my makeshift warehouse.

The old, scarred floor creaked beneath our feet as we walked inside. The space was all open and spanned the entire square footage of the floors below. Rows of organized boxes sat in neat lines, each labeled with what was in them and the year and season they were. I also had some spare furniture and display pieces.

Julian had been up here before, but not in a long while. He glanced around the space, staring up at the tall ceiling and then back at me. "Where do you want this, boss?"

I wrinkled my nose. "I'm not your boss," I quipped. "But I want them right over here."

He carefully unloaded the boxes where I indicated, and I was about to thank him, when my phone went off.

My stomach flipped at Dawson's name on the screen.

You better be leaving now, or you won't have time to get ready. This is a wedding. You're supposed to look fancy, and I hear that takes you girls a long time to do.

I gasped as I looked at the time. He knew me well.

I'm leaving now. I texted back.

He sent me an eyeroll emoji. I chuckled.

I mean, it. I'll be home soon.

At least you had your phone on you.

I'm getting better!

When I looked up from my phone, Julian was watching me, the dolly empty. I blinked, shaking my head to clear it.

"Thank you," I said, slipping my phone back into my pocket. "I'm really sorry I can't stay and talk, but I'm running late, and Dawson is waiting for me."

"He's waiting for you, huh?" Julian waved a hand. "Don't worry about it."

We left the storage room and walked back down to the shop where we said a quick goodbye.

Once Julian had left, I practically sprinted to my car and drove up to the cozy little cabin to get ready for my first ever date.

I was both excited and terrified. If things didn't go well tonight, I didn't know how we were ever going to go back to where we were before.

Chapter Twenty-Eight

FAYE

KNOX AND SHILOH'S WEDDING was breathtaking.

They said their vows under a flower-covered pergola in front of the pond on the Willow Hope Ranch property. The ceremony itself was small, no more than family and friends to witness the two of them promise their lives to each other. It was intimate and so beautiful.

Ty Ranes was the best man, standing proudly beside Knox as he took his bride. Annabelle and Ellie were the only two bridesmaids wearing gorgeous, classic black dresses. Ellie had a black ring sling where sweet Amelia lay tucked against her mama's chest, sleeping away as the ceremony processed.

Knox had asked Dawson to stand in his wedding, but Dawson refused. Not out of anger, but because he didn't feel like he deserved to stand up there next to his brother. He said they were just getting to know each other again, and he didn't feel right about it.

So, he sat next to me and held my hand as I cried happy tears for the beautiful couple.

After the private ceremony, we were all invited up to the Evans estate where the reception and public fundraiser would take place. I'd never been to a wedding like this one, where the couple took the spotlight off themselves and used their reception to raise funds for charity.

Dawson squeezed my hand as we approached the massive, colonial style mansion he'd grown up in. Masses of people streamed through the towering double doors of the front entrance. I'd been to the mansion several times before. Most of the town had since the Evans family held a yearly gala to fundraise for the ranch for as long as I could remember.

I stepped closer to Dawson's side, glancing up at him. Throughout the ceremony, he had remained stoic and reserved, making it difficult to discern his emotions. He was trying to mend his relationship with his brother, but so many hurt feelings surrounded it all.

"You all right?" I asked.

He tore his eyes away from the house, meeting mine. The corner of his lip tipped up. "Yeah," he dipped his chin. "I'm good."

He stepped forward, leading me toward the house.

If I thought the wedding was beautiful, Annabelle had outdone herself with the reception. Stepping into the marble entrance of the house, I audibly gasped in awe.

The decor seamlessly blended rustic and dark romantic aesthetics. Tall brass candle holders, each with lit tapered candles, adorned the space and gave it a warm glow. The grand staircase's banister was draped entirely in lush, dark greenery, punctuated by large dark crimson and purple roses. Rustic lanterns with flickering flames graced every stair.

I gaped at all the attention to detail. Everywhere I looked there was something beautiful to admire as Dawson led me through the crowd in the entryway and to the ballroom. Tables were set up inside with dark linen tablecloths and natural wood chairs.

"This is all absolutely beautiful," I mused, as Dawson brought us to an empty table.

Dawson pulled out a chair for me, raising his brows. "Annabelle sure knows what she's doing."

The room buzzed with life and excitement as people mingled around the space, eating and drinking and laughing. Near the right end of the room was an elevated stage where a live band played soft background music. A dance floor separated it from the rest of the tables. On the opposite side of the ballroom from the stage was a large buffet with all kinds of food and hors d'oeuvres.

Dawson grabbed us each a glass of wine from the open bar at the end of the buffet tables, and I thanked him as he took a seat next to me. He'd picked one of the smallest round tables, and at the moment, we were the only two sitting at it.

I was almost finished with my glass of wine when the band momentarily stopped playing as someone entered the stage, walking up to the microphone stand near the middle.

Annabelle Evans smiled at the crowded ballroom as she readjusted the microphone down to the appropriate height for her small frame.

"Hey, everyone," she said, her voice booming and gaining everyone's attention. "I am so incredibly happy to welcome you all back to the Evans estate for another amazing event. We're so thankful y'all came out not only to celebrate Knox and Shiloh but to help support Paws and Pastures, a local rescue and vet clinic that is near to their hearts."

There was a round of sparse applause from the crowd.

Annabelle nodded. "I wanted to thank everyone who helped make this event such an amazing success already."

She unfolded a small piece of paper in her hand, and she listed off all the vendors and businesses that had donated items or assisted with the food and decor. It was a surprisingly extensive list, and reminded me that though I didn't like the small town gossip train, there were so many more positives than negatives about living here.

"I'd also like to thank my father, Robert Evans, for letting us use such an iconic venue." She paused at the next name of her list, pulling in a deep breath. "And I want to thank my brother, Dawson. Some of you might have misguided opinions about him, but I want to thank my brother for all his help with this event, including his very generous monetary donation and his gorgeous painting for the silent auction." She beamed with pride. "Y'all will have to take a look at it and put in a bid because it is stunning."

As the applause started, I threaded my arm through Dawson's, hugging him tight. He stared at his sister, a small smile pulling at his lip.

Annabelle folded up her paper again. "Finally," she said, her eyes sparkling. "I want to thank Faye." My heart thrummed at the sound of my name. *Me? Why was she talking about me?* "She has given her limited, precious time to help organize the silent auction even with all the work she's had on her own shop. Which is why Knox and Shiloh, in collaboration with Paws and Pastures, have decided that a portion of tonight's donations will go to her to help with damages to her building."

There was a beat, a fraction of a second, of silence as I processed what she'd said because there was a thunderous applause. I gaped at Dawson who was grinning from ear to ear. A few people who were milling around our table patted my shoulder and congratulated me and I was so overwhelmed with the kindness and generosity. I didn't deserve it, but it sure was going to help. The sense of being cared for and loved washed over me.

"Did you know about this?" I asked Dawson in stunned disbelief.

Dawson shook his head and wrapped an arm around my shoulders. I buried my face in his neck as the tears started coming.

"I can't think of a person more deserving of this, Faye," he whispered in my ear.

Chapter Twenty-Nine

DAWSON

I PULLED FAYE AGAINST me as her body shook with overwhelmed sobs. I had no idea my siblings, and Axel, had decided to do this for her, but I was eternally grateful.

I planted a kiss on the top of Faye's head as the applause for her died down, and shifted my gaze back toward the stage. My sister had disappeared, and Knox stood in her place, a guitar slung across his body, repositioning the mic back up.

Knox cleared his throat, and the lingering noise died down as everyone's attention went to the stage.

"Hey, y'all," Knox said, sounding a bit off kilter. He adjusted his cowboy hat, which didn't look as ridiculous as I thought with his gray tux. "I'm glad everyone came tonight. I give my thanks to my sister, who made all of this possible."

Faye popped her head up from my shoulder as the applause started again, and she clapped her hands so hard and so fast I thought she might hurt herself. I chuckled softly.

"Anyway," Knox continued as the clapping died down, "Annabelle told me it was time for Shiloh's and my first dance, or something like that. Well, if you don't know this about me, I don't like being the center of attention. But mostly, I sure as hell can't dance." A quiet rumbling of laughter spread through the crowd. "Instead of all that, I'm gonna play a song that I wrote for my wife." His lips tipped up in an almost involuntary smile. He shook his head. "I still can't believe I'm lucky enough to call her that."

Knox strummed a chord on the guitar. "So, yeah, I'm gonna sing to my wife and let y'all dance instead of me."

Knox looked back at the band, and they started playing, a catchy melody that was country, with a twist of something else. It was very Knox. He played his guitar, and then he started to sing. I'd seen my brother perform only one other time, and even when I'd hated his guts, his talent impressed me.

Tonight was no different.

As the song progressed, people pooled onto the dance floor. The song wasn't exactly slow, but it wasn't upbeat, either. It held a steady and catchy rhythm that coaxed couples to lock hands and sway to the beat.

I glanced at Faye. Her palm was pressed over her heart, listening intently to Knox's song.

My hand reached for hers. "Come on," I said, standing from the table.

Faye blinked up at me. "What?"

I leaned down and whispered in her ear, "My brother might not be able to dance, but I can."

With a gentle tug, I pulled her onto her feet and guided her onto the dance floor. Her lip caught between her teeth as we joined the small crowd. I faced her, resting my hand on her waist and drawing her close. Tentatively, she circled her arms around my neck.

"Just go with it," I said softly. "The song won't last much longer."

As we moved back and forth, she eventually relaxed into me. The sensation of her warm body pressed against mine brought a sense of comfort and peace that was entirely new.

She looked up, her smile so bright and pure that I couldn't help but return it.

All I wanted to do was kiss her, but making out on the dance floor was probably in poor taste and I was only beginning to get my reputation back. Instead, I pushed a stray strand of hair out of her face and cupped her cheek.

"You've changed everything, Faye," I said. "You changed me for the better."

Her small frown confused me. "I didn't change you, Dawson," she said, shaking her head. "You changed yourself. *You* did that. I was simply the encouragement."

I swallowed, resisting every urge I had to kiss her until I couldn't breathe. Instead, I crushed her against me, wrapping both my arms around her.

Her arms tightened around my neck. We stood there as the love song my brother wrote for his bride came to an end, and the dance floor cleared.

Faye and I were the last ones. She pulled back, and we grinned at each other like the fools in love we were. "I should probably go hunt down my sister. I haven't gotten to hold my niece yet today, and I really want to."

She pushed up on her toes and pressed a kiss to my cheek. "I'll be right back, and we can resume this."

"Promise?" I held up my pinky finger.

She smiled and curled her small finger around mine. "Promise."

I watched her walk away, enjoying the view in the dark blue lace dress that hugged every dip and curve.

The band started playing again, without my brother, and I walked off the dance floor. My head was on a swivel as I wandered through the crowd in the ballroom. I wanted to thank my brother for what he'd done for Faye. I'd congratulated him briefly after the ceremony, but other than that I hadn't spoken with him. He'd been busy.

As I waded through the people, it was so stark how much had changed. Everyone I accidentally met eyes with, smiled. There was barely any disdain in people's faces or judgment. Some even stopped to compliment my work and were excited for my upcoming gallery. It was almost surreal. I never expected to be...accepted again. Not in this town.

A sudden feeling of overwhelm welled in my chest. The crowd, though friendly, felt like it was pressing in on me. I was getting better at being social, but I wasn't the best, and it frustrated me that I couldn't find my brother.

As more and more people pulled me aside to ask questions or give accolades on my work, it all became too much. I smiled and nodded as much as I could, but headed toward the exit.

A crowd lingered in the entryway by the auction tables, but I focused on the set of double doors on the opposite side of the space. I knew this house like the back of my hand, having grown up here. A small lounge was off the entryway, and though the doors were closed, they weren't locked. Crossing the marble floors, I hurried in front of the staircase and slipped inside the dim, quiet room, taking in a few deep breaths.

I closed the door behind me. It was mostly dark, the soft evening seeping in from behind the drawn curtains. There were two leather chairs and a couch facing a wall of books that almost no one ever read. They were mostly for decoration, unfortunately.

I inhaled the scent of paper and leather. The noise from outside could barely be heard here, and it soothed my anxiety. I approached the couch and sat down, letting out a long breath.

After everything that had happened with my family after our mama was attacked, I never thought I'd be able to come into this house again and feel...at peace. I leaned my head back against the couch, letting myself relax for a moment.

So much had changed. Knox's wedding had been beautiful. I didn't think I'd feel so happy for my brother again, but I was. Watching him marry the love of his life had thoughts running through my mind...thoughts involving Faye.

I didn't know if she was ever going to want something like that with me, but I had to be alright with whatever she was willing to give. I could be whatever she needed.

Everything was because of her. She'd saved me in more ways than one. I wouldn't be here at all, mending broken relationships and living a life I never dreamed of, if it wasn't for her.

Faye was my everything, and though I wanted her in every possible way, I'd take her friendship if that's all she could give me.

I owed her everything.

Chapter Thirty

FAYE

"All right, let me give that baby one last hug then I really should find my date." I turned back to Ellie, who handed me Amelia for one last squeeze. "I still can't believe you're here after just having a baby."

"Yeah," Ellie said, shifting uncomfortably in her chair. "I love Knox and all, but I don't think the best man and I will be staying much longer."

"Fair enough."

What had first started out as me saying a quick hello to my sister ended with us surrounded by a group of people who wanted to chat. We talked about how exciting it was that the boutique was getting some of the donation money. Julian had stopped for a while, completely surprising me. But I'd eventually walked Ellie over to a table so she could have a seat and rest.

I handed the baby back, who'd been a complete angel the entire time, and glanced around the ballroom. It was still crowded, and hard to see, but I found the table where Dawson and I had sat. He wasn't there.

"Am I finally going to get a chance to meet my little grandbaby?"

Ellie and I froze, our eyes meeting in panic at the familiar voice neither one of us wanted to hear.

I glanced over, meeting my mama's pale blue eyes. She was wearing a black, tight dress that was much too skimpy for a woman her age. Her hair was pulled up into a slick bun and her makeup was a little too heavy, making her look even older than she was.

She was staring at little Amelia, a strange expression crossing over her face. Something like—longing, maybe?

Ellie pressed the baby closer to her chest. "What are you doing here?"

Mama's lips thinned. "It's a public event, sweetie. I can be here if I want. You can't hide away indefinitely."

Ellie leaned away from her, her eyes darting around the ballroom. She was probably searching for Ty. The look of anxiety on her face had my chest tightening. I stepped between her and Mama.

"You should probably go," I warned. This wasn't the time or place to do this. It was too public.

Then again, that was probably what she was banking on. Hoping we wouldn't make a scene in such a public venue. My own eyes swept over the crowd around us, wondering where Dawson had disappeared to.

"I just want to meet the baby. She's my granddaughter. You don't have the right to keep her from me."

Rage rose in me, but Ellie's voice came from behind me before I got the chance to speak.

"She's my daughter, Mama. I have the right to protect her."

243

"Protect her?" Mama spat. "From who? Me? I'm not going to hurt an innocent baby, honey." Her tone was exasperated like we were the ones being ridiculous.

I glanced over my shoulder at my sister. Tears brimmed in her eyes as she clutched onto Amelia, who for once was starting to fuss.

This was enough.

I stepped toward our mama, grabbing hold of her wrist. She gasped and tried to pull back, but I didn't let her go. "You're leaving," I demanded.

"Let go of me," she hissed.

Instead, I started walking, dragging her away from Ellie and Amelia and toward the ballroom exit.

"My God, Faye, let me go!" Mama struggled to get free, but she was weaker than she looked. The bones in her wrist jabbed into my palm and though she dragged her feet, it wasn't hard to get her out of the ballroom.

I didn't let her go until we were near the front doors. "Get out!" I said, voice low and firm as I pointed to the exit. "You don't belong here anymore. We don't want you here."

Her chest heaved as she stared at me, her eyes sparking with anger and something else I wasn't expecting...desperation.

She wrinkled her nose as her lip curled in a snarl. "What? You get all that donation money and now you think you have the right to throw me out of my own damn town?"

My stomach twisted. Had she known about the money I was getting? How could she?

I shook my head. At this point, I didn't care. All I wanted was my sister to feel safe again. "Is that what you want? You can take all my money if it means you'll leave town and never come back."

Mama's jaw tightened. Her eyes assed me carefully up and down. As if she was looking for an indication that I was lying. She wasn't going to find anything. I meant it.

"I don't want your money," she eventually answered, almost in a whisper.

"Then what do you want?"

Her hands balled into fists at her sides. "I want *you*, Faye. You and Ellie. I don't have anything left."

I blinked at her, taking in her words. "What are you talking about?"

"I'm all alone," she spat between clenched teeth. Her eyes started watering and my heart constricted. I've seen my mother cry over lost lovers, but not much else. "You're all I have left."

I shook my head, unable to make sense of what she was saying. She'd never looked at Ellie and me as anything but pawns before. "Why don't you just settle down with someone else like usual? Some place far away from here?"

That anger flashed again in her expression. "Look at me, Faye," she said. "I'm not exactly young anymore. No one wants me and I can't be alone."

I stared at my mother as something finally clicked and became clear. She *had* come back to Cypress Falls looking to get something from my sister and me, but it wasn't money or control this time. It was love.

A low laugh escaped me. Humorless and hollow. I crossed my arms over my chest, suddenly aware that we were making a bit of a scene in the entryway. We weren't being loud, but people were noticing the tension between us.

"What's so funny?" Mama snapped.

"Nothing," I said. "It's just...my whole life I wanted this from you. Ellie and I always loved you despite all the shit you put us through."

Mamma swallowed hard. Her jaw clenched like she was biting her tongue, but she didn't interrupt. "You've always been so desperate for love, Mama. You sought it at every turn, but you never realized it was right in front of you the whole time."

"I always loved you girls," she said, defensive.

"No, you didn't." I shook my head. "I'm not sure you even know what that means."

My entire life, I feared turning into the woman standing before me. I thought that by shunning the idea of love would save me from that fate. I'd convinced myself that love was an offensive, four-letter word that brought nothing but pain and heartache in the end.

As I stared at my mother, it was clear that I was nothing like her. She looked for validation in love. She was desperate to fill a hole in herself that couldn't be healed by another boyfriend or another husband.

My mother left me with trauma and scars, but I chose to make a better life for myself. I wasn't my mother.

"Don't just shake your head and laugh at me. You don't know what I've been through!"

"No, I don't." Her life couldn't have been easy. It was obvious she had trauma, too, but that wasn't my fault. It wasn't my younger self's fault, either. "But it's the choices you made that sealed your fate, Mama. I'm not sure if the damage you've done can be repaired, but in order to start, you have to be willing to change. I don't know if you are."

"Stop talking to me like I'm a child." Mama planted her hands on her hips, her face reddening. "I *have* changed."

"Then prove it. I can't speak for Ellie, but if you really want to change, I'd be willing to consider trying to build a relationship with you. But if you're not willing to work on yourself, you might as well just leave now because I can't fix what's broken in you. Only you can do that."

Her body was vibrating, her fisted hands trembling as she stared at me. She stepped closer, and the pure venom in her expression had the hair on the back of my neck raising.

"Don't you talk to me like you're better than I am. I raised you. I sacrificed for you and fed you and this is how you repay me?" She glared, her eyes icy and cold. "You're nothing, Faye."

She spat the last words and then shoved me aside as she opened the front door and strutted out.

My heart raced as the sting of her last words sank in. It wasn't as painful as I expected. Maybe because I've finally realized that she didn't define who I was. Not anymore.

Still, my chest felt tight. My lungs struggled to suck in oxygen as I stared at the people milling around the entrance, shooking curious glances my way.

I wanted Dawson, but I didn't know where he was. I didn't want to go back into the crowded ballroom to look for him, either. I needed some fresh air.

I turned on my heel, heading outside into the cool evening.

Sudden tears were hot and wet trailing down my cheeks as I crossed the porch and headed toward the massive lawn. It wasn't because of the words Mama had said to me, my tears were because of all the choices I've made that led me here.

If I hadn't been so desperate to convince myself I didn't need love my whole life, where would I be right now?

I took in deep breaths, trying to clear my head and wrap my mind around the truth that had become clear to me. Love didn't bring pain and heartache. Choices did. Selfishness did. Hate did.

I meandered toward the forest that boarded the Evans' property, desperate for some solitude while I processed everything that went done in that entryway. I wanted time to think before I went to find Dawson again. A shiver wracked through me, the warmth from the sun not touching me in the shadow of the trees.

My body stiffened at the sound of footsteps behind me.

"You look like you could use a drink." The voice was familiar, but unexpected. Julian came up beside me, holding out a slender glass of champagne.

I made a noise, something between a sigh and sob, as I tried to wipe the tears from my face. "Did you happen to see all of that?" I asked, my cheeks heating as I took the champagne. I hadn't seen him in the entryway, but assumed he'd seen the confrontation between Mama and me.

Julian shrugged. "It wasn't that bad."

I stared down into the pale, bubbly liquid, not believing him. "My mother is a real charmer," I said, rolling my eyes. I pulled in a shuddering breath, needing to get a hold of myself.

"I'm sorry, Faye."

I let out a breath. "Yeah, well, it's not your fault." Then, I tipped the flute of champagne up to my mouth, draining the whole thing in one go.

"You gonna be alright?" Julian asked.

I turned to him, holding the empty glass toward him. "Yeah," I said, nodding. Truly meaning it. "I think I will be. I just needed some fresh air."

"Can I do anything to help?"

He didn't take the glass, and as I stared at him, a dizziness came over me. My eyelids got so heavy it was hard to keep them open. My legs suddenly started to feel wobbly and I stumbled, dropping the champagne flute onto the grass as Julian grabbed my elbows.

"You feeling okay?" His voice sounded strange, like it was far away instead of right next to me.

With more effort than it should've taken, I turned my head up toward him. His form swam in my vision, and no matter how many times I blinked, I couldn't get the dizziness to go away.

"Oh, Faye, you don't look good."

I frowned at Julian. "I'm...dizzy," I said, my words slurred like my tongue wasn't working right.

What the hell was going on?

Julian laughed quietly, and the hairs on the back of my neck rose. "It took me a long time to figure out exactly what I was going to do with you, Faye. Lucky for me, tonight worked out perfectly."

I blinked again, my heart pounding, but my eyes wouldn't open again. Once they fluttered closed, my world went black.

Chapter Thirty-One

DAWSON

I COULDN'T FIND HER.

I'd spent too much time trying to decompress and when I came out of the lounge, there was a crowd milling around the front door. Axel had been there, and he'd told me that Faye and her mother had some kind of fight right there in front of everyone. I hadn't heard a damn thing.

If Faye's mama had been here, it couldn't be good. She would need someone to talk to and I'd desperately searched the whole damn house, and found no sign of her.

Out of breath and on the edge of losing any of the composure I'd managed to keep, I ran back into the too crowded house after searching the entire outside perimeter. There were too many people in my way as I hurried into the ballroom. I pulled my phone, calling her again for the thousandth time.

I'd already checked the ballroom, but there were so many peo-ple, I wanted to try again. I slowed down as I passed the table we'd shared earlier, my eyes latching on to her small purse. She must've left it.

I snatched it off the table, opening it like it would somehow give me a clue as to where the hell she'd gone.

The only thing inside was a tube of lipstick and her phone. Of course she didn't have her damn phone with her. My fingers clenched around the flimsy purse as the frustration welled.

Part of me thought that I shouldn't be so worked up that I couldn't find her, but something felt off. A sense of foreboding had washed over me when I couldn't find her right away.

"Hey."

I whirled around as someone's hand came down on my shoulder.

"Whoa," Knox backed away from me, palms up like I was going to punch him or something. I didn't blame him. I probably looked as feral as I felt. "What's wrong?"

I closed the purse, but kept it in my hand. Faye would want this back once I found her.

"I can't find Faye," I said between clenched teeth.

Knox pushed back his hat. I had no idea how he saw anything in this dark room with that hat on. "What do you mean?"

I cursed. I had no fucking desire to retell the story, all I wanted was to find Faye and make sure she was alright.

"She had some kind of fight with her mother. She's probably pretty upset. I need to find her."

Knox's brows drew together. "What did she see? Is she okay?"

I raked a hand through my hair. "I just need you to trust me, Knox. Please. I need to find her."

He stared at me, his gray eyes assessing. I wouldn't blame him if he walked away and called me an idiot. I could be freaking out over nothing, but I needed his help.

251

"Okay," he finally said, and the relief made my knees weak. "What do you need?"

"I don't think she's in the house anymore. I've searched the whole place, outside and in."

Knox's eyes widened. "The whole house?"

I nodded.

He whistled low. "Damn, okay." He held up a finger. "Give me a second. Stay here."

Before I could question him, he had turned and disappeared into the crowd. A few moments later, he returned, dragging Annabelle by the arm who was holding on to the hand of Colton, her husband.

Annabelle frowned at me. "What the hell is going on? I was enjoying a dance for the first time all night, and Knox pulled me off the floor in a panic."

I pulled at the tie around my neck like it was choking me. "I can't find Faye."

Annabelle stared at me blankly. "What do you mean?"

I huffed out a sigh. "Exactly what the hell I just said. Look, I'm worried. She had some fight with her mama and then disappeared. You know the weird stuff that's been going on involving her."

My sister paled. "You think she's in danger? You think her own Mama wants to hurt her?"

God, I hoped not. "I don't know, but I can't find her anywhere on the property, and I was the one who drove us here. She either started walking back home or someone else picked her up."

I didn't know what I was hoping for more, that she was walking alone on the side of the road or someone had given her a ride. I tried to keep the image away of her father coming out of the shadows while she was totally alone and vulnerable.

"Did you call her?" Colton chimed in.

My eyes cut to his. He was a local police officer, so he knew everything that had happened to Faye these past couple months.

I held up her purse. "She left it."

Colton's mouth tightened. "Okay, let's not panic before we know for sure that something is wrong." He glanced at my brother. "Knox, you stay here and take another look around the house. Make an announcement asking for anyone who has seen Faye recently to let you know."

Knox nodded.

"Annabelle and I can drive around the ranch and the surrounding roads and see if we see any sign of her. Dawson, why don't you go check your cabin in case she found a ride there."

My fingers drummed nervously against the side of my leg. I nodded, trying to calm myself and focus on the plan. "What if she's not there?"

Colton stepped closer. "Then keep looking. I'm sure she's around here, and we'll find her."

I let out a long breath. I glanced at the people around me, at my family. We had been so broken for so long. I was thankful they were willing to help. Especially since this night was so important to both of them.

"Thanks," I said, my voice thick with emotion. "I really...I appreciate it."

Annabelle reached out and touched my arm. "It's what we do, Dawson. We have each other's backs, all right? It doesn't matter anymore where we've been. We're family."

I glanced at Knox. He dipped his chin in agreement.

"Okay," Colton said, grabbing Annabelle's hand again. "If we're going to find her, we should go now."

With those words, I didn't hesitate. After one last glance at my siblings, I turned and headed out of the house I'd grown up in and back to my Jeep to find the girl I loved to remind her just how much she meant to me.

I FLEW UP THE front steps of the cabin, praying she was waiting for me inside, that she was safe.

I punched in the code to unlock the door, yelling her name before I set foot inside. My voice echoed through the quiet cabin. No one called back.

After running upstairs, I knocked on her bedroom door, hoping she'd yell back at me to leave her alone. Nothing but silence answered again. I opened the door to a painfully empty room. I turned before the sight brought me to my knees and flew back downstairs and to my bedroom.

Meatloaf huffed at me as I stormed through the door, jumping up from his dog bed. For once his tail wasn't wagging. I had no words to comfort him because instinctively, my very soul warned me that something was wrong.

No matter how mad Faye was, she wouldn't disappear.

Not even her sister, Ellie, had seen or heard from her, but she also confirmed that their mother had tried to corner them. Ty had gotten Ellie and the baby home safe and they were staying put where it was safe.

It was going on over an hour since Faye went missing, though.

I crossed the room and entered my closet, heading to the gun safe. Since the day of the shooting, I'd added a few to my collection, one being a Glock pistol. I took it out of the safe, along with the belt holster and secured it on me. If someone did anything to hurt a damn hair on Faye's head, they wouldn't get away with it unscathed.

I gave Meatloaf a quick stroke on the head on my way out. He looked up at me with so much concern, like he knew, too, that something was off.

"I know you're worried," I whispered to him. "But everything is gonna be okay."

Maybe I was saying that more to myself than the dog.

Meatloaf huffed through his nose, and I scratched him under the chin before heading out the door.

My phone rang as I hopped back into the Jeep. It was Annabelle.

I answered the call. "Anything?"

The pause that hung on the line made my stomach clench. "We've been all around the ranch and some of the side roads, and we haven't seen her."

My brow furrowed. "There's no sign of her at all?"

"No. I'm sorry," Annabelle said. "We're going to keep looking, though."

My jaw clenched. *Where the hell could she be?*

I put a hand on the steering wheel, gripping it hard as I tried to think through my muddled thoughts. "I'm going to check one more place."

Chapter Thirty-Two

FAYE

A SHARP, OVERPOWERING SCENT cut through my haze of unconsciousness, jolting me awake. I coughed, my chest tightening as my nose stung. A pungent, chemical scent—like smelling salts—had the back of my throat burning. My head whipped around me, eyes wide as I tried to orient myself in the dim room.

I jerked my arms up, but something stopped them, pain lacing across my wrists. I glanced down, horror drowning out all other thoughts as I took in the ropes binding me to the wooden chair.

"You're cute when you're afraid, did you know that?"

My heart pitched at the sound of his voice. I tensed, my gaze drifting to his. He stood directly a few feet away. His jewel green eyes were fixed on me. His arms were crossed over his chest, his head was tilted to the side.

Pure fear coursed through me, mixing with a sense of confusion. A sense of betrayal.

"Julian?" My voice sounded so quiet. So weak. "What's going on?"

The corner of his lip curled up into more of a sneer than a smile. "What do you mean? I brought you home."

I frowned at him, and then my eyes started to take in the room around me. It was cold but also somehow stuffy. Dust hung in the air as the last of the daylight was fading through the tall windows behind Julian. All around us were rows of neatly ordered boxes. In the far end, were the boxes Julian had just helped bring up here hours ago. I looked down and studied the chair. It had once been a piece I used in the changing room of the boutique.

We were on the third floor of my building.

"I'm surprised it took you this long to realize it."

"Why did you bring me up here?" I shook my head, none of this making sense. "Did you put something in my water to knock me out?"

My brain was waking up as I remembered the strange taste of the water.

Julian's smile widened. "I told you, I've been trying to figure out what I was going to do with you for a long time, Faye. Tonight just happened to work out in my favor. It was perfect, really."

My heart beat so fast it was hard to breathe. "You need to untie me," I demanded, trying to sound braver than I was.

He flat out laughed. "God, you're pathetic."

Heat rose in my face, his words stinging. Julian had been my friend for over a year, closer to two. None of this made any sense. "I don't know what is going on, but whatever it is, we can work it out. I just need you to untie me."

Julian rolled his eyes. He took the few steps that separated us. He leaned forward, resting his hands on top of the chair, his head lowering toward my ear. "Faye, you can ask all you want but I am not untying you. I'm afraid only one of us will be walking out of this building tonight."

His breath smelled like stale wine. A shudder ran down my spine. "What do you mean?" I asked, my voice wavering.

Julian's eyes shot up to the ceiling above me. I followed his gaze, my blood running cold at the sight of the rope I saw hanging there, a deadly loop tied at the bottom. Bile burned the back of my throat, but I fought it down.

I looked back down, and our eyes met at the same time. "It's finally time that I get this job done, Faye. I've played around with you enough."

My mind spun. Everything that has been happening to me the last two months ran through my head. "Played around with me?" I asked, dread filling me.

He cocked his head to the side, licking his lips as he studied me. I wanted to squirm under his stare, but I wouldn't give him the satisfaction.

"I have a confession to make," he said softly, and then he leaned closer. He was so close I had to turn my head before our lips met. His breath echoed in the shallow of my ear. "Your father killed my mother."

Shock reverberated through me, tensing my muscles and making my hand numb. Julian wasn't smiling anymore. No hint of humor lingered on his face. His eyes were hard and cold and calculating. Nothing like the warm human I'd known.

I shook my head. "That's not true."

His hand shot out so fast I had no time to react before the splitting pain burst on the side of my face. I yelped, my head whipping to the side as the skin on my cheek burned and throbbed.

"That woman your father was sent to prison for killing, was my mother. She was married to that son of a bitch for years before their toxic relationship killed her. Or rather, your father decided to fucking kill her."

Tears burned in my eyes. Not only from the pain of his slap, but from the pain of his words. Marc had said that his wife, the wife who died because of him, had a son. I clenched my teeth, cursing myself for never thinking of the little boy who had lost his mother. I was so focused on getting to know my father, I hadn't let myself think much of his past at all. Of the family that was ruined because of him.

Slowly, I forced my gaze back to Julian. Rage reflected back at me in his eyes.

"I'm so sorry."

"Shut up," he snapped. "You have no right to be sorry. You knew what that man had done, and you welcomed him into your life. You gave him a home. You gave him a purpose. He never deserved any of that. He doesn't get to have any family if I don't. He took mine away, and now, I'm going to take away his."

Oh, God. No. No, no, no. This was not happening. This was not real.

I pulled in a trembling breath, trying to remain as calm as possible. "Yeah, I did give him that. But he didn't give a damn about me. He doesn't care, Julian. He left me, and he betrayed me."

Hurting me wasn't going to bring my father any kind of pain.

Julian's lip twitched again, a ghost of a sneer. He shrugged one shoulder. "Yeah, I got a little carried away. I probably shouldn't have done such a number on the boutique and everything, I couldn't help myself."

My stomach fell through the floor. I blinked at him, struggling to wrap my mind around the revelation. "It was you?" The words slipped from my lips, my mouth hanging gaping. "If you're the one who vandalized my building, then what happened to my father?"

259

That full smile returned, so cold that it chilled my blood. "I got carried away with him, too. When you first told me that he was upstairs in your apartment, it took every ounce of self-control not to run right up there and bash his head in. So, I waited. I thought I'd have to do it while you were asleep. Lucky for me, you left the apartment. I waited for a while, and when you didn't come back, I snuck inside and came face to face with the man who ruined my life. I had wanted him to suffer first, but my restraint only goes so far."

A surge of nausea churned in my stomach. A while passed before I could open my mouth without puking. "Did you... Did you hurt him?"

"I hadn't planned on doing it that night. But he didn't deserve to live anymore, Faye."

His form swam as my vision blurred with tears. This whole time, I blamed my father for everything. I thought that he wanted to ruin me. I believed he wanted to kill me. Shame and grief and guilt washed over me in an overwhelming wave that I barely formed the words, but I needed answers. "If he's dead already, then why are you doing this to me? Why did you ruin the shop? Why did you try to shoot me?"

He sighed and shook his head. As if I was some child asking stupid questions. "Because even in death, he doesn't get to have a legacy. His blood runs through your veins. Who knows what little spawn you could bring into this world someday. No, his family line has to end." His eyes lit up as if the thought excited him. "And if there is some kind of afterlife, I'm hoping that he's looking down as I torture and end the daughter he loved."

A sob escaped me, the tears running down my throbbing face. "He—he loved me?"

Julian shrugged. "They were the last words out of his mouth. I assume it was true."

It felt like someone had taken a red hot poker and speared me right through the chest. "Why the hell did you ever pretend to be my friend?" I cried, struggling against the ropes binding me "If you hate me, if you hate my freaking lineage so much, how the hell could you ever be nice to me?"

He leaned toward me, his lips pulling back from his teeth an ugly grin that made me want to crawl out of my skin. "Because it was fun." The utter callousness in his voice grated against my heart. "Because of the agony etched all over your face. It brings me pleasure. I couldn't draw out your father's death, but I could draw out yours."

His teeth caught his lower lip as he inhaled sharply. I flinched at the pleasure in his expression. "For a long time, I thought I could move on and live my life. I thought that the pain would eventually go away. Isn't that supposed to happen? When people are in pain they eventually heal, right?" He slammed his palm against his chest, the hollow thud jolting through me. "But that never happened." He shook his head. "People don't heal. The pain just festers and rots and ruins your life again and again. I'd had enough of it. I decided it was time to make the person responsible for ending my life lose theirs. That's when I found you."

"Me?"

"The man I wanted to kill was in prison. I couldn't get to him. But I could get to you. When I was young, he didn't mention you much, but a few times when he was drunk he would babble on about the daughter he had in Cypress Falls. He'd curse your mom for keeping you away from him." Julian rolled his eyes. "With the name of your mother and the place you were born, it wasn't difficult to find you. What I hadn't been expecting was that he found you, too. The first time you told me about him getting out of jail, I honestly thought I should buy a lottery ticket because it seemed too good to be true."

A fresh wave of tears cascaded from eyelashes. I opened my mouth to reply, but a noise disrupted us. I froze, both hope and fear coursing through me as the bell above the front door of the shop twinkled as the door opened.

Then, his voice rang out so loud and clear that we heard it clearly on the third floor.

"Faye! Faye, are you here?" Dawson's voice echoed up to me, making my pulse spike.

Julian's hand clamped over my mouth, crushing my lips against my teeth. He hissed in my ear, "If you say one word or make any noise at all, I will kill you and him." To punctuate his threat he reached into his back pocket and pulled out a knife. My eyes zeroed in the sharp blade glinting in the last bits of light crawling through the windows.

Dawson's voice called my name again, the desperation in it breaking me. Everything in me longed to call out to him. In this moment, with a knife near my damn throat, I cursed myself for never saying the words that he deserved. Because I was in love with Dawson Evans. I had loved him for a very long time, a love that was deeper and brighter than friendship.

He was my best friend, but he was so much more. I had forced myself to be alone because I was scared to get hurt. But that all seemed so ridiculous now.

It was very clear to me now that the place where I'd always belonged was with Dawson.

I pulled in a shuddering breath through my nose. The fact that I might never see his face again hit me hard. Regret and sorrow filled me like sand, almost drowning me.

Dawson's footsteps moved, his voice coming closer as he exited the shop and climbed the stairs.

Julian stepped nearer, his hand pushing down on my mouth harder, bruising my mouth. His body draped over mine, his scent and heat suffocating me, as if he was trying to keep me from moving any part of my body.

My heart jumped into my throat as the door to my apartment burst open and his steps ran inside.

"Faye!" He was all but screaming. "Please, I need to see you."

My fingers dug painfully into the wooden arms of the chair. I prayed he never even thought to come up here. He needed to stay safe, which was far away from Julian.

We listened as Dawson continued to search through my apartment, calling out for me the entire time.

And then, he went silent.

Julian's eyes narrowed as he listened, waiting.

A sudden, loud growl of frustration pierced the air.

"Where are you?" Dawson cried, sounding so defeated.

The door to my apparent slammed shut, and I held my breath as his footsteps began to fade instead of getting louder. Relief and disappointment washed over me with equal measure as we heard the door to the shop closed.

Julian waited longer, his hand over my mouth. When the building remained silent, he eventually straightened, pulling his hand back from my mouth. His lip curled as he wiped something wet dribbling down my chin.

Blood.

He stared at the crimson smear on his thumb, a look of satisfaction playing on his features. "Dawson is always so close to ruining my fun," Julian said, letting his hand fall. "I wish I'd actually shot him all those weeks ago."

A sudden overwhelming anger blazed inside my chest. After everything Julian had done, and everything he'd broken, his only wish was that he had killed Dawson the day he tried to shoot me?

"You're nothing but a coward," I spat, putting every ounce of hate and rage into my words. I was coming to terms with the fact that I probably wasn't going to make it out of this alive. But I wasn't going to go easily.

Julian's brows rose. "What?" he hissed, surprise and annoyance warring in his expression.

I set my jaw. "You're nothing but a weak, cowardly little boy." I pulled against the ropes around my wrists. "You're so threatened by a woman that you have to tie me up in order to get your way."

My words seemed to hit him slowly, the color of his face changing to beat red. I snickered at that, soaking in the satisfaction. Maybe that was the only thing I had now.

"You little bitch," Julian screeched as he raised the knife.

I closed my eyes, letting out a small cry as I anticipated the sharp sting of the blade...

But it never came.

"Get away from her," Dawson said, in that deep, threatening growl.

For a moment I thought that maybe Julian had already killed me somehow.

My eyes popped open. I wasn't dead because all I saw was Julian. But the rage and hate had vanished from his eyes, replaced with panic.

Julian moved fast, placing the knife at my neck. "Come any closer and I'll slit her throat."

I winced as the blade kissed my skin.

"Get the fuck away from her, Julian," Dawson spat, his voice coming from directly behind me where the door was. I couldn't see him, but I sensed him.

"Dawson, just go. He's not worth it," I said, glaring at Julian. I didn't want Dawson getting hurt.

The distinct sound of a gun being cocked echoed through the quiet.

"Don't worry, I can deal with him."

The hair on the back of my neck rose. If Dawson had a gun, that changed things.

Julian's tall body was bent at the knees, like he was crouching to hide behind me. Damn coward.

"I said stop!" Julian shouted, digging the knife in until a bead of blood rolled down my neck.

"And I told you—twice now—to let her go," Dawson bit back, but I heard the pinch of panic in his tone.

My heart raced as I tried to get my brain to think of something, anything, to help Dawson. I wished I could see him, I wanted to look into his eyes.

I bit my lip, staring at Julian. He was so close, the knife stung at my throat. I needed him off of me.

I carefully moved one of my legs. Julian didn't notice; his attention was focused on Dawson, sweat beading on his brow.

Julian had only tied my wrists down, my legs and feet were completely free...and he was so very close. Before I talked myself out of it, I moved. I brought my knee up swift and hard right between Julian's legs. The pain registered on his face, and he folded forward. I lifted my other leg, kicking my foot hard into his gut.

Though I'd used all my strength, he stumbled back only a step, the knife leaving my skin as his arms flailed to keep his balance.

265

That one step was enough.

An ear-splitting crack echoed off the walls. Julian stumbled back and then crumpled onto the dusty floor.

In the next breath Dawson was there. The tears overflowed as the adrenaline pumped through me. Dawson grabbed the knife off the floor where Julian had dropped it and turned to me, cutting the ropes from around my wrists.

I sprang from the chair, wrapping my arms around Dawson, holding on to him for dear life. It took me a moment to realize he was saying my name over and over, asking me a question.

"Are you all right? Faye, are you hurt?"

I pulled back, and he cupped my face in his hands, his eyes scanning me, focusing in on the blood dripping from my mouth and down my neck.

My head bobbed up and down frantically. "I'm okay," I said. I needed to assure him because the fear and panic in his eyes was too much. "I'm okay, and I'm so sorry I was too weak to tell you sooner, but I love you. I love you so much, Dawson."

His eyes widened. "I know, Faye." Then he leaned in, smashing his lips against mine in a hurried, but passionate kiss. When we broke apart, his eyes scanned my face again. "I love you."

He hesitated a half a second longer before he thrust a phone into my hand. "But I need you to call 911 right now," he instructed before kissing me on the forehead. Then he was gone.

I blinked down at the phone, and then back up at Dawson as he approached the heap on the floor that was Julian.

"What are you doing?" I hissed, panic shooting through me.

Dawson's sharp eyes met mine. "Call 911, get an ambulance over here and the police." He looked down at Julian who wasn't moving. My stomach clenched, and bile burned the back of my throat.

"Is he dead?" I whispered.

Dawson shook his head. He ripped off his suit jacket and pressed it against Julian's side. "He's not going to be if I have anything to do with it," he snarled.

A low, pained moan came from Julian as Dawson pressed against the gunshot wound.

I startled at the sight of the blood glistening on Dawson's hands. Finally, I dialed 911. As I held the phone up to my ear, Dawson grabbed Juian by the jaw, yanking his head around so that he was staring him directly in the face.

"You hear that? You do not get to die here and make me a killer." His voice was a low warning. "After I save your damn life, you're going to pay for what you've done."

Chapter Thirty-Three

FAYE

Two Weeks Later

I WALKED THROUGH THE large stone archway of the Cypress Falls Cemetery, a woven basket dangling from the crook of my arm. As I wandered down the concrete pathway, the sense of foreboding and sadness I'd experienced the first few times here, had begun to wane.

The gravestones lined up in neat rows were becoming more than a sense of sadness. Yes, death was sad. Grief was utterly painful. But while every stone, every carved name, meant some-one had grieved, it also meant someone had loved. Since the cemetery often brought a sense of gloom, I was choosing to re-member that every grave had a story. And every story, whether romantic or not, was about love at its core. Because that was what the human heart longed for—to be loved.

I turned off the path and trod through the crunchy, stiff grass. The sunshine was warm on the back of my neck, the weather finally beginning to warm up from the bitter chill that clung to winter. We were right on the cusp of spring.

I slowed, approaching the farthest row of graves. My heart panged like it always did when I got this close. A sense of grief and guilt washed over me, lingering on even though I was working through them every day. I stopped at the small temporary grave marker, my eyes staring at the name written there.

Marc Lawrence.

Taking in a deep breath, I knelt down on the grass, my long flowy linen skirt pooling around me. I set the basket down and opened it, taking out a fresh bouquet of spring flowers. My hands clenched around the bound stems as I held them a moment. I focused on their sweet perfume and bright colors, not on the war of feelings stirring up inside of me.

We'd only been able to bury him a little over a week ago. Julian was out of the hospital and in police custody and had taken a plea deal. I was glad for that, in a way. A trial sounded exhausting, and even though I had no doubt it would've been worth it, Julian was going to prison for a very long time regardless.

As part of the plea, though, he had to reveal where my father's body was. I was thankful he hadn't dumped him in the water or something. We were able to recover his body and put him here, so he could rest at peace.

I finally placed the flowers onto the fresh dirt of his grave. Then I sat back, clutching my hands in my lap. I'd told him many times already how sorry I was for thinking he'd done all those things that

Julian was responsible for. I liked to believe that wherever he was now, he could hear me when I spoke to him.

"We had the grand reopening of the boutique earlier this week," I said, a smile pulling at my mouth. "So many people came to support, it was wild."

The shop looked amazing, too. Even better than it had before. I'd designed a custom graphic tee specifically for the reopening event, and I had sold out of all of them. My boutique had been flooded with people all day, and though I'd been thoroughly exhausted by the end of the night, I'd felt so loved, too.

My Mama hadn't made it to the opening, though. Shortly after our confrontation at the wedding, she had skipped town. I was both relieved and disappointed. It hadn't surprised me, I'd expected it, but I felt bad for her. Even though she probably didn't deserve my sympathy, she'd never know how good life could be when you accepted change. When you started healing yourself from the inside out.

"Dawson is opening his gallery tonight," I said, pride swelling in my chest. "I'm so excited for him. I know that you'd like him if you'd gotten the chance to meet."

Dawson had been my rock these past two weeks. Not only had he saved me from Julian, but he'd never left my side though the many rough nights after. I was still struggling with the nightmares Julian had left me with, but Dawson had been with me, my steady support.

A breeze ruffled the hair around my face. I liked the icy bite, and it felt soothing over my skin. I stared back at my father's name. It hit me that for most of my life I hadn't known that name, and I wished I'd had more time. I wished we could've gotten to know each other better.

270

"I know I say this every time I come to see you, but I'm sorry." I placed a hand on my chest, over my skittering heart. "You deserved better than what happened to you, no matter what you'd done in the past."

I placed my hand on the dirt, pressing my hand into the soft soil. Though it was a tragedy how things ended with my father, I took some solace in the fact that I'd been right about him. His last words had been those of love and not betrayal.

"I love you," I whispered, tears welling in my eyes. "I'll never forget you."

I HURRIED DOWN THE street, the large pink box cradled in my arms. Dawson's open house for the gallery's grand opening was going great, better than expected, and I'd had to run over to the bakery to grab more cookies.

As I approached the gallery space around the corner from my boutique, pride blossomed in my chest. The large display windows were covered in his art. We'd been through so much these last years—the last few months in particular—but we'd made it out. It had all been worth it to get here, achieving our dreams with the entire town rallying around us to support us.

I slipped inside the crowded gallery, heading to the small table of refreshments we'd set up near the back. The scent of frosted sugar cookies made my mouth water as I opened the box and situated them on the empty plate. I checked the coffee and water to make sure they were still plenty full, and then I spun around to toss the bakery box away.

I gasped as I accidentally stumbled into someone.

"Whoa, sorry about that."

As I looked up, Axel Roberts blinked down at me.

Let out a breath, shaking my head. "No, I'm sorry. I should really slow down and watch where I'm going." I let out a nervous laugh.

Axel glanced at the table behind me. "You're working hard. I shouldn't have gotten in your way."

I waved a hand. "I'm really glad to see you. Thank you for coming."

"I'm happy to be here." His eyes flicked to where Dawson stood with customers in the corner talking. "He really has changed, hasn't he? I had no idea how talented he was."

"Yes, he is." I followed his gaze, a grin pulling at my lips.

I looked back at Axel. "Hey," I said, my tone shifting. "I haven't gotten the chance to talk to you since the wedding. I wanted to thank you for agreeing to share some of the fundraising money. I wouldn't have been able to open as quickly without the help."

Axel tucked his hands into the pockets of his jeans. "It was the least I could do. I'm glad it helped." He stared at me a moment longer before he cleared his throat. "Anyway, how's Meatloaf doing? I'm hoping well since I haven't seen him in a while."

I nodded, my smile widening. "Yes. He's doing great. He's really become a part of the family."

"I'm glad."

I was, too. Meatloaf had been part of my therapy since everything happened with Julian. He never left my side, always a constant comfort and making me feel safe. I'd be forever grateful for the day Dawson had rescued him. Because as much as we saved him, he saved us, too.

"Well," Axel said, leaning around me and grabbing a cookie from the plate. "I'll see you around, Faye. Take care of yourself."

I nodded. "You too, Axel. Enjoy," I said, glancing at the cookie.

He held it up and nodded with a smile before he walked away.

The rest of the night passed quickly. Dawson sold more paintings than he was expecting, and made agreements to take on some commissions. As things began to wind down and the gallery cleared out, the exhaustion hit me.

As Dawson ushered the last customer out the door, I started cleaning up the refreshments table. There wasn't much left; the second round of cookies had also been entirely eaten. As I threw some trash away in the can, something near the back of the room caught my eye. There'd been so many people in the gallery, I hadn't noticed it until now. A painting hanging on the wall was covered by a black cloth, and I frowned at it, getting closer. I tilted my head to the side as I studied it.

I jumped as Dawson wrapped his arms around me from behind. He nestled his nose into the crook of my neck, inhaling deep and sending chills across my skin.

"It's been a long night," he said, sounding as exhausted as I felt.

I put my hands on top of his. "You had an amazing opening. I'm so proud of you."

He sighed happily. "You didn't have to stay the whole night, but I'm glad you did."

I smiled, and my gaze caught again on the hidden painting. "Why is this one covered?" I asked. "None of the rest are."

Dawson paused. He unwrapped his arms from around me and stepped toward the painting. He glanced back at me, a nervous expression flitting over his face. "This one is a surprise."

"A surprise for who?"

He pulled in a deep breath. "A surprise for you."

Before I could say anything, he grabbed the cloth and pulled it off.

I gasped at the masterpiece underneath. It was the painting I'd seen in his studio—the one with the dancing girl in the middle of the forest. It was breathtaking then, but now that it was finished, it was exquisite. The layers of paint created a unique texture, the colors vibrant and so true to life the whole thing looked real. The girl lifted off the canvas, her arms raised toward the golden sunlight streaming down on her as she danced between the trees.

I forced my gaze away from the painting to stare at Dawson. "I thought that was a commissioned piece?"

He shrugged. "I lied." He reached for my arm, trailing his fingers over my skin down to my hand before he wrapped it in his. "I started this painting when you first came to live with me. I don't usually paint humans, but that's the funny thing about you. You always inspire me to get out of my comfort zone."

I bit my lip. "I...inspired you?"

He nodded. "The girl isn't exactly you," he said, glancing at the girl he'd created on the canvas. "But you did inspire her. You bring so much happiness and light...and the freedom there is in choosing to see the good in the world. I wanted his piece to convey that."

Tears welled behind my eyes as I gazed at the painting. "Thank you."

Dawson shook his head. He stepped toward me, his eyes holding mine. "Don't thank me. If anything, I should be thanking you. All of this..." He gestured around the gallery. "It wouldn't exist without you. Being with you has been the best thing to ever happen to me, Faye."

My breath caught in my lungs. "Dawson—" I started, but he placed a finger on my lips, silencing me.

"I'm not done yet," he said, a smile pulling at his mouth. "I wanted to give you something, but I always wanted to ask you something."

My heart thudded against my ribs.

"Faye, you never left me, even when I deserved to be left. When things were hard and dark, you were always by my side. I want you to know that I love you to the very core of my being."

"I love you too, Dawson."

He brought up his hand, holding out his pinky finger toward me. "Promise?"

I grinned and curled my pinky finger around his. "I promise."

His finger tightened around mine, and he didn't let go as he stooped down onto one knee.

My eyes widened, my heart leaping into my throat as Dawson stared up at me. "Then will you marry me, Faye?"

My mouth fell open. Our pinky fingers were entwined as I took him in, not believing what I'd heard. "Marry you?" I breathed.

Dawson nodded. "I want to be by your side forever. I want you to be my last and only promise."

My cheeks heated as happy tears slid from my lashes. After so much pain and heartache, I never imagined my life would come to this.

Dawson reached into his pocket with his other hand out something small that glinted in the studio lighting. My heart melted as my mouth gaped. Pinched between his thumb and pointer finger, was my grandmother's ring.

"Now, this isn't your real engagement ring, but I thought you'd appreciate having it back," he said with a smile. "Faye Liles," he continued. "Will you be my wife?"

I nodded, an elated, overwhelmed sob bubbling up from my chest.

"Yes," I said, meaning it to my very soul. "I'd be honored to marry you, Dawson."

THE END

If you loved this book, I'd be honored if you left a review!
Make sure to join my newsletter for bonus content!

Also By Abbey

Cypress Falls Series

To keep up to date with all of Abbey's releases in this series please visit:

www.authorabbeyeaston.com

Connect with Abbey

To access exclusive bonus scenes, AND be the first to know about new releases, sign up for my newsletter by visiting:

www.authorabbeyeaston.com

Email: Aeaston@authorabbeyeaston.com

Printed in Great Britain
by Amazon